Nothing's Forev[er]

The later years
Series two
Book # 1

BY

STUART MICHAELS

Chapter one

Thursday, 24 September 1987

At long last! Six months of tough negotiations and almost feudal arguments with the local council's Planning and Building Department, they have finally given me the go ahead to start work on my extension. I will admit that it's not entirely all their fault. We've changed our minds several times, but insisting we resubmit the plans every time there was a minor or major alteration has worn exasperatingly thin. Especially when the little Hitler of a planning officer informed me on final agreement that I was lucky to have my plans passed so quickly. If I worked in that institutionalised manner I would have gone out of business many years ago. I firmly believe the hiccups I've endured are because I'm an Englishman owning a house in the man's native Wales, and he's gone out of his way to be obstructive on purpose.

Right from the conception of adding rooms to my home, I've had reservations about having the work done because, deep down, I still miss my old flat in the centre of town. Having the money to better myself was burning holes in my pockets, and with this place coming onto the market at the right time - with its obvious potential and position - the temptation to spend my hard-earned cash became too great.

For two years now, I have lived high above the town looking down over the small harbour, and out over Carmarthen bay toward the Gower Peninsula. It is a magnificent setting with stunning views. It was love at first sight and I couldn't resist the temptation of buying the chalet bungalow-style property when the opportunity arose, but, stuck up here, I miss the hustle and bustle of town life. Not that Saundersby is a particularly busy, vibrant town through the depths of winter, but I could at least stroll the few yards to the local pub for a beer or two and touch base with my friends and the locals. Up here I'm isolated, and transport of some kind to get down into the town is a necessity to enjoy those same few beers with the lads.

Jenny, my live in girlfriend, pushed hard to get things moving. The extension was initially her idea. Somewhat naively, at the time, I called the builders in to quote for the work, just to please her; but, silently, I liked some of her ideas, such as an indoor swimming pool, and once I'd got used to the idea of extending the house I then went to town with ideas of my own.

What started off as simply making the kitchen and lounge considerably larger - with the mandatory conservatory on the rear of the house, naturally - plus the twenty-metre length pool with all the trimmings, has ended up with extras too numerous to mention, but I'll give it a go: Two more en-suite bedrooms, for a start, making a total of five, once the work is complete; a games room with a fully fitted, functional bar, a large double garage for our cars, and of course, the huge patio at the rear of the house for barbecues and entertaining purposes. Then there's the six-foot high, front garden wall, to keep out unwanted guests, finished off by the electrically operated wrought iron gates, complete with remote control. The cost of this work far exceeds the price I originally paid for the house. A lot just to please one woman.

Jenny is twenty-two; I'm thirteen years her senior. The age difference doesn't bother us, but she can be very immature at times. Jenny stands around five-six in her stockinged feet, has shoulder length brunette hair, and wide green-brown eyes. She has a small, white pigment birth mark on her neck, just below her left ear, on her otherwise perfectly tanned, smooth complexion. Jenny looks after herself - hence the request for the indoor swimming pool - eats sensibly and takes regular exercise. If I had one criticism, it would be that she drinks way too much, but then we're all capable of doing that from time to time!

At thirty-five, I'm putting on weight where I shouldn't be, and take little or no exercise other than what I do during a normal working day. Hell, the good life suits me; why should I worry over putting on a few extra pounds?

The builder I've commissioned to do the work comes highly recommended, and he's ready to start when I give him the nod. Next Wednesday is October 1st and my builder says he'll need to get started very soon to avoid the deep excavation work required for the pool being swamped by the deteriorating winter conditions.

Following a lengthy telephone conversation, making quite sure that he has the latest drawings to hand, Mac, the builder, promises me that his men will be on site first thing Monday morning. That's brilliant, because I'm not a patient man and want this work done as quickly as possible. I don't want to hear excuses about the weather holding up work; this is South Wales, man, what do you expect!

Mac – Alan McKenzie - has agreed to a six-month contract, bullied by my persistence, in truth, which means he must be finished and off site by the end of March next year. Mac tells me he's confident he'll meet the deadline. Perhaps the finishing date clause - where he starts to pay me if he hasn't - has got something to do with that!

The work on the house isn't the only building works I'm currently involved with. The business - my business - has for some time, had a requirement for an office in the Birmingham area. We are busy; overloaded with work, in fact. It's an ongoing, successful, business growth plan, but currently my company is expanding at an alarming rate, and we haven't enough space or the right personnel here to cope with the demand. I use the word 'alarming' because we're in danger of spiralling out of control, and we need to be pro-active to combat the situation.

I discovered that as a city Birmingham is an expensive area in which to either rent or buy, and I have no desire or need to locate further north. Because of those reasons, we've concentrated our search for new premises south, and predominately west, of that fair city.

Our head office here in Saundersby, is idyllic. Situated right in the harbour, it nestles in one of the most beautiful settings you could wish for. Because of that, it makes for a happy office, and a happy office, in my view, is a productive office. We couldn't mirror that setting in the city of Birmingham, but as we scoured the surrounding area looking for potential sites, we bore the ambience of Saundersby in mind.

When we - the board of directors, comprising of myself, Graham Kingsman and Richard Strike, my junior partners in the company - stumbled upon Great Malvern, we instantly knew it was right for our needs. Taking in views from all sides of the building, out over the hills and wonderful countryside, we snapped it up then and there, and the task of converting the office to suit our requirements is underway.

I go up there at least once a week, checking on the progress and conducting interviews with Graham, who, for his sins, will oversee proceedings until we find the right person to manage the new business office. He is working to a deadline too. The building works are to be completed and the new office fully staffed and operational by the 1st January 1988 - three months from now. Sounds do-able and it is, but there's a deep routed culture amongst country folk - as I've discovered here in Saundersby where I live - and that is, 'Yes guv, we can do that for you…tomorrow'.

Jenny is beginning to bitch about the amount of time I'm spending away from home, and she's unable to, or doesn't want to, grasp the importance of the Great Malvern project. I have run my own private detective business for almost eighteen years, and apart from when I acquired the Saundersby office, this is a first. I am taking a huge gamble expanding in what has been a tough decade; a decade where many businesses have gone to the wall because of the high interest rates and inflation levels forced upon us. This is a massive step to take, and one that could ultimately determine the success and future of the company. Naturally I worry that everything has to be just right.

Jenny doesn't see it that way. She's not capable of understanding, and to avoid her progressive level of moaning, I've started to stay away from home more frequently. She has no need to moan or worry, but she does and much of what she whinges over is of little consequence; like whether or not the hole the builders have dug is in the right place, and if it is, is it deep enough for what they're doing?

Jenny is driving me to distraction, and to appease her I have set up a weekly, Monday morning, site meeting with Mac to sort out potential problems. I needed a builder I could trust because before I engaged Mac's services I knew I was going to be away on business a lot, and I was incredibly selective when choosing Mac's company to do this work. That's why this folly is costing me way more than I could have got away with. Jenny doesn't understand that.

Frankly, I could do without this unnecessary time being wasted, because I am a very, very busy man. My time is not dedicated to the Great Malvern project alone, or my personal building project. The Saundersby office is busy and I'm hands on, right up to my elbows, and with Graham away, I have his workload to oversee as well as my own caseload. I charge my clients good money for my time, and they deserve a good service in return. I pride myself on that. It's what I built my business on and it's very important to me to deliver the very best service.

With favourable weather conditions on his side, Mac has done well in the first couple of weeks. His gang of burly builders have worked hard and, contending with the limited space down the side of my house restricting mechanical assistance, they have completed the digging for the pool. What pleases me most is seeing all the footings for the house extension completed ahead of schedule. Yet Jenny moans, despite my site meetings with Mac.

She is really trying my patience, and distracting me from the more important issues. I'm seeing a side of her I don't much care for and I'm beginning to question our relationship. This extension is for her and yet she isn't content with the progress Mac is making. The more Jenny stamps her feet, throwing her tantrums, the more I withdraw.

The pressures of work are building, and I need Jenny to be on my side to help me through this period. The way things are going presently between us, I'm predicting that we are heading for a major conflict.

Friday, 16 October 1987

I've had the best drive back from Great Malvern since the chore began. Traffic was light and my journey home wasn't delayed by one single traffic snarl-up. Listening to the news on the car radio as I drove back into Wales, it seems that there could be a knock on effect from the so-called storm last night. It appears that the south and southeast of England was hit by a hurricane during the early hours, which has brought southern England to a virtual stand still by fallen trees and power cuts. It was a little gusty at times last night in Great Malvern but not strong enough to cause damage. Checking in with head office before I set off, thankfully, the storm missed us in south Wales. I shudder to think how long that could have set Mac back.

Arriving back at the office right on lunchtime, I talk Richard into buying me a pint in our daytime local on the other side of the harbour from the office while I update him on the progress.

Richard is twenty-nine. He is a tall, stocky man, muscular, not over weight, with short-cropped fair hair and a sun-bronzed complexion. He is powerfully built, and works out regularly in the gym at his club with the weights, keeping himself in tiptop condition to play his beloved rugby.

Richard is the most junior of the partners in my business and is an absolute wizard when it comes to electronics and surveillance techniques. His artistic flair was obvious from an early age, and his passion for photography blends nicely with his line of work. Unlike me, he is a patient man, except when he plays rugby - as I have witnessed - or has to deal with his mother. Richard is the son of my surrogate mother, Jan.

Our so-called daytime local is almost opposite the office and no more than a couple of minutes' walk away. Called the *Harbour Lights,* it is a typical tourist seafront haunt, catering for and ripping off the unsuspecting holidaymaker. Inside it is tacky, cheaply decorated, and cluttered with those nasty brass ornaments and fake first-addition books you see on sale in copious amounts at the flea market. Sadly, the bar prices don't reflect that, but there's a reasonable menu and the food is palatable.

Walking in through the main bar entrance I get a shock. Sat directly in my line of vision, at the far end of the bar, is Jenny. She's in the company of a guy called Tony Morris and they look very cosy. Richard sees what I see and drags me by the arm to the bar.

'What the hell is she playing at, Richard?' I say, venting my immediate anger on him.
Tony Morris is an old flame of Jenny's. She gave him the big heave-ho to be with me - or did she? It appears they may have been stringing me along all this time.

I have never liked Tony. Not because of Jenny, but because of what he is. A suave bigheaded man of twenty-four, he has the reputation locally of being a bit of a ladies' man, capable of charming the pants off any woman with his smooth talk and cheap jewellery. He is trouble with a capital 'T', the local jack the lad who wheels and deals, mainly deals, and is crafty with it. Tony has never done an honest day's work in his life. I go to confront them but Richard's superior strength, and technique for restraining a person stops me from making a fool of myself.

'He's not worth it. You know that. Now get that down your neck,' Richard says, placing a pint of bitter on the bar in front of me.

'What's she doing with that tosser?' Suddenly I don't fancy the pint Richard's bought me. 'Some other time, perhaps. If I stay here and drink that, I'll end up doing something stupid.'

I stay late in the office trying to catch up with my work. I'm fooling myself by hiding behind the pretence. The work can wait, but I know that the minute I walk through my front door and see Jenny sitting on the settee, drinking wine and watching television, we will argue. I no longer want her living in my house sharing my bed if she's messing around behind my back with Tony. On the other hand, for nothing more than selfish reasons, I don't want her to leave. I would miss the company. I don't know what to do for the best.

It's around eight o'clock when I open my front door. The TV is blaring away in the back room and I find Jenny sitting on the settee as predicted, glued to the box, with her feet up on the coffee table, drinking a large glass of white wine.

'You're late babe,' she murmurs, without taking her eyes off the set. 'Have a good trip?'

'I got back at lunchtime,' I inform her, which provokes movement on her behalf and she turns to look across the room at me with horror on her face. 'I called in to the *Harbour Lights* for a pint with Richard, but when I saw the clientele they let in these days I decided not to stay.' No sooner have I reached the open-plan kitchen area, than Jenny rushes in behind me.

'I can explain,' she says, nervously.

'I don't want to hear it.'

'It was nothing. You've been ignoring me recently and I wanted some company. Tony's just a friend.'

'You've been seeing him behind my back, haven't you?'

'No! That's not true. I would never do that to you. Tony and me were just having a quiet drink together that's all.'

'Are you still sleeping with him?'

'No!' Jenny screams at me.

'You looked very cosy together.'

'We were just talking, having a laugh. More than we've done for a while, that's for sure.'

'Oh, so now this is entirely my fault? Look around you, Jenny, what do you see? Take a good long look, will you, and then if you dare, ask yourself where all this comes from. If it helps, I'll tell you where it doesn't come from, and that is sitting in a pub with friends all day drinking alcohol and having a good old laugh. Work, Jenny, that's what I do, and working hard allows me to buy the things I want, and it pays the bills. I do that pretty well and if you don't like it, Jenny, you know where the door is.'

I've said my piece, got it off my chest, and conveyed my feelings. Slipping out of my jacket, I hang it over the back of a kitchen chair, open the fridge door and reach inside for a cold beer.

'I know what you do for me, and I love you for it. I don't want to leave you.'

'Then stay away from Tony!'

'Why can't you spend more time with me? I hate it when you're away and I get really lonely here on my own.'

I open my bottle of beer, lean back against the old work surface and take a long refreshing slug. I am jealous of what I saw at lunchtime and I'm sparring for an argument. It dawns on me as the cool beer hits the back of my throat, that Jenny is right. When we are together, we don't laugh and talk like I saw her doing in Tony's company.

'This isn't working, is it? You and me want different things from life.'

'Stop it, Nick, you're scaring me.'

Jenny walks over to where I'm stood, puts her arms around my waist, and pulls herself into my body, whispering into my ear as she does, that she loves me. I say nothing in return, because I can't return the compliment. There is something missing in our relationship. I've realised I don't love her, and after what I saw at lunchtime I'm not convinced she really loves me.

'Let's get married?'

I freeze at the thought, and her words send shivers down my spine. Marriage is not for me. I should push her away and tell her what I really think.

'We'll do it proper,' Jenny continues. 'Get engaged first. We could go into Swansea tomorrow and look at rings, if you like?'

'I'm working,' I tell her, which is crazy. Why don't I tell her the truth?

'You can miss one day, can't you?'

'I can't, it's important.'

Jenny lets go and steps away, pleading with me to change my mind.

'All my friends are getting married, I hate it when they show off their engagement rings and I can't.'

'Is that all marriage means to you, being able to flash a diamond under your friend's noses?'

'Of course not,' she snaps back at my suggestion. 'I love you, and I want us to get married.'

I figure that now is as good a time as any to tell her and place my left hand on her blushing cheek to comfort her while I deliver the crushing news. 'I like you a lot, you're a great girl, but I can't marry you. I can't give you what you want.'

'What do you mean by that?' she asks softly.

She has a right to know. This is going to be painful for her to hear and I have no wish to hurt her feelings, but I can't let this talk of us getting married carry on. I grab myself another beer from the fridge, pour Jenny a fresh glass of wine, and lead her by the hand through into the lounge.

'What is it, Nick?' she asks while I switch off the television.

'I should have told you this before now, but I really didn't think that we'd get so serious.' I warn her, joining her on the settee.

'You can't have kids, can you?' she says, raising her voice. 'You're infertile aren't you?'

'Just listen, for once in your life, please, Jenny.' I demand, and settle back into the settee making myself comfortable. 'When I was eighteen years old I made a large amount of money, virtually overnight. I made that money because I took risks, and I've been taking those self-same risks for almost eighteen years now. Out there, outside my front door there are a great number of persons extremely pissed off with me. Any one of those said persons, at any time, could be waiting around the next corner for me with just one thing on their mind: to take revenge. I live with that threat every day of my life and as far as practical, I take precautions. That relentless pressure comes with the job, and over the years, I've got used to it. You see, Jenny, getting married complicates that, and a complication of marriage is children.'

Jenny, I notice, sits perfectly still, staring at me; her eyes follow my hand while I take a drink from my bottle of beer. For once I don't think she knows what to say. 'If we got married and had kids, how could I step outside my front door knowing that there was a chance I wouldn't come back? I couldn't, and I can't live my life like that. I've given this a lot of thought over the years and I know I'll end up a lonely old man, but I made the decision not to get married eighteen years ago when I started up, and I'm going to stick by it!'

We sit in silence for what seems an eternity. I wish Jenny would say something, even if it were to tell me I'm wrong in my decision, and that life doesn't have to be like that. I think it's fair to say that had I thought differently, Jenny wouldn't be sat here with me now. Linda would.

'You don't love me do you?' Jenny asks nervously.

I shake my head. 'I'm sorry, Jenny. It's not that I don't, I can't let myself fall in love. I'm sorry, I've been very selfish, and I should have told you right from the start. I guess in a way, I'm already married.'

'Yes, to your bloody job!' she screams at me. 'How do you think that makes me feel? I hope you're proud of yourself. How can you be jealous of me and Tony after what you've just told me?'

'Because I do have feelings for you.'

'Like hell you do. I'm just a bit of fun, another notch on your bed post.'

'Not true, Jenny.'

'You bastard; how can you be so cold?'

What wine is left in her glass ends up in my face. No more than I deserve. In tears, Jenny runs off upstairs. I see little point in going after her. Instead, I head back into the kitchen for some paper towel to dry myself off.

Jenny has every right to be upset and angry with me. I shouldn't have let things go so far. I don't know why I let her move in with me in the first place. Perhaps I thought I had changed, or could change, and that I was ready to settle down. Clearly not. I'm not ready to. Now look what I've done, and all because I haven't the time, or perhaps the inclination, to make our relationship work. Jenny deserved better than that.

Despite a night of wild, passionate love-making, and what I took to be making up, Jenny surprised me this morning by packing her bags and leaving without saying goodbye. I am confused to say the least by her walking out like this, because she didn't have to leave.

I'm being very selfish as per normal, because I want her to stay here with me, albeit on my terms. Jenny wanted far more from our relationship than just being lovers, and I'm not prepared to give her that. Money, ambition and success drives me, and very little else in my life carries the same level of importance.

I'm not sure where to go from here, or what's best? Part of me wants to go after her and ask her to come back, but the greater part of me says no. I'll certainly not compromise myself and go down on bended knees; that will show an insurmountable level of weakness in my character and give Jenny a green light to push me into marriage.

I don't want to be on my own, that I know. I also don't want a house full of people getting under my feet and making unreasonable demands, especially the variety that sleeps all day and cries all night, shits in nappies, and pukes up on your clean shirt as you're on the way out to an important meeting.

I guess the least I should do is talk to her, but what would that achieve? I'm not going to change my mind. I don't love her enough to change my life for her - if I loved her at all! Callously, in a moment of denial, I consider offering her money so she can get herself straight, but with due consideration who will that make feel better about the situation: Jenny or me?

And what was last night all about? Was Jenny showing me what I would be missing if she left? Did she hope that by showing me it would persuade me to change my mind? Maybe she was right when she said that she was no more than another notch on my bedpost. I certainly didn't view our relationship that way, and if I did subconsciously think like that, I'd have to look very hard for another notch. Jenny is - was - my first real relationship, although she's not my first love, and even that's not strictly true because I don't think I've ever actually been in love with her.

I am very negative toward dealing with those things I don't want to deal with, that's why I like my line of work. I'm not being big-headed, but I'm good at what I do and it comes easy to me. Living in the fast lane with schedules to meet I've become very set in my ways, and being a single man for so long has made me incredibly insular. I've realised I don't like, and can't handle, the stress and upheaval that comes with the package of a personal relationship. I do like people being close, but not so close that they find it necessary to dictate to me, and that is exactly what I have allowed Jenny to do: get too close and try to dictate my life. I think if I'm honest, I saw Jenny as a 'girlfriend' that I slept with and who I enjoyed a social life with. I treated her like a business partner and not a lover, a housekeeper or a partner.

Monday, 19 October 1987

Looking up from reading a set of work- related notes I see Mac at the patio door. He knocks on the glass and beckons me over once he's attracted my attention. I've forgotten all about the builders after what's gone on, and all the time Jenny was here, I didn't have to worry about giving them access. Another problem to sort. My house is an extension to my office, and from time to time, I leave private paperwork lying around. I trust Mac, but I have files here that I don't want anyone to see.

Sliding back the old patio door and stepping outside to see what Mac wants, I think of Jenny again. Did I see her as a glorified home help? Is that what I really want?

Mac doesn't actually need access to the house for a few days, possibly longer if the weather holds, he says, so I will do what I've always done in times like this, and that's bury myself in my work. The only question I didn't ask Mac was why he felt the need to tell me. I can only assume he has spoken to Jenny.

I'm later than usual arriving at the office, but my morning routine is exactly the same as it always is. The only part of the office complex on the ground floor is the reception and waiting area. First stop of the morning is to collect my mail and chat to the lovely ladies who man the reception desk before I head on upstairs.

My office is directly above the reception area, and with windows on two sides facing south and east, respectively, I have the best all round view of the harbour and town. Who wouldn't want to come to work with views like this?

My private place of work is a mess, a shambles, a veritable mixture of discarded and vitally important paperwork, and a total disgrace. Sounds daft but I'm not proud of my untidy world, and I'm not as bad as this at home, housekeeper or not. By arrangement, the cleaners have long since stopped bothering to step inside. I have a workable system with them now. Only those items left outside in the corridor are to be thrown away as rubbish.

Dropping today's mail and newspapers onto the least congested spot on my desk, I turn straight around and walk down through the main office; it's a ritual I've carried out since the day I first employed someone. I like to be seen, and if anyone has a question to ask, and wants to talk to me on a work-related problem, then this is their chance to do so. To a first-timer, this may seem snobbish, aloof perhaps, but once I've started my day's work I don't like being disturbed by petty everyday matters. It can be frustrating and unnecessary in my opinion. They all know the routine, and generally it works very well.

Once I know they're happy, coffee is made in our small kitchenette and I return to my desk to flick through the papers and open my mail. Reading the morning papers is another of my daily tasks, and as old as the business itself. I buy every local, regional, and national paper available. I skip through them all, highlight anything I think that might generate business, passing leads onto whom I think needs to follow the stories up. In the early days - while living with Jan in the village - I did it all myself. It proved to be a very successful tool in the expansion of my business. Today, the same thing can be said. This simple daily task still generates around three percent of the annual gross income. Cold-calling, as it's affectionately called, is to me an upside down pyramid. Once you've hit the target it just goes on growing and growing. Hence the need for the office in Great Malvern.

My level of concentration is poor this morning. Jenny is on my mind and I should do the decent thing, and at least find out if she's all right. Jenny is a local girl, and has probably gone home to her parents, but I should find out. Her relationship with her father is strained, and although I've only heard her side of the story, she told me that they don't see eye to eye. I can relate to what she said about him and there's a chance she may not have gone home. However, thinking about the alternative is driving me to distraction.

Mac and his building works are playing on my mind too. I know he doesn't need access to the house just now, but if I ignore the problem for too long it will become a major issue. What I need is a house-sitter. With the business I'm in you would think that I could pluck someone off the shelf, dust them down and install them in my house as a minder this very day. I probably could, but it's knowing whom I can trust.

That person, like Mac and his builders, will have the freedom to roam inside my house amongst the potentially revealing and delicate paperwork I have lying around, and that is a problem.

The frustration of being left in the lurch is beginning to make me angry, and I'm looking to blame everyone else for the predicament I'm in. Let's face the facts here; this is Jenny's fault. She wanted the extension work done. Personally I was more than happy with the way things were, but in the end, it was her interference in what we'd embarked on that was the cause of the friction between us. Her walking out has left me with a huge logistical and financial headache.

Checking my messages and mentally noting that nothing is urgent - or at least can it wait until later, probably much later - I convince myself that I'll be better off out of the office doing something constructive.

I drive around the coast the short distance to the village - as I often do when I'm feeling this low - for a quiet chat with Jan and a chance to catch up with the local gossip. As much as the shop drove me mad, I liked the camaraderie it provided. This morning I have another reason for being here.

When I first arrived in South Wales, I lived with Jan and Richard for two and a half years in the small flat above her shop, post office, and later, her coffee shop. I moved out when the adorable white witch, Beth Rhys, put the flat of my dreams on the market and promised me first refusal. I've often wondered what she actually meant by first refusal, but I got the flat all the same. That seafront apartment overlooking the bay in Saundersby was my home for twelve wonderful years.

Living with Jan in the village was a special period in my life. I grew up there, became a man. While we strove to reconstruct our personal lives and rebuild her business, the pair of us became very close friends. She became my surrogate mother, a real friend, and I hold her very dear to my heart.

Jan sold the old post office in 1982 and we shed a few tears together over its passing. That was a sad day for all of us, but Jan could no longer cope with the shop by herself. With the proceeds from the sale, Jan bought a small two-bedroom bungalow in the same village. The dutiful son Richard takes good care of his mother and still classes her home as his. Retired now, Jan can always do with some extra cash in her purse. That's why I'm here.

Jan is in her late fifties now. A stern looking woman - much as we all remember our first schoolmistress to be - she's tall with it. Her rounded face and piercing eyes for most part cannot hide her mood, and I've learnt the hard way what to say to her, and how to say it before she speaks; but we have a terrific understanding and I can get away with more than most.

As is normal, Jan is pleased to see me, and soon we're sat in her lounge, which looks down across the beach, chatting, drinking coffee, and eating chocolate digestive biscuits.

'I have a favour to ask of you,' I say, while watching the biscuit crumbs loop through the air from my untimely and embarrassing spitting contest.

'I thought you might have. You only come to see me these days when you want something,' she replies, noting the exact spot the crumbs landed.

'You know that's not true,' I reply, fudging the truth.

'So what's this favour you want me to do?'

'I might as well tell you now before Richard does. Jenny left me on Saturday morning.'

'I'm sorry to hear that, love. I've said to Richard on numerous occasions that she wasn't right for you. Perhaps it's for the best in the long run.'

Why don't you tell it like it is, Jan, I want to say, but then she's always been like that, outspoken, and not one to hold back on expressing what she's thinking. At least one knows where one stands with her.

'She hasn't run off with all your money has she?' Jan asks with some concern. 'I wouldn't put it past her… That's it; you're after a loan.'

'No, nothing as serious as that. Jenny wanted to get married and have kids, and you know my feelings on that score. Simple as that really.'

Jan is aware of my feelings. We've discussed the subject of marriage on many occasions, mainly because of Linda, and she doesn't hold with my views, but she does understand my reasons. We certainly don't need to open the subject up again and discuss the matter further.

'Jan, as you know I've got the builders in, and I don't trust them enough to let them have a free run of the house when I'm not there....'

'And you'd like to ask me to baby sit the house for you?' She butts in.

'There are no flies on you. I'll pay you for your time of course.'

'You know you don't need too,' she says, half-heartily.

'Oh, I think I might. There's about five months of work left, and most of that is inside the house now.'

I've lit the fuse for her and sit back to see what she comes up with. Five months is a long time to make the daily trek from her house to mine. It's almost exclusively through the dark miserable days of winter and quite a commitment to make.

'Heavens above! What on earth are you having done? Knocking the place down and starting again?'

'You'd have thought so with the amount it's costing me. So what do you think?'

'I don't know, love. For a start my car isn't all that reliable.'

Nice one, Jan, and she has the cheek to worry whether Jenny has ripped me off.

'Some mornings it just won't start. It's not good in the damp, my mechanic tells me. Well, it is nine years old now,' she adds.

She can stop now. I've got the message.

'That could be a problem for you, couldn't it?' I suggest, playing along with her little game. 'Being there early to let the builders in while I'm away is important. Never mind, I thought I'd ask you first. Doesn't matter; if you can't help me out I'm sure I'll find someone.'

'I could borrow Richard's car.' Jan suggests with renewed interest, knowing full well that it's a company car and Richard needs it.

'Richard is very busy, and with Graham away in Great Malvern for a couple of months he's going to get a lot busier,' I inform her, cutting the ropes on her sail.

Jan offers me a cigarette. She started smoking again seventeen years ago when I turned up, and she blames me for encouraging her every time she coughs. She says it's her one and only vice. Jan conveniently forgets whom she's trying to convince. I've seen the white wine flowing on many an occasion.

'Five months did you say?'

I nod my head in response while Jan offers me a light for my cigarette.

'Every day for five months could cost you a pretty packet,' Jan states as she winds herself up to the big finish.

'It may not be every day. I'll only need someone there when the builders want to get into the house. Whoever takes the job on will need to be flexible,' I respond, taking the wind out of her sail again. 'What if I were to put you on the company payroll? I can then justify buying a company car for you,' I suggest, putting her out of her misery. 'Nothing very special mind.'

'That's sweet of you. I was sitting here thinking of ways around this, but I never thought of that!' Like hell she didn't!

'What will happen to the car when the work is finished? Will you take it away?'

'We'll write if off to tax. The car will be yours to keep.'

'Oh, that's wonderful! A new car; thank you so much,' Jan says excitedly and then pauses for a moment while she takes a sip of her coffee.

I can tell by the look on her face that she's not quite finished.

'How much will you be paying me for this house-sitting?'

Despite the cost, I'm pleased to have Jan on board. I know I can trust Jan and she will have my best interests at heart. She will moan about the state the house is in and the way I live, but that's nothing new to me. She will describe every brick they've laid, and every hole they've dug. I can stomach that because she won't be ringing me up at work every five minutes.

On the way back to the office, I swing by Jenny's parents' place. They haven't seen or heard from her and they weren't aware that we'd split up. Strangely, I'm not surprised by what they've told me because I've had my suspicions. I suppose that's why I've called into the *Harbour Lights* public house.

Jenny and Tony are sat in exactly the same spot they were in on Friday lunchtime, laughing and joking in much the same way as I'd seen them. Jenny hasn't wasted any time in moving on - or is that backwards? In my opinion, it is. I can't be jealous or cross with her now, all I feel is pity toward her. If she thinks she's happy then who am I to say she's not, and why should I worry? I just wonder if she really knows what she's getting herself into?

While downing a quick pint of best, they parade themselves - for my benefit, no doubt - as the happy couple. If they think I am jealous of what they have then they are wrong. They are welcome to one another and I hope they'll be happy together, even if it is only for an hour.

Chapter two

Thursday, 14 January 1988

Sitting amidst the debris of what was once my small, but perfectly formed, kitchen, eating the cooked breakfast Jan has prepared, she brings the morning post through and drops it down on the table in front of me.

Jan is in my home virtually full-time because Mac and his lads are way ahead of schedule. There are no more 'just holes in the ground'. The exterior brickwork is finished and the roof is on. The extension is dry and Mac is in the process of breaking through into the main house ready for the final push.

Amongst the normal amount of junk mail, one particular, white, glossy envelope stands out. Eager to see what's inside, I open it up first.

'They know what they can do with that!' I say out loud, in disgust. Jan is standing where all women should be stood, and that's at the sink washing and drying the dishes, listening to me impassively while I rant and rave. 'They've only sent me an invitation to their bloody wedding,' I snap, waving the invite around in front of me before slinging it across the table.

'Who are they?'

'Jenny and Tony; who do you think?'

'It obviously bothers you?'

Shovelling the last mouthful of breakfast down my throat, I rise to my feet and take my empty plate over to Jan so she can wash it up. Under the circumstances, it's the least I can do.

'No, for your information, it doesn't bother me. What I fail to understand is why they've included me on their guest list. Why should I want to celebrate them getting married?'

'Would you have been cross if they hadn't invited you?'

'I would have preferred it if they hadn't, and to be honest, I'd rather have not known. What they do together from here on in is none of my business.'

I slide my empty plate into the soapy dishwater in the sink. Jesus, Jan uses a lot of washing up liquid. I miss my old dishwasher, although Jan's doing a good job on a temporary basis. It's so much easier to press a button.

'I take it you're not going then?' Jan adds.

'Not a chance!' I reply. 'I'm way too busy, anyway.'

'When is the big day,' Jan asks, passing me the tea towel? I think that's what you call it.

'Two weeks. Saturday, 30th January at midday. Why do you ask?'

'Aren't you just a little bit curious to know why they're getting married?'

'What exactly do you mean by that?' I demand, staring at her, because that is a very strange comment to make.

Jan takes the tea towel from me, dries her hands, and switches on the electric kettle.

'If there's something you're not telling me, Jan, you know you might as well spill the beans because I'll find out, anyway, from somebody else.'

'Me and my big mouth,' she sighs. 'There's a rumour going around that Jenny is pregnant. And it is only a rumour.'

'Why should that bother me?' I respond, hoping she will elaborate on what she has just told me, but as those words leave my mouth, I think of Jenny and our last night together. *No, don't go there Nicholas*, I say to myself. That was three months ago and Jenny would have told me. Oh, Jan! What have you done?

I try to convince myself that this is nothing more than pure coincidence, and that what I now fear to be true is all in my mind. Jenny left me and moved straight in with Tony, so anything's possible. *Exactly, Nicholas!* Anything is possible, but Jan has sown the seeds of doubt in my mind.

Surely they wouldn't be that cruel, inviting me to their wedding and gloating over their happy news?

I'm being paranoid, and considering my views on fatherhood, do I really want to know if this baby is mine? Sometimes questions are best left unanswered.

What would I do if Jenny told me the baby is mine? To satisfy the situation I'd have to completely change my life-style. I don't want to, that's where the problem stems from. I certainly don't want kids, or to get married, but if the baby is mine, do I really want Tony Morris bringing it up, surrounded by his crime-riddled life-style? Talk about a Catch-22 situation!

How can I satisfy myself that the child she's allegedly carrying is Tony's, and not mine?

'Sorry,' Jan says, interrupting my thoughts. 'I shouldn't have said anything to you.'

'I'd have found out sooner or later if it's true. It's easier coming from you.'

'I'm not suggesting for one minute that this baby is yours, but I detect by your reaction that you have your doubts.'

'As far as I'm concerned, the baby Jenny is carrying is Tony's. Good luck to the pair of them, I say. They'll need it…especially Jenny.'

I'm putting on an act in front of Jan. This is far from over, and I will find out who is the father of Jenny's baby…with or without her help!

Richard is working hard at expanding his side of the company's business. He is making steady progress into the visual and electronic aspect of personal security to the rich and famous. Richard has a good hand-picked team around him - many of whom we, as a company, headhunted to land their services - and their drive and expertise is beginning to pay dividends. Generally, I let him do his own thing because I trust his judgement. When it comes down to things technical I'm way behind Mr. Average. I simply don't understand the jargon, and as long as Richard makes money, I don't need to understand.

This morning, though, he's asked me to go with him to meet a very wealthy potential client. After my conversation with Jan about Jenny earlier today, I'm not at the races, and I could do without the added pressure of selling our business, but a promise is a promise.

Once at the office, I go through my usual routine and retire to my office with a cup of coffee to scan through the papers while I wait for Richard. An advert in the back pages of the local newspaper catches my eye, and intrigues me. 'Find out who you really are…'it starts. 'Could you live and survive off the land if you had to…?' the advert continues as the print becomes smaller 'Do you have what it takes to become the complete person?'

For some unknown reason, the advert fascinates me. Why it should is beyond me. Perhaps it's because I think I have a need to rediscover myself. I am under a lot of pressure at the moment, both personally and professionally, and anything to boost my flagging morale can only be good for me.

I've always led from the front, that's what I'm good at, and the last thing I want is my lack of enthusiasm to rub off and influence those around me. I fold the paper in half and stuff it into my already crammed desk drawer, with all the other 'I'll look at that again' items.

We've got to be in the Ross-on-Wye area by two o'clock. From our base in Saundersby, it isn't one of the easiest journeys to make, and unless Richard pulls his finger out, pretty smartish, we'll not make it on time. In the future the new Great Malvern office will cover that area but Graham is having huge problems employing the right staff, and much to my annoyance, we're nowhere near completion.

We're already two weeks behind our opening deadline - that includes the building work - and I'm beginning to think that this venture is a bridge too far. I should be more involved. I had a lot of faith in Graham delivering the goods but the facts are there to see. It's not happening, and the longer he's away from his desk here in Saundersby, the more pressure there is on me. Ideally, we should change places. Graham would jump at the chance because his wife is becoming very vocal about his continued absence, and she's unhappy that there's no end in sight. She's blissfully unaware that she's not the only one.

I have the builders to worry about and it's not practical for me to be away right now. Apparently - as Richard pointed out recently - any excuse is good enough for me not to do something, lately. People are noticing a change in me and that's not good. That's worrying. On top of all that, I now have Jenny to worry about.

I drive, allowing Richard to brush up on his notes for the meeting. The fact that he's a terrible driver has a huge bearing on that decision. Not as bad as his mother, but he runs her a close second. Richard's map reading also comes into question. He manages to get us temporarily lost in the country before gleefully announcing that we've arrived, which has me asking him if he'd taken down the address correctly. What we're looking at doesn't belong to the landed gentry; it belongs to the nobility! The Queen would be proud to own a place like this. It's not in the same class as Buckingham Palace, but what I'm casting my gaze upon would put Sandringham and Balmoral in the shade.

A frail old man, who looks to be in his early eighties, stops us at the gatehouse while he verifies our appointment. Whilst he picks up the phone, no doubt to call through to the main house, I stroll a few paces along the gravel drive toward the house and pause to look across the open countryside at the imposing view of the palace. Most country houses of this stature are owned and run by a trust of some nature these days, but to be looking at one still in private hands, and at first glance in such fine condition, is quite remarkable. The old man soon gives us the nod to proceed at an absurdly cautious maximum of 10mph. We're expected, he informs us. At his recommended speed the drive from the gatehouse down the gentle slope to the main house takes us a full five minutes to complete. Words fail me.

I'm gob-smacked, genuinely speechless, and sit in the car for a few moments staring at the grandeur that surrounds me. Even the granite stairway, which leads up to the pillared and arched entrance is magnificent.

I have a passion for old houses. My dream is to one day own a country home of stature. Not on this scale, this is way out of my league. Through my interest, I know without being told, that the original building is Elizabethan, and similar in its look and layout to Longleat House. The honey coloured, Cotswold limestone frontage must be at least fifty yards in length, and with it's castellation of capping stones topping the construction it's clear the original owner built this house as a statement of strength and power.

Christ, when you live in a place like this you know you've arrived.

'Do you think we should use the tradesman's entrance?' Richard gulps in awe.

Slowly ascending the steps past the two ferocious-looking weathered stone lions - sitting proudly on pillars either side of the stairway, loyally guarding their master's castle - I've forgotten why we're here.

'Remind me, Richard; what are you and I doing in a place like this?'

'I had a call from their secretary a couple of days ago. She was a bit vague over the phone but she mentioned a security contract for some sort of highbrow bash they're planning to hold. She gave me the impression, when we spoke, that a more permanent deal was up for negotiation. This could turn out to be a nice little earner if we play our cards right.'

'You can do the talking; I'll just sit and observe, if you don't mind.' I tell Richard, and I'm not going to elaborate just now on why I'm taking a back seat, today. Richard doesn't need to know my head is a mess, and this is neither the time nor place to lose control. I have strong views, and in my experience, people from a wealthy background come with a superior attitude. Challenged, I may forget my place. 'I bet the butler earns more than I do.' I say, pressing the doorbell button.

While we wait, I continue my assessment. I'm bemused by the whole thing. Why would someone with this obvious wealth want to deal with a tin pot firm like mine? Perhaps that's a little unfair on Richard. His team have done sterling work in bringing the company thus far, but if I were the owner of a place like this, I would want to deal with an established, household name for important matters such as security. It's a peculiar attitude to have, knocking ones own company. However, where the security side of our business is concerned, we are in the fledgling stage of growth, and my main concern revolves around whether we have the necessary resources to fulfil, successfully, a contract of this magnitude. As a follow on to those thoughts, I find myself asking if we, as a company, have insurance policies large enough to cover ourselves in situations like this. I'd rather Richard didn't commit us today until I've had time to check, especially on our public liability policy.

The large oak door swings open. Again, we're told we are expected, and a young man of around twenty-five invites us inside. Smartly dressed in casual clothes - a light brown pair of chino trousers and a fawn coloured Ben Sherman shirt - he's not your classical vision of a butler. He leads us across the huge, tiled floor entrance hallway into the most enormous and magnificent reception room. My eyes don't know what to look at first. The paintings hanging from walls alone would buy my company three or four times over. Our potential client not only has money at his disposal, he has the class and style to match. Inviting us to make ourselves comfortable, the young man leaves us alone to peruse.

'Christ, Nick. Take a look at this place!' Richard blurts out. 'I bet there's not a single item in this entire room worth less than a grand.'

'Worrying isn't it?' I reply, slowly walking the length of the room, giving every item a wide berth, just in case.

I'm drawn to the beautiful, open, stone fireplace. It's not lit, and doesn't look as if it's used all that often. I've always longed for a real fireplace, but not one as big as this mother. Think of the cleaning! On reflection, I should have included one in the building works I'm having done. I can see myself relaxing at home on a cold winter's night in front of a roaring log fire – all by myself. Mulling it over in my mind to where I could fit one in, and how it would look, I decide to ask Mac when I see him next, about the possibility, before he progresses too far with the interior work.

The door behind us opens. When I hear the sound of stiletto heels on the wooden floor echoing around the large room I turn to see who is joining us. A tall, shapely, blond woman strides purposefully toward us across the highly polished wooden flooring.

'Good afternoon, gentlemen,' she says, in her well-heeled voice. 'Thank you for coming at such short notice.' She stops in front of me. 'Beautiful, isn't it?' she adds, referring to the fireplace I've been admiring. 'I'm Victoria Jackson. Please call me Vicki.' Vicki holds out her hand and without pausing for a breath she continues. 'You must be Richard?'

'I'm Richard,' my younger colleague butts in, hastily joining us by the fireplace. 'This...' he adds, referring to me whilst they shake hands, '…is Nick, a business colleague of mine and my driver for today.'

That's worth a response. In fairness, I have told him I'll take a back seat, and hopefully it will give Victoria confidence in Richard's ability to deliver the goods. While we seat ourselves, at Victoria's invitation, she questions Richard about whether or not I should be privy to this meeting. I look at him, daring to him to ask me to leave - he doesn't.

I like making character judgements on people the first time I meet them. In my experience, you can tell a lot about a person by the clothes they wear. Victoria is tall and slim, and, like the butler, she is wearing smart, but casual clothing. Work clothes with designer labels. Her white roll-neck jumper has a crisp appearance - new perhaps or rarely worn - and her black slacks hug her legs perfectly. She is pretty, not stunningly so, and there's a very distinctive sixties style about her hair. A Lulu or Cilla Black look. Victoria isn't the sort of woman that would turn my head for a second look, and she's wearing far too much make up for my liking. Tastefully done, but I've met numerous secretaries to powerful men over my working career and I think it cheapens them. Why pretend to be something you're not?

The huge, leather armchair folds itself around me as I sit back and eagerly await Victoria's reason for summoning us here today. For her part, she wastes little time.

'What are your views on blood sports, Richard?' Victoria asks.

'I don't hold a particular view,' he quickly responds.

'Do I gather from your answer that you're neither pro nor anti?'

'No. My answer depends on whether the person I'm working for is either pro-or-anti blood sports.'

'Very good. I like that attitude.'

Victoria reacts positively to Richard's quick response. By saying what he has, he's proved to her that he's flexible in his approach to matters, and will work to her specific requirements.

'My late husband, Sir Aubrey Jackson...'

Bang goes my theory of tarty looking secretaries, but it does explain the twenty-something butler.

'...did, for many years, before he so tragically passed away last summer, hold one of the country's largest fox hunts.'

My heart bleeds for her, left alone in all this poverty.

'Aubrey affectionately called his grand event the "March Hunt", that had a guest list likened to a Who's, Who. My wish is to continue with my late husband's tradition, but I have a problem - several to be exact.'

It beggars belief that a thirty-something, pretty, blond, rich girl can possibly have several problems. The hoards of eligible upper class gentry-type males must be falling over themselves in the stampede now she's single and available, and I bet she loves every minute of their attention.

'With the help of my estate manager, Joseph,' Victoria continues. 'I've brought the hunt forward to coincide with my birthday, which incidentally is the same date Aubrey I married on. I've scheduled the hunt to take place on Sunday 14 February in his memory.'

How thoughtful.

'Joseph and I, have kept the new date a closely guarded secret. My guest list, Richard, has many important and powerful dignitaries on it and they rather insist on their private lives not becoming public knowledge!'

Victoria scoffs, which instantly makes me want to vomit, thinking of all those toffs bragging over the latest millions they've made. I may have to change my attitude if Graham's last quarterly figures are correct. The company's annual turnover forecast for this year is expected to be in excess of three million pound. Very nice, of course, but heaven forbid that my company's financial success should turn me into someone from Victoria's background!

'Problem one,' Victoria goes on. 'Despite all our efforts, the date of the hunt has unfortunately become common knowledge. Our theory is that one of my own staff gave that information to the local newspaper. The press are having a field day with the information at my expense, and our proposed plan to hand deliver the official invitations tomorrow has been suspended until we find out who that staff member is. I'm taking that precaution because until I announce the date officially, the gossip the papers are spreading is no more than speculation.'

'Doesn't necessarily have to be someone on the inside,' I butt in. 'Where did you have the invitations printed?'

'Messrs Parker and Dobson, finest designers and printers in London, and very discrete. They wouldn't let me down.'

'I'm just wondering, here, how many people they have working for them, assuming, of course, that they actually do their own printing and that they don't sub-contract. Bearing that in mind, I would suggest you ask them, because if they do sub that work out, then any number of people could have seen the closely guarded date of your hunt.'

'Oh, dear,' Victoria sighs. Her mood rapidly changes from a positive lively one to a negative dour one. 'I hadn't considered that possibility.'

Serves you right, you stuck up cow, I think.

Realising I've overstepped the mark; I look to Richard for continuation. I had promised to keep quiet and just observe. I've already poked my nose in where I shouldn't and I sense tension brewing between Victoria and myself.

'Nick's only trying to make you aware of all the possibilities here, and that not everything we see is black and white. If you hire us, Victoria, we can look into that. 'Now...' Richard adds, 'you said you had several reasons for asking us here today.'

'Quite! I have a problem with my new neighbour and this could be connected to the date of the hunt being leaked. When I say to you, he's my new neighbour, that isn't correct. He has in fact lived in the cottage adjoining my land for nearly two years now. The gentleman in question is an anti blood sport protester, and in the short time he's lived next door, he has managed to become the leader of the local hunt saboteurs. He's an obnoxious man, pig-headed and very arrogant and I don't much care for him, or, I might add, what he stands for. He can be a real charmer when he wants to achieve his goal, and a very convincing man, especially when it comes to, how should I put it, the less educated.'

'That's a personal opinion, Victoria, and not a fact.' I comment, getting myself involved, again. 'Why don't we stick to the facts?' I deserve the look of horror Richard throws in my direction. Victoria reacts angrily, verbally blasting my questioning her.

'Let me make things quite clear to you, Nick! When I have to drive out of the area to shop and fill my car up with petrol because the local community won't attend to my needs, that's when I know I'm right. The simple truth is, he has turned my community against me and I live in constant fear of what they might get up to next. Please don't suggest otherwise to me.'

Suitably put into my place, Richard jumps in and tries to rescue the deteriorating situation between Victoria and myself. Fact is, I don't like her, or what she represents. There are always two sides to a story and when the feelings are running high, and fox hunting is an emotive subject, I want to hear both sides of the argument before making a judgement.

'What exactly is it you want from us, Victoria?' Richard asks. 'And as a passing interest, what is the name of your neighbour?'

'His name is Reginald Moss.'

I know that name and immediately look across at Richard who has the same frowning, memory-searching look about him. Not a recent connection, but a name from the past and rather annoyingly I can't immediately place him to anything. Victoria is so far up her own rectum that she doesn't notice our momentary deviation, and continues with her pitiful, hard-done-by bleating.

'I've heard some disturbing rumours about this ghastly man, and I'm making it my public duty to name and shame him. Put simply, Richard, I want you to dig up as much dirt as you can on Reginald Moss, and get him out of my life, once and for all.'

'Why, and for what purpose?' Richard asks.

'To discredit him; to show the local community what sort of man he really is, and that they shouldn't trust him. I want him hung out to dry,' she adds with venomous feeling.

Now it's my turn to ask. 'Why? So life can return to the way you want it to be?'

'And what is wrong with that?' Victoria snaps.

'You're no better than he is, dictating your own views and principles to ordinary decent folk.'

'How do you justify that statement? This is country life. All I'm doing is protecting the age-old right of country people to control the pests by hunting. Reginald Moss has no right telling me what I can and cannot do on my own land. Without people like me, investing millions of pounds in this countryside, thousands of ordinary people would suffer great hardships. Unless they travelled great distances, they wouldn't have work to go to. They certainly wouldn't have suitable housing to live in, and they would go without food on the table. Would you like me to go on?'

'That won't be necessary, Victoria, I think Richard and I know where we stand. I am concerned, though, that you believe it's all right for you to impose your lifestyle, opinions, and rules on the ordinary person, but its not all right for someone like Reginald Moss.'

'Good God, Nick! I'm talking about the freedom to hunt when I like, and as often as I like. Hunting is a born right, and man has hunted to feed his family since time began. What we are doing is making sure those basic survival skills are not lost, and by doing so keeping a country tradition alive.'

'Victoria, when my ancestors decided not to climb trees, they didn't have such luxuries as butcher shops and supermarkets, and I understand why they did what they had to do in order to survive. I don't know how your personal circumstances affect the way you live because we clearly live in separate worlds, but I find trotting along to the local corner shop far more convenient than running across a field, up to my arse in mud, to get something to eat. And strange as this may sound, I've never seen fox on sale in my local supermarket.'

'Now you're being ridiculous! Hunting is a right, and as a landowner I'm exercising that right.'

'Look, this is getting us nowhere,' Richard butts in. 'Perhaps it would be a good idea, Nick, if you wait outside while Victoria and I finish off.'

His suggestive, raised eyebrow look at me makes me realise that I've over stepped the mark - again. Fox hunting is an emotive topic and there are a great number of people, from all walks of life, against the barbaric slaughter of innocent animals. Particularly fox hunting. I allowed myself to become personally involved and in my position, I should know better. Supposedly, I am a professional man, and personality clashes should not influence my thinking and decision-making.

On my way out, I pause in front of Victoria. 'Everyone is entitled to an opinion, Victoria. They call it democracy.'

Had Victoria Jackson not mentioned the name Reginald Moss, I would tell Richard to forget the whole deal. I have never knowingly involved myself, or the company, for that matter, in personal vendettas, and my heated discussion with Victoria has led me to believe that this is the case here. What she had said in front of me was all hearsay, her side of the story, and she failed to come up with one shred of evidence to suggest that Reginald Moss was doing anything wrong. It is, however, his connection to the past that interests me.

I've let Richard down badly. Actually, it was a pretty good effort without really trying too hard. When I left that room to stroll up and down outside, chain smoking as I did, I left him with a mountain to climb. Richard has little chance of redeeming the situation, and if by sheer fluke he does, he will have little room in which to negotiate a sensible contract.

Our silent journey home gives me time to reflect on today's events. A day that started badly when Jan told me about Jenny, rapidly went down hill from that point onwards.

Richard is extremely cross with me. From the few words he did utter before falling asleep in the car - and subject to further discussion - I gather he secured a contract with Victoria. I'm over the moon at the prospect of working with, and seeing, the delightful Victoria, again. Strangely, Victoria and her problems are not uppermost in my thoughts, nor for the moment are Jenny and her alleged pregnancy, or Mac and the building works. It is the advert I'd seen in the local paper this morning causing the most concern. Something about it doesn't sit comfortably in my mind.

Dropping Richard off to collect his car from outside the office, the only words of note we exchange as we go our separate ways are, 'we'll talk about this in the morning'. While I'm here, I decide to go into the office and take another look at the bloody advert I'd seen. I know if I don't do this now, I will end up driving back down here in the middle of the night to satisfy my curiosity.

Much to my surprise, because it's well after 8 p.m., several of my employees are still hard at work. I like that, especially as they are all salaried. It shows a level of dedication.

Making my presence known, I make a coffee and retire to my office. I might as well be here working rather than moping about the house feeling sorry for myself, worrying about the building work and Jenny.

Done correctly, wading through all the papers takes time, but I wanted to carry out this exercise and make sure that the thoughts bugging me for most of the day are correct - and they are! The one un-answerable question I had nagging away has been answered – is the advert I saw in all of today's papers? It isn't and it only appears in our local, twice weekly rag, *The Advertiser* - why? From the thirty odd papers I've scanned through, that particular paper will have the lowest circulation. That is what bothers me. Why would someone spend that sort of money on an advert of that kind knowing the returns will be minimal? I doubt they will recover their costs.

Another small fact gives rise to my suspicions. We, as a company liase closely with the paper and often fill their pages with relevant and up-to-date news and gossip. Occasionally, I give them interviews, or factual statements on local issues to print, should they wish, and I have recently been quoted by them as saying that I was putting on weight and needed to work on my fitness level. Coincidence maybe, but I think the advert is aimed at me, and to allay my suspicions I'm tempted to find out.

The reply address is a box number, which immediately throws up the warning signs. I have desk full of names and addresses where past clients have used box numbers in good faith, and found themselves on the receiving end of fraud, or some sick prankster's idea of a joke; neither of which is a good enough reason to willingly place oneself at the mercy of an unknown source. My curiosity, however, far outweighs any dangers that may lurk behind the box number, and a simple, non-committal reply won't do any harm. I already know what I'm going to say: *Governor NTI awaits response.*

If the advert is aimed at me, they will know who I am, and they will know that the bold blue *NTI* lettering on the front of the office stands for *Nicholas Thompson Investigations*. Let's see what happens.

Friday, 15 January 1988.

Richard left a message on my answer phone last night asking, no, insisting I arrive at the office early this morning. He says we have an urgent need to discuss my crass behaviour yesterday. He sounded really hacked off, and after a night to think things over I know I was out of order yesterday. My own movements today dictate an early arrival and I'm on site way before the time Richard had suggested.

I turned the house over last night, going through all my old case files, searching for the name Reginald Moss. So far, I haven't come across what I'm looking for, so now it's a case of ploughing through the office archives to see if they'll reveal any secrets. I have no current recollection of why his name means something to me but I have a nagging feeling there is some un-finished business. Despite my repentant mood I'm not doing this on Victoria's behalf; I'm making it a work priority of my own.

The morning papers haven't arrived, which slightly alters my normal morning routine. A walk down through the office to the archives at the far end, though, is not an inconvenience.

Very quickly, it becomes painfully obvious that finding a particular file, without a scrap of information to hand, will take a long, long time. The filing system is in a mess. Although, the files are numbered, and should be in numerical order, they are not. No singular person is responsible, we all are. It seems that none of my staff has either the time or the inclination to put things away neatly behind them, and given the state of my own office, I can hardly moan about the condition of the archives.

Knowing where to start is pure guesswork. The lowest numbered section I've found is marked 61,000 to 61,500. On my desk, I have a file marked with the number 92,153. This could take me days, weeks even, and where, I wonder, are the files marked 1 to 60,999? Searching in this manner for a particular file is futile.

We have a system of bullet cards in the office for easy reference but this is client-based, and from recollection, I'm fairly sure Reginald Moss wasn't a client of *NTI*. The more I think about that name, the more certain I become that as a company we had no actual dealings with him. If that is the case, why does his name mean so much?

'We need to talk.'

Standing, holding the archive door open, Richard barks his words of wisdom in my ear. I could do with a break from this fruitless task, and make myself a coffee before joining Richard in his office.

His office is different in every way to mine. Clean and tidy with not a speck of dust visible to the naked eye, there's not a single thing out of place. Absolutely nothing, other than what is supposed to be in his office, is! His level of cleanliness is not normal for a man, and I feel obliged to remove my shoes before entering his office, it's that clean. What he needs is more work to fill his spare time.

'You were out of order yesterday. What was that all about?' He continues to bark while I draw up a chair and sit down on the opposite side of his desk.'

'I'm not sorry, Richard. People like Victoria Jackson live on the cusp of reality and they believe they're the superior race. She wound me up big time because I let her get under my skin.'

'Not good enough. The future of our business relies on clients like Victoria Jackson; clients with real money, money that pays our wages and our overheads. If that had been me yesterday, you would be crucifying me now.'

'We must sort the archives out; I'll never find what I'm looking for with it in that state,' I reply. 'There must be a better system on the market for storing information.'

'You don't give a shit, do you?'

'About Victoria Jackson? No.'

'Since when have we been in the position to turn clients away?' Richard asks with concern.

'Did we get the job? Not that I care, you understand.'

'No thanks to you; you know we did.'

'So where's the problem?'

'I don't have a problem, but I think you have. Do you want to talk about it?'

'Which one in particular, Richard? The Great Malvern office, or the lack of it? The fact that I'm weeks behind with my work and invoicing, or maybe the thousands of pounds I'm spending unnecessarily on my house, or could it be because Jenny is getting married to Tony and I've been told that she's pregnant, and who knows who the father is!'

Leaving him opened-mouthed, I return to my disorganised, lived-in office where one could play cards with the amount of messages I have left on my cluttered desk. It's high time I prioritised, but how the hell can one concentrate on work-related matters with all this other shit going on in one's life?

Richard appears in my office doorway. 'Why don't you take some time off?' he suggests.

'To do what exactly?' I ask him. 'Sit at home and worry about the work I've got sat on my desk? Look at this lot!' I say, waving a fist full of messages at him. 'And that's only two days' worth. I can't afford to take time off, Richard; what I need to do is work harder.'

'Let me take some of your work from you. I'm pretty busy myself but I can farm some of that work out to the guys,' Richard offers.

'What we need is for Graham to sort the fucking Great Malvern office out and get his arse back here. Not only is he driving me insane with his moaning about his wife, Melanie, moaning, I'm still doing all his work for him. If he put as much effort into staffing the place as he does his moaning, he would have been back in the fold weeks ago.'

Richard removes a number of dust-covered files from the leather chair opposite me, drops them on the floor, and sits himself down. 'The fact that Jenny's pregnant is really getting to you, isn't it?'

'Jenny's got nothing to do with the work load.'

'I'm not talking about your workload. You need to take a holiday, or the stress will kill you. How did you find out she's pregnant?'

I stare silent at him with a look of surprise gracing my haggard features. 'You are joking with me, aren't you?'

'No!'

'Well, for your information your mother told me, and you're now going to tell me you didn't know?'

'My mother told you?' Richard replies, sounding as surprised as I am that he didn't know. Something must cross his mind, because he laughs nervously. 'I know where she might have got that from,' he announces. 'Mum goes to the same WI as Jenny's mum. When you and Jenny were living together mum often came home with tales she'd been told about you two.'

'Charming! Is there no part of my life that's private?'

I think I already knew that, being constantly in the public eye has its drawbacks. Knowing that other folk are talking about you behind your back makes one feel vulnerable. I don't much care for that.

'Do you think the baby could be yours?' Richard probes. 'Is that what you're upset about?'

'The baby can't possibly be mine.' I respond, conveniently forgetting as I do the last night Jenny and I spent together. That last night was three months ago. I know that's a long time, but it brings into question how long has Jenny known, and why she hasn't opened her mouth before now? I think I have good reason to question the baby's parentage. Rising to my feet, I walk over to the window, and deep in my own thoughts, I gaze out over the harbour.

'Our relationship had been rocky for some time. We weren't…if you know what I mean?' I need to deflect Richard's interest; he'll bug me forever and a day if there's a merest hint that the baby could possibly be mine. I do have my doubts, but I will deal with the problem my way, without outside interference. 'Jenny and Tony are getting married two weeks from now. I think she's making a big mistake and I'm worried about her. That's all.'

Turning around to face back into the room, I park my backside on the narrow windowsill. 'I'm cross with her too, because I only agreed to the extension work being done to keep her quiet. When Mac's finished, I'll have a five- bedroom house, a twenty metre indoor swimming pool, a games room, and a huge garage for "his and hers" cars. A bit much for a single man, don't you think? I could live in one room, and I hate fucking housework!'

'It'll be worth it in the end, you'll see.'

'Will it?' I say, getting to my feet. 'Enough, hey? We've got work to do.'

'Let me take some of that work off you; at least until Graham comes back.' Richard asks again.

To be honest, it's worth considering under the circumstances. 'I'll have a look at what I've got on the go, and let you know. And thanks for listening.'

Our accounts lady is one of the old school. Maggie Davies likes to do things the proper way, by longhand. That's being disrespectful. Her office is the most modern and up to date, gadget-wise, in the building. Maggie, has at her fingertips, the one computer the company currently owns. She doesn't like it and what it stands for, but she is wise enough to recognise the advantages and tolerates its use.

I've sat with Maggie for over an hour - directly after talking to Richard - watching her working and seeing for myself the computer's capabilities. What we have is very basic, and after two years of use, the system has become dated.

Hearing and seeing the tape spinning back one way then the other would send me crazy after a while, but there is no doubt in my mind that these things will become an integral part of business in the future. I want it to do much more than just our accounts. I read somewhere recently that the development for networking systems is moving so fast that my idea for greater business use is not so far-fetched. For all I know, a usable system may already exist, and I wasn't aware because until very recently our business hasn't had the need. Wouldn't it be nice to simply type in a name and within seconds, have all the information you require displayed on a screen in front of you.

Hearing the name Reginald Moss has sparked off this urgent search. I've instructed Maggie to investigate and price the latest, most up-to-date office computer system currently available. I want to set the pace, enhance my capabilities, and be the first in my field to maximise the use of the new technology coming available. The money saved in time alone will give me the edge over my competitors. Just imagine the savings one could make if the office here in Saundersby could communicate from computer to computer directly, and instantly with the new office in Great Malvern.

I realise the initial costs could be prohibitive, but the long-term benefits are far more attractive. I'd rather type in a name and let the computer do the work than spend hours wading through dusty old files in a hot archive room.

Maggie used our time together well – ever the typical accountant, she moaned about our escalating running costs and lack of invoicing this quarter to cover them. I made it her job to point out the company's financial position and although not serious, I had to concede that she was right voicing her concerns. Our latest phone bill is horrendous, and over the last three months that cost alone has risen by a staggering twenty-five per cent. The Great Malvern office is the main cause of that huge rise, and communicating by computer in the future is becoming a far more attractive prospect. In the meantime, I've asked her to look into different phone tariffs to see where we can make some savings. I didn't dare mention to her that I've been looking at one of these newfangled mobile phone units. The phone's physical size puts me off - with its car sized battery to carry around - and I'm not sure I want to be at everyone's beck and call twenty-four hours a day.

I've managed to concentrate for the rest of the day, catching up on my work and completing almost three-quarters of my outstanding invoices ready for Maggie to process on Monday morning. I should stay on and make a start on Graham's invoicing to put the smile back on Maggie's face, but going home late last night to an empty house didn't solve my loneliness. I don't have someone waiting at home for me whether it's five o'clock or ten o'clock, and I've got to get used to that. Burying myself in my work doesn't alter that fact.

At dead on five o'clock, I clock off when everyone else does. It's Friday and I'm off down the pub a little later to meet the lads for a drink. Arriving downstairs on my way out, Sue, my secretary and company receptionist, calls me over to the main desk and holds out a faxed message for me to read.

'Does this mean anything to you?' she asks.

Taking the message from her I read the simple note: *Governor. KO. County.*

The message is a reply to the one I sent yesterday, and one I understand perfectly. I thank Sue, stuff the message into my trouser pocket, and step outside into the dark, cool evening air. One thing's for certain: whoever this is knows an awful lot about me.

Since Jenny left, instead of going shopping or whatever it was we did when we were together – which wasn't a lot - I've spent my Saturday afternoons watching football. To avoid the stick I would otherwise get from my friends, knowing I watch Haverfordwest County play, and the intrusions into my private life that may bring, I've not told a soul. No one knows about my Saturday afternoon excursions - or at least I thought not. Tomorrow, County are at home to Kidderminster Harriers in the fourth round of the Welsh Cup, and kick-off is at two o'clock. So somebody knows. That same person could be watching me, right now. That thought has me looking around but there's nothing to be gained by that, because I don't know if the person concerned is male or female. Will I go to the game tomorrow and find out? Of course I will!

Richard, Graham and I, along with several of our closest drinking pals, are well into a good, Friday night, drinking session when Reg Wallace finally puts in an appearance. Reg being late has become a regular thing, and so is a heavy Friday night session. After a long and sometimes difficult week, whenever possible we all meet up and unwind over a few beers. A week just like this one has been. To begin with, we made a pledge not to talk about work, but most Friday nights are now dedicated to just that.

Reg is always late, and the standing joke aimed in his direction suggests that he's not allowed out to play until his chores at home are finished. Reg is not under the thumb he's just fucking tight when it comes to spending money, and always times his entrance to perfection. If he's unlucky, he might have to buy one round. On a good night - for him – he'll get away with not standing a round at all. Strictly, that's not true; Reg does a lot of 'standing around'. Being an educated man, Reg uses the situation to his advantage, telling those who care to listen that their remarks are true. I know differently.

Reg is fast approaching the ripe old age of forty and really beginning to show his age. Once a stocky, powerfully built man of average height, his muscular build now bulges and sags in all the wrong places. His receding hairline, once neatly parted down the middle, is now a bloody three lane motorway across the crown of his skull, with enough room these days to add another three lanes - in both directions!

I like Reg, and over the years, we've become firm friends. At least once a week we play darts together for our local club, and as pairs partners we've not been beaten for nearly three years. When we play darts, Reg likes to drive, and to be honest I let him so I can have a drink. A long-standing and unwritten tradition says that the driver isn't expected to buy drinks - my point proven I think.

For several weeks now, Reg has tactically avoided questions concerning his fortieth birthday, citing the fact that it depresses him too much to even think about it, and he doesn't want to celebrate his coming of age by having a party. I tell him he's a tight-fisted, bald, fat old git! There's little point hiding the truth from him.

Last summer, when the board took the decision to expand, I asked Reg to join the company. To be fair on him, he did give my offer serious consideration, asked all the right questions as expected, and weighed up all the pros and cons available to him at the time. In the end, he made what he thought was the right decision for him, and that was to stay in the police force. On reflection, I now believe he made the right choice. Reg is very opinionated, strong-willed and likes having his own way. Sound familiar? Because of that, there's no doubt in my mind that we would have eventually clashed, and over something quite trivial, I expect. I value his friendship, and working together would have placed a strain on that friendship. It's also very useful having an Inspector in the local force as a personal friend; the very reason I join him at the bar when he's caught out, and forced to stand his corner! The man's in a cold sweat.

After exchanging the normal pleasantries, Reg brings up the subject of my house. I insist he doesn't go there, and assure him that I'm only at the bar to make sure he buys everyone a drink. I apologise to him for not being quick enough to catch the moths escaping from his wallet when he opened it in front of me. The time lock on the damned antique can't be working.

'Piss off,' he grunts. 'I always buy my fair share.'

I say nothing, but muse instead that it's high time he spent some of those frayed white fivers nestling neatly in his brown leather wallet before they really go out of date.

'What do you want?' he adds, checking his change carefully.

'What makes you think I want something?'

'How long have we known each other?' Reg asks in return.

Am I really being that obvious? 'Does the name Reginald Moss mean anything to you?'

Reg stares at me; he's thinking. I know he's thinking because he always grinds his teeth when he's thinking, although, in this particular case, it could be because he's parting with his money.

'No. Should I have reason to?' Reg responds.

'Possibly not. His name came up in conversation, the other day, and I thought I recognised it, that's all.'

'Means nothing to me, but I'll run it through the database on Monday if you like; see what it throws up,' he offers.

The information he has at his fingertips is one of the reasons I'm thankful he didn't join us when I gave him the opportunity. I hope to change all that soon with a system of my own, and not rely on his generosity, because despite our friendship, he isn't always this helpful.

Chapter Three

Saturday, 16 January 1988

Mac arrives early for work and I'm still in bed. Last night was an exceptionally heavy session - no thanks to Reg - and I'm not ready for my day, or the builders. The noise they're making outside my window forces the issue. Slowly easing myself out of bed to the sound of machinery starting up, I stagger downstairs, half awake, to open up the house and let Mac get on. In a brief conversation, Mac informs me he made a point of watching the weather forecast this morning, which he hinted wasn't favourable. I gather his aim is to complete the roof today before the expected wet and windy conditions sweep in and slow him up. Once the roof is on and the interior secure, he wants to start knocking through to the main house. The knock on effect of that means I've got to clear the spare bedrooms of my rubbish. Not what I wanted to be doing this morning, but in fairness to Mac, I promised to make a start weeks ago.

Having a large caffeine intake, with nicotine chasers, to get my morning underway, I struggle back upstairs and stand pondering over the task ahead. Box after box of paperwork lies stacked three-high in places, covering almost half the floor space of the second bedroom. How can one individual own, and be responsible for, so much rubbish? I haven't the time now to sort the paperwork out, and opt for the least brain-taxing method: physically transferring the mess from this room across the hall into my room.

It isn't long before last night's efforts catch up with me and I need a rest. Sitting on the edge of my bed, I use my time casually flicking through several files to see what's in them. I know what I'm hoping to find, but that's just wishful thinking.

A female voice, calling my name, stops me. Odd, I'm not expecting Jan, today. Curious, I wander back downstairs into the lounge at the rear of the house.

'Jenny, what are you doing here?' She's the last person I had expected to see.

'I got your message about collecting the rest of my stuff,' she informs me.

Not being totally with it, this morning, remembering that I bumped into Jenny's mother a few weeks ago, in town, and left a message with her for Jenny, takes a little time to register.

'I hope you don't mind me dropping in like this. Is it convenient?'

I don't respond, because I'm not interested in her idle chat. My gaze and thoughts, not surprisingly, are focused on her tummy, and it's not until she rubs her hand across her stomach and speaks again that I realise what I'm doing. 'You've heard my good news then?'

'Is it good news, Jenny? Is it what you really want?' I ask her, knowing full well that it's not my place to be doing this, but I just can't help myself with the doubt I carry.

'Tony and me are very excited with our news; it's what we both want.' Jenny informs me.

'Then, may I wish you the very best of luck, because, Jenny, you will need it!'

'Don't be like that. Please be happy for me.'

Rather foolishly, I dismiss Jenny and leave her to her own devices. I know the cow could get up to anything upstairs on her own, but for some reason I trust her to carry on and do what she came here to do. Perhaps that's because I'm not dealing very well with seeing her in my house. Since we split up, I've removed myself from the equation and thrown up the defensive barriers to protect myself. Like a fool, instead of asking her personal questions about the baby's parentage - as I should - I've clammed up.

Jenny is upstairs an hour or more sorting her stuff. Eventually, she appears back down in the lounge struggling with four black bin liners, full of her rubbish. Her arrival coincides with Mac appearing at the patio door to speak to me. Like a knight in shining armour, he offers to carry her stuff out to her car and my pregnant ex-girlfriend takes him up on his offer. Stopping by the patio door she tries to engage me in conversation.

'Will we be seeing you at the registry office?'

'I have no intention of coming. Sorry. If you find the time, pop a present list into the office, if you've got one.'

'If I'm passing I might,' she snaps at me, and turns to leave.

'Jenny?' I call out, stopping her. On the tip of my tongue is the all-important question I must ask before she leaves. I pause for a second while she stares at me. 'Good luck,' is all I manage to say.

Mac goes over his revised build plan with me, and providing the weather is reasonable, he forecasts that he'll be finished approximately three weeks ahead of the original schedule. That, in turn, means my stage payment dates will alter. The money is in place and paying Mac on time isn't the problem. He's asked me to start thinking about the internal décor - which is something Jenny would have done, had she stayed - and I really haven't the first idea how I want the finished article to look. There is an awful lot to consider. At this late stage, I think I'd be best advised to find myself an interior designer. Let someone else worry about the bloody colour schemes.

What with Jenny, then Mac making demands on my time, the morning has passed me by. It's past midday before I know it, and I need to quickly shower, change, and make my way down into town for lunch before driving over to Haverfordwest to watch the football.

At the top of the stairs, Jenny has left two black plastic bags - full of what is presumably her rubbish - for me to dispose of. One of the two bags leans awkwardly against the top banister. In her haste, Jenny hasn't tied off the tops of the bags and the contents are perilously close to spilling out down the staircase. Stopping at the top of the stairs to make things safe, my inquisitive nature has me looking inside. My heart misses a beat when I see three, thin, oblong boxes prescribed by her doctor and dispensed by the local chemist, lying on the top for all to see. I know what they are and none has been opened. Each box contains one month's course of medication. Someone had taken the time to neatly scribe the dispensary date on each box, 3 September 1987, and it doesn't look like Jenny's handwriting. Jenny had stopped taking the pill at least four months ago. To be pregnant now, she must have done at some stage.

This discovery - in my mind anyway - brings into question the parentage of her unborn child. I'm not that naïve to believe accidents don't happen, but I have tried to convince myself that in our case, one hadn't. In her own way - by leaving the boxes where she knew I'd find them - Jenny is telling me accidents don't happen. Why should she want me to know? What does Jenny want from me?

Finding the pills is not absolute proof of the baby being mine. Jenny may have had a number of valid reasons for not taking them, but what finding them here in my house has done, is to cast doubt in my mind. Doubt had prepared me to overlook the problem for the benefit of all concerned, which is why I didn't ask her the million-dollar question.

The bloody cow! She gambled on me looking into the bags, and she knew if I did, I'd find the boxes of unused contraceptive pills. What the fuck am I going to do about this?

I sit at the top of the stairs for a long time, clutching the three cartons, emotionally shattered and close to tears. My hurt slowly turns to anger. Jenny is getting her own back, and in her eyes probably no more than I deserve, but what a way to go about it!

I'm ready to confront her. I'm going to thrust the pills under her nose and ask her what the hell's going on? She and Tony are tying the knot two weeks from now and I deserve to know the truth before they take their vows. I doubt, however, if I approach this with her, that she will be honest with me. Considering what I have found in these bags, I guess she has told me; but why, and like this?

Parking at *Haverfordwest County FC* is limited, and I like to be early to claim my normal spot. I have an expectant apprehension about this afternoon, which has nothing to do with the football. Someone wants to meet me. That someone knows a great deal about me, and that is a little worrying. I want to place a face and name to the unknown person, so I know whom I'm dealing with, and establish the real reason behind why they've gone to all the trouble.

I see no reason to change my normal routine. Through the turnstile, I take a quick look at the condition of the playing surface, purchase a match program from the vendor, and head toward the snack bar for a coffee, and bacon roll, while I digest the latest club news. The one variation I am making to my normal match-day routine is to watch closely what is going on around me, and the people that involves.

The attendance today - because it's a Welsh Cup game - is expected to be above average, and Mac's concerns over the weather conditions appear justifiable, which may affect the number of paying customers through the turnstile. The day's weather has deteriorated into a steady period of rainfall – with worse to come according to the latest forecast – and that could reduce the expected bumper crowd to a good crowd. Games like this for Haverfordwest, against Kidderminster Harriers, are lifeline to clubs struggling to survive, and I hope the weather doesn't spoil it for them - or the game as a spectacle for us.

Maintaining my routine, I stand close to the snack bar until kick off - buying a second cup of coffee in the meantime - and study the passing faces. A larger than normal crowd today will hinder my attempts to identify those faces I don't recognise.

At this level of football, the away supporters - and therefore total strangers – are more usually few and far between. Attending on a regular basis as I have recently, one comes to recognise the other regular die-hard supporters. That will help, but I believe that unless this person steps forward, I will have very little chance of identifying my contact today.

The direction County are playing in the first half is determined by the toss of the referee's coin. Once decided, I walk around behind the goal they are attacking and join my old match-day buddies, Baz and Mal. They've repeatedly told me they are retired, and that they are both over the age of seventy, without being too specific. Baz and Mal are good, uncomplicated company who claim to have watched County play, both man and boy. Their combined knowledge of County's history is indisputable, and goes back to a time well before the beginning of the last world war. In fact, Baz has really dated himself by telling me that he remembers *Haverfordwest Athletic Football Club,* as they were then called, turning semi-professional. I gather that was in 1936, when they joined the Welsh Football league. That shows incredible loyalty to the football club, and it could be argued that after fifty years or more, watching week in, week out, between them, they must have bought the football club in entrance fees alone. The amount of money they've claimed to have spent across the bar in the clubhouse after every home game would probably pay the current players' wages for several seasons - or buy a player like Paul Gasgoine. I'd settle for a pound for every time I've heard them say, 'I remember when' and 'poof's game these days'. I'd be a rich man.

I think Baz is the older of the two men; he certainly looks it. Every game, without fail, he drifts into his favourite story about laces in footballs - usually as a result of a striker heading the ball incorrectly, and high and wide of the goal - adding for good measure that, that would have hurt in his day. The pair of them make me laugh with their dated comments. What I really like, is that there's no pressure watching the game with them, and as far as I know they don't know who I am - or what I do for a living. If they do, they've never said, and I'm not going to spoil an afternoon's enjoyment by volunteering that information.

With the score 0-0 at half time, Haverfordwest are more than holding their own in a keenly fought contest. Harrier's keeper, Paul Jones, has made several fine saves, which, in my opinion, has denied County a deserved halftime lead. With fifteen minutes to kill, I head off to the snack bar to buy the teas and coffee while Baz and Mal sprint down to the other end of the ground hoping to see the 'Bluebirds' score in the second half. I always buy the half-time refreshments, and despite their retrospective offers, I've never seen either of them with their hands in their pockets - let alone the colour of their money. I guess that's already behind the clubhouse bar. Buying the half-time teas and coffee doesn't actually bother me. After all is said and done, they are pensioners, although they both could just as easily be millionaires, on the quiet.

The chat in the queue at the snack bar - while I patiently wait my turn - is similar to that of Baz and Mal's: County are impressive and a touch unlucky, today. One man, just in front of me, has nothing to say. I haven't seen him before and he looks a little out of place at a football match. With half the game over without incident or contact of any sort, this man's general appearance gives rise to my suspicions.

Baz and Mal thank me for the drinks and dig ravenously into the bag of jam doughnuts I purchased at the same time. Taking a doughnut for myself before they all disappear, I turn to watch the teams re-emerge for the second half. Standing only feet away, to my right, is the guy I clocked in the snack bar queue. We lock stares and he speaks.

'First time I've seen Haverfordwest mate,' he says. 'Are they normally this good?'

His accent tells me he's not a local man; Midlands, probably, but not a Brummie. South of the city, I would guess. Ridiculous, why am I questioning his place of birth? The Bluebirds are playing Kidderminster Harriers!

'This season they have been,' I reply. 'I just hope they put one of their chances away this half, or they might live to regret it!'

Without being obvious, I take in what information I can about him as we exchange views on the game. He's about six-foot in height, stocky, with an athletic build. The bobble hat he sports partially hides his face, but his clean-shaven chin highlights a very prominent, powerful jaw. He's dressed in a waist length, black, leather jacket, Levi jeans, and what looks to be a Ben Sherman shirt - casual attire, but very smart. My initial assessment of him points me in the direction of the services, a military man; a practical man of simplicity. Two further minor observations of him compound my theory. On his feet he wears shoes, not trainers, and they are highly polished - to over-perfection. The second and more significant factor is the lack of identifiable baggage. He has an air of sophistication about him; a cool customer who enjoys earning and spending money. A mark of a person's status can be obvious by their attire, but more usually identified by the quality of jewellery they wear. This man has none of that self-gratifying extravagance - not even a wristwatch. An educated guess would place him in the SAS or SBS. My hunch is the SAS.

County concede half way through the second half; 1-0 down, my old mates, Baz and Mal, raise their game, shouting encouraging praise to the players at the top of their voices.

'That was against the run of play, governor,' the stranger turns and says to me.

In response, I light a cigarette, weighing up in the time it takes me whether or not that was a deliberate use of the word *governor*.

'You'll need to give that filthy habit up if you want to better yourself,' he adds.

'What do you want from me?' I ask, stepping a couple of paces toward him.

'Your help.'

'I would have thought, a man with your obvious background was more than capable of looking after himself, without anyone's help,' I suggest to him.

'I'm looking for a front man, someone the public knows, and someone who the public respects.'

'Why?'

'Not here,' he whispers.

'Then not at all,' I inform him, and add, 'because how do I know I can trust you?'

'You don't, Mr. Thompson, but I know you like earning money, and that's the carrot I need to get you interested.'

'Really?'

'I'm talking about earning money beyond your wildest dreams, here. You have a good business and a comfortable way of life. What I have to offer you will treble your earnings within a year.'

'Sorry, I'm not interested.'

'Why,' he asks?

'Because you strike me a desperate man. Why else would you come to a football match and offer me, a complete stranger, the chance to earn riches beyond my wildest dreams? And I don't know who you are, or anything about you.'

'For your information, the name's Brad. Give my offer some thought, Mr Thompson, because I can make you a very rich man. You know how to contact me,' he says, and casually walks away.

He's right; money does make me sit up and listen. Always has done and always will, but beyond my wildest dreams? What did he mean by that, and what would that involve?

As always, Baz and Mal invite me to join them in the clubhouse for an after match drink, and as always, I politely turn them down. One day I'll surprise them, and when that day comes, I'll make sure I'm carrying enough money. I'm going home, content in the knowledge that County gave a good account of themselves today, but annoyed because they lost - to an England-based football club playing in the Welsh FA Cup!

If I wasn't so busy, I might be tempted to join Baz and Mal and drown my sorrows, especially after the week I've had. Unlocking the door of my car and sliding into the driver's seat, I start thinking over what this Brad fella had to say. There's no doubt that curiosity has got the better of me. His suggestion of earning big bucks - money way beyond my wildest dreams - is, as he said, a big carrot, and cannot be totally dismissed. The green stuff is a passion of mine, it's what drives me, and I'm tempted to find out more; and I hate unanswered questions.

While I settle myself in for the drive home, my gaze falls upon the glove box in the front of the car. I'd put Jenny's surplus contraceptive pills in there before I left for football, fully intending to return them to her at the earliest convenient opportunity. I know that if I drive back to Saundersby in this mood, I'll seek her out and confront her over the baby - not a smart idea with Tony around. With that thought fresh in my mind, I turn and look at the football clubhouse. Bollocks! What the hell, you only live once.

Sunday, 17 January 1988

The sound of a phone ringing wakes me up. God, I feel awful this morning. Slowly coming to in response to the prolonged shrill of canned, bell ringing, I force my eyes open and become aware that my room has changed overnight while I've slept. This isn't my room! This isn't my house! Sitting bolt upright, I look around the room. Where the bloody hell am I?

That horrible, intermittent, penetrating noise stops as I scan the room for clues. Thank God for that, someone has at long last answered the phone. Who?

The curtains in the room are drawn but there's enough daylight seeping through the drapes to check the time on the working, alarm clock ticking away on the bedside cabinet. Bloody hell, it's half past ten. In that case, it must be Sunday morning. What the hell happened to Saturday night?

My trainers are sat neatly on the floor next to the bed, and my jacket hangs on the back of what looks to be an Edwardian style chair. Apart from that, nothing of mine appears to be out of place in this large bedroom - except me!

Dragging my weary body and heavy head out of bed, I slope across to the window and throw back the curtains. Hell, it's still raining. There isn't much to see through the glass apart from fields, hedgerows, and the bare, winter carcasses of trees; certainly nothing to give away my whereabouts. Wherever I am, it's very quiet.

Slipping into my trainers, I take my jacket off the back of the chair and head for the door. Beyond the bedroom door, a magnificent, dark stained, wooden-clad hallway greets me, leading to a similarly magnificent and stunning wide staircase. My mind is racing as I gingerly descend the stairs; actively trying to recall where I was last night, and whom I'd met. This is no ordinary house, and although I started out drinking with my two, old, retired mates, Baz and Mal, at the football club, I must have bumped into someone else - someone important.

At the bottom, the grace and splendour of the entrance hall reminds me of Victoria Jackson's place, only on a much smaller scale. Several piles of leaflets, neatly stacked on a small, half-round, wooden table attract my attention. They look like visitor guides, full of information.

Brock Manor, the very first one I pick up informs me. I know where I am now, but I still don't know how or why?

Instincts tell me to head toward the rear of the house to find the kitchen. A coffee intake is an absolute must in combating a thumping headache, and a mouth that is as dry as a kangaroo's jockstrap. Finding the kitchen is a task easily executed, but one that holds a surprising result. Sat at a large, wooden table, placed dead centre of the large, modern kitchen, is Mal.

'Wonderful'! he utters when he sees me, and rises from his seated position to greet me. 'I trust you slept well?'

I'm a little surprised to see him and that must show on my face.

'Fantastic night at the football club wasn't it?' he continues, heading for a jug of percolating coffee bubbling away on the side.

I wish I could remember last night.

'Come, come,' he adds, gesturing in my direction for me to sit down at the table. 'Make yourself comfortable. I'll pour you a coffee; then rustle you up some breakfast.'

I do exactly as I'm told while Mal attends to his promise.

'If you don't mind me saying,' he says, 'you seem a little surprised to see me?'

'I'm a little surprised by every thing I've seen this morning.'

'Ah, yes,' Mal starts, returning to the table with my coffee. 'You thought the two old men you watched football with were retired, old, farm hands, or something of that nature, I dare say.'

'To be honest, Mal, I've never given the matter much thought.'

'You haven't!' he replies, seemingly surprised by my admission. 'Even when we let you to buy the teas at every home game?'

'So, are you Lord of the manor, or just the hired help?' I ask him.

'You're the detective; what do you think?'

Reaching over and gently stirring two teaspoons of sugar into my coffee, I sink back into the high-backed chair. This weekend is turning out to be one I'd rather forget. Jenny's mum giving our secrets away is merely the tip of the iceberg. What with Brad knowing more than I want anyone to know, and now Mal disclosing his hand, it's becoming painfully obvious that no part of my life, private or not, is sacred. What's even more disturbing for me to learn is that people are making it their business to know.

'Someone has been doing their homework' I sigh.

'Surprised?'

'Disappointed, more.'

'Why? Because by doing a little research, your two old football mates have found out who you are?'

'I'd like to know why you felt you had the need to?'

'So, what's your professional opinion?' Mal asks, sitting down opposite me, avoiding my question. 'Am I lord of the manor, or just the hired help?'

'Rumour has it that Lord Brock is a recluse. Keeps himself locked away because he's mad.'

'Fact or fiction?' he asks.

I stare long and hard at him. 'Fiction,' I tell him.

'Based on what evidence?'

'Based on the fact that I'm sat talking rationally to him.'

'You're suggesting that I am Lord Brock?'

'Yes, but why you had to keep it a secret rather baffles me.'

'Why do you go to football, Nick?' Mal asks, slapping the palm of his hands down onto the table. 'Is it because you simply want to be yourself for a while, without all the pressures of everyday life?'

'That's exactly why I go to the football!'

'Then you will appreciate why I keep my identity secret. All the time people believe I'm mad and lock myself away, I have, in effect, total freedom. Being rich or famous has its drawbacks, and I take great care maintaining those splendid rumours one hears. Something you should pay more attention too. Being constantly in the public eye, like you are, makes you an easy target.'

'That's the nature of my work.'

'Nonsense, that's the way you like it. You see…' Mal adds, rising from the table and walking a few paces across the kitchen before opening a sideboard cupboard. Removing an A4 lever arch file he returns to the table. '…I know quite a lot about you.' Mal places the lever arch file down on the table so I can easily see the contents.

'How long have you known?' I ask?

'Several months. It was Baz who first recognised you, and it was he who came up with the idea.'

'What idea?'

'I write for a living. The money I earn from my writing helps to pay for the upkeep of this horrendous family heirloom; mainly stuff for the tourist industry, and books of historical interest on Wales. Baz, incidentally, is my publisher, and he suggested I wrote your biography. With your permission, that is. Like it or not, you are a fascinating character, and the research I've carried out on you makes splendid reading. Tastefully compiled, we're quietly confident that we have a potential best seller at our disposal. What do you think?' he asks, opening the lever arch file.

'Who the hell would want to read my life story?'

'You'd be surprised, and we'd pay you for your troubles. Strike a deal that suits both parties. Baz is good at what he does, and he wouldn't take a book on unless he knew he'd make money.'

'You're winding me up!'

'Why should I want to do that? I want to make money out of you, not alienate you. What do you say?' he adds excitedly.

In my delicate state, Mal is pushing me into making a decision. Those who know me well know that that is not a good idea. He obviously hasn't done his research thoroughly enough. I don't like pushy people. Door-to-door salesmen, for instance, don't stand a chance with me.

'How far are we from the football ground?' I ask, rising to my feet. 'I assume that's where my car is?' Mal looks at me in disbelief. I get the impression this hasn't gone the way they had predicted, and he and Baz wrongly assumed that I would jump at their offer. They don't know me at all.

'I'm sorry. I thought you'd be pleased with the idea.'

'I'm very disappointed in you, Mal. The fact that you only spoke to me at the football because you wanted to make money out of me really stinks. I'm not interested, and don't try to do this without my permission or you'll really find out what sort of person I am. I hope I'm making myself perfectly clear.'

Discovering that Mal only wanted to be my mate to make money out of me has really hit home. Watching football in good company without complications is one of the few pleasures I have, and he has taken that away from me. I feel let down and betrayed by him. Above all, I don't want my life story on the shelves of every good book shop for people to read!

By the time I reach home, the events of the past two days have wound me up like a tightly coiled spring, and I'm ready to explode. I'm so disappointed by this morning's development that it isn't measurable. I know I can't sit around the house all day on my own seething over Mal's disclosure; I will go mad, so despite the awful weather, I take the decision to freshen up and walk down into the town to get totally rat arsed.

Drinking alone at lunchtime is about as low as one can sink, but I stick to the task as if my life depends upon the challenge. The worsening weather gives me an excuse to stay. All the signs are there for me to see: working too much, drinking heavily and snapping at people for no good reason; the pressures of everyday life are affecting me, yet I chose to ignore the signs!

Chapter four

Monday, 18 January 1988

I'm broadening my horizons. I've noticed that my ability to upset people is becoming second nature. Jan is less than impressed by the fact I'm still in the house when she arrives to let the builders in, and as sure as eggs are eggs she lets me know her feelings in her own unique style.

I have a massive hangover from yesterday's over-indulgence, and a little sympathy here wouldn't go amiss. Not a chance, and because of my extra-curricular activity I'm unusually late for work. I don't care, but Jan wants me out from underneath her feet so she can crack on unhindered, and forcefully drags me to my own front door to get rid of me.

'I'm going, I'm going,' I tell her, if only to get away from her nagging voice.

There's no routine at the office this morning. The very moment I walk into the chaos, Sue intercepts my unsteady progress and drags me across to the reception desk. Men dressed in blue overalls are milling around, their tool kits, and materials, left unattended in the waiting area as if tomorrow will do. It's cold in here too, colder in fact, than it is outside. The wearing of extra layers of warm clothing in here is definitely the order of the day.

'I would have thought, that this plumbing work would be better done over a weekend,' Sue snaps at me, and I can't help but to agree with her.

What bloody plumbing work? I ask myself, looking at the mess. I have absolutely no recollection of ordering any work in the office, being undertaken. I apologise to Sue straight away and promise to investigate.

'I don't understand why we need extra radiators and a new boiler fitted. There was nothing wrong with the old system,' she adds.

'Where's Richard?' I ask her.

'Typically, on the one morning you're late, he left early to attend a meeting. I understand that he will be out for most of the day,' Sue informs me, which is one more thing I have no knowledge of, or have forgotten, perhaps.

'Where's he gone?'

'He has an eleven o'clock appointment with Victoria Jackson.'

Richard kept that quiet, but then I guess that's his prerogative.

Scanning the mess scattered around the normally quiet and tidy reception area, trying to make sense of what is happening, a familiar face beams a smile at me from across the other side of the room. Mal! Just what I need on a morning like this?

I bark at Sue to get Graham on the phone as an older man dressed in his company's blue overalls arrives at the bottom of the stairs. I reach out and grab his arm as he ignorantly tries to push past.

'What's going on here?'

'You may well ask,' he responds?

'I think I just did.'

'We've got the wrong sort of radiators, and the boiler is nowhere near big enough to heat this place. I'm just going to phone my boss to find out what's happening here,' he replies, and walks off toward the main exit door.

'Graham for you, Nick,' Sue says, waving the receiver in front of my face.

The penny has dropped. 'Graham! Are you expecting a plumber today?' I shout down the phone. 'Because if you are, he's going to be several hours late. Now get it sorted!' I yell, and slam the receiver down.

Graham is back in the Great Malvern office this morning. What I'm witnessing going on here is for that office, and either he or the plumbing firm has messed up, big time. He needs to get this sorted quickly or my staff will walk out because it's too damn cold to work.

'You look like you could do with some help?' Mal whispers into my ear.

'What are you doing here?'

'I had hoped that you could spare me a few minutes of your valuable time, but I can see you're busy. I'll come back another time.'

'We've got nothing to talk about, Mal.'

'That's where you're wrong. I'd like you to give me the opportunity to explain.'

I stare at him for a moment. I'm puzzled. I made my position perfectly clear yesterday and nothing has changed. What on earth does he think I've got to offer?

'Give me a few minutes to sort this plumber out and I'll give you five minutes. If you can't sell it to me in that time then you must back off,' I tell him, and storm off to confront the plumber.

He isn't difficult to find in his brand new, white, Ford Escort van, which is sign-written in bold blue numbers and lettering, advertising the company he works for. I find him sitting in the driver's seat with the door open and his legs hanging outside, and I'm not jealous he's using one of these new fangled mobile phones. His boss must be doing very nicely, thank you. That could change quicker than he knows.

'We've got a slight problem,' he informs me, replacing the hand set on completion of his call.

'Let me guess: you're in the wrong place?' I snap.

'Someone in our office put the wrong site address on the works order,' comes his feeble excuse for the cock up. 'I've driven all this way for nothing.' He sighs loudly, expecting me to be sympathetic. 'My boss wants me to meet him in Great Malvern at one o'clock, so I need to get going.'

'And I've got an office full of cold people dodging your tools and materials. Get it sorted before I cancel the contract. There's a good man.'

'Sorry mate; no can do. My boss will get someone back here tomorrow to sort things out for you. That's the best we can offer you at the moment.'

Calling me his mate is his first mistake. Telling me he's leaving without fixing the heating is his second. While he turns away from me to secure his new phone, I whip the van's keys out of the ignition. Shaking them in front of him with a big grin on my face, I walk off, back towards the office.

The plumber's protests fall on deaf ears. I'm not interested in his problems, only mine, and he's not getting his keys back until the heating is up and running again. Stepping inside the office reception area, I come across Mal talking to Sue, not a situation I feel comfortable with. Who knows what they're discussing?

'Give me my bloody van keys back!' The plumber shouts at me, alerting everyone in the vicinity to our problem.

'You'll get them when the heating is back on.'

'You can't do that,' he protests.

'Watch me,' I tell him, and turn to Mal. 'My office.'

Closing my office door behind us, I remove my rubbish from the client's chair, dust it off, and offer Mal a pew. He's not impressed, and I'm not bothered that he's not impressed.

'As you rightly observed, Mal, I am a very busy man and I like my anonymity. You've got five minutes to say your piece, and remember, I'm not interested in earning you money. So please don't waste your five minutes, and my time.'

'Nick?' He starts, and the way he questions my statement suggests that this is all about money. 'I can't deny that writing this book may well make me money. It's what I do, but this isn't about what you can do for me, this is about what you can do for South Wales. The very place you call home.'

'Now you have lost me.'

'Let me explain.'

'I can't wait!'

'I told you yesterday that most of what I do is for the Welsh tourist industry. It's an industry, which is in a rapid decline and one which requires a much needed boost.'

'So write about Dylan Thomas,' I suggest.

'Dylan Thomas has, and always will have, his place in local folklore but his appeal is limited. Literary buffs love him and many pay homage to his brilliance. South Wales needs something new, something which is both exciting and real. A present-day icon, if you like, to promote not only the beauty of this country, and what it has to offer, but to tell people that this is a vibrant, buzzing, fun place to visit. There's plenty to see and do here; we need to let the public at large know that it's not just a sleepy backwater where coach companies bring the over sixty-fives to escape the hustle and bustle of suburbia.'

When he stops to take a breath, I can't help myself, slowly clapping my hands at his opening statement - which rather annoys him.

'I don't believe you Mal. You can't seriously want to use my life story to promote the Welsh tourist industry?' I scoff. 'Live in the real world, will you. A lot of what I could tell you would scare holidaymakers away; not encourage them to visit these shores.'

'Why did you come here in the first place?' Mal asks, leaning forward. 'You're not married, so it wasn't for love. Was it because you fell in love with the place while you were on holiday all those years ago?'

Mal has got me cornered. Sitting back in my chair, I stare back at him, wondering what he'll come out with next. I'm not about to help him out by telling him he's wrong.

'There had to be a reason, for you to leave home. If nothing else there must be a story there?' He pauses again, to gather his thoughts. 'You're a successful businessman, but have you taken the time recently to look around you? If you have, then you will have noticed just how many local family businesses have closed down. Gone and lost forever, and that trend is increasing almost daily.'

As he speaks, his voice trembles with passion. He's angry too and I don't know if that's a good or bad thing. You can be blinded by your own beliefs - I should know.

'Families are moving away because they can no longer make a decent living in their homeland. Nor can the current generation afford to buy our houses. With the lack of work, they cannot afford the inflated house prices in this area. City folk are snapping them up as second, or, in some cases, third homes, which they might use once or twice a year and rent the rest. That's no good to us!' Mal mumbles, shaking his head in disgust. 'What will become of our local community? I tell you what; twenty years from now, genuine locals will be an ethnic minority. We all need to support our community before it's too late, and you can help to do that!'

I find myself sitting quite still, listening intently to him. My hands stretched out behind my back, clasping the back of my head, which the body language experts would tell you, means that I'm open to suggestion or comment. For me it's simply a way of relaxing, I find it comfortable.

Life in South Wales isn't as bleak as Mal pretends. Admittedly, there is a trend amongst the younger generation to move on in search of work, but the country in general shares the problems we all currently have. We in South Wales are by no means unique on that front. Mal is right to some degree because those lost businesses won't be replaced - not necessarily a wholly tragic loss in my opinion. Tacky and overpriced goods being offered to prise money from unsuspecting holidaymakers no longer has a place in our society.

There are exceptions, of course, and some businesses will be missed, but caught in a world of spiralling overheads they realise there is no long-term future. Jan sold her shop for that very reason. Her profits were in a steady decline, and she sold up before the business got into real financial trouble.

Reasons for the decline aren't black and white as some believe, and although the high interest rates of the eighties shoulder most of the blame, the above national average unemployment in this area doesn't help. There wasn't, and still isn't, a whole lot of spare cash available to lavish on luxuries. I can see his point of view, but I don't see how writing a book on my life can help stop the decline, or bridge the financial deficit.

My own business has survived relatively unscathed through this decade. When we tried, several months ago, to analyse the reasons for this, the indicators led us to just one area: insurance. Fraud investigations have almost trebled in recent times. Put simply, a vast number of ordinary folk are making false insurance claims to bail themselves out of trouble. Some are taking drastic measures too, and it's difficult to comprehend why people are prepared to take huge risks, such as arson, just to survive; but it's happening and we are being paid handsomely to find out. In this hostile economic climate home security is fast becoming a 'must have' accessory. The more fortunate amongst the populous want to protect what they have.

Using logic, the decline in the home tourist industry can be blamed on the readily available, affordably cheap, package holiday to the land of continuous sun, sea, and sangria. Sadly, Wales cannot compete with that.

Writing a book on my life story isn't the answer. I don't know what is. The way I see it, Wales needs to sell Wales - not me.

'Mal, I'm well aware of what's going on around me, and what you are trying to do is admirable. It's just not for me. Sorry,' I inform him, after such a wonderful speech.

'I'm sorry too. Our small but perfectly formed principality needs a helping hand to rejuvenate itself,' he says, standing up. 'As a local man with influence, I thought you might want to help us achieve that goal. One day, this glorious country of ours will be a place everyone wants to visit. The big country, don't you want to be part of that?'

'I already am.'

'Then why won't you help?' he adds, walking over to my closed office door.

Mal has pricked my conscience with his plea. I am part of this community, and the community as it stands is slowly falling apart. Selfishly, what will be the implications on my business when it finally does? Can I afford to ignore that, and is it all right to think, *I'm all right Jack, sod all the others*?

'Mal, County haven't a fixture next Saturday. Lets do lunch and talk about this?' I suggest, which brings a smile to his face. 'This doesn't mean I've changed my mind. I just want to know what you're proposing to do. I'll be in touch.'

I hate failure. Over the years, I've learnt to accept that it happens. Failure is, after all, part of everyday life and it makes one more determined. That doesn't mean I have to like it! Mine is a risky business, where solutions are dependent on many variants. Sometimes a good result is down to pure luck, and not the hard work one as an individual may put into a case.

Financial constraints, too, play their part. Working for a private client often means there is a limit to what one can achieve under an agreed contract. A valuable lesson I learnt very early on. The sad fact is, that to run a successful, profitable business means you can't - and one doesn't - work for nothing. A degree of flexibility should always be considered, and each case should be judged on its own merits. At the end of the day, an extension to a contract - in search of a solution - is the client's decision. When negotiating with a client at the outset, that is the most important factor to disclose, because in some cases, there may never be a satisfactory conclusion.

In the past, because of my business practice, I have been accused of preying on people's emotions. To suggest that I'm taking advantage of someone when they're mentally unstable, or worried out of their minds; is an unfair comment. It works both ways. I'm sure a client wouldn't thank me for taking on a job, have me tell them I will resolve their problem and then spend the next ten years working on the case. Both parties have the right to be protected from the other - that's why I like the use of contracts. Everyone involved has a choice, and know where they stand.

Stopping - giving up, if you like - when the money has run out is a hard line to take. On numerous occasions, I felt guilty when informing a client that the money they've invested in me has gone, and I've nothing positive or conclusive to tell them. I personally hate that moment, but who was it that said life was fair, and as long as my conscience is clear, and I know I've done all I can for my client, I'll live with it!

Bragging about my achievements isn't my forte; however, an average eighty-five percent personal success rate isn't to be sneezed at. It is, in fact, the foundation on which my business has been built.

This morning is one of those occasions when failure sucks. Opening my mail, a cheque made out to the value of three-hundred and fifty pounds slips out of an envelope onto my desk. Final payment for work I had done for old Mrs. Williams. What hurts is, I know she will be happy for me to cash it.

I allowed myself to be out-manoeuvred by a very clever lawyer who not only knew his stuff, but also knew how to work the system. I failed Mrs Williams and I'm going to give her the money back. Being your own boss gives license to bend the rules, and no one can question my motives.

Mrs Williams is a sixty-seven-year old widow. She needs the money far more than I do and I'm cross with myself for sending her the invoice in the first place. In hindsight, had I not been so rushed and preoccupied with my own troubles, would I have taken more care? This oversight is down to me and I don't intend ripping Mrs. Williams off. I won't post it back to her; I'll return it personally and explain my reasons for doing so. I quite fancy a trip out to get away from the chaos in the office.

Leaving the plumber's van keys with Sue - with instructions not to give them back until the heating is on - I jump into my car and set off along the coast toward the Gower Peninsula. Not an area I'm familiar with, although trips into Swansea aren't uncommon. I do know, roughly, where I'm going, until I get there, that is.

I have been to Mrs. Williams's home in Llangennith a couple of times but I always struggle to find her place. She lives in a small cottage tucked away on the road to Cockstreet. I always manage to drive past her house without seeing the small cottage at the first time of asking, and have to turn around in the campsite a little further up.

With my music playing softly in the background, relaxing my mood as I drive through Llanrhidian, Stembridge, and on in the direction of Burry Green, towards Mrs. William's house in Llangennith, I really start to take notice of the countryside I'm passing through. The raw, rugged beauty of the Gower Peninsula invokes pleasant thoughts, and Mal's plea drifts through my mind. 'The big country, don't you want to be part of that?' I've woken up to what he's saying and he's right; I live here so I should be part of the future of Wales.

His words are reinforced by Mrs. Williams when I take her out for lunch in Rhossili. What a stunning place - even in the depths of winter. Out on the tip of the peninsula is Worms Head, and although I've not set foot in this place before, Worms Head is no stranger to me. Many an hour has been spent gazing across Carmarthen Bay from the village, or Saundersby, at this rocky outcrop.

Behind us, the land rises steeply, forming Rhossili down, and below – from our window seat in the pub – we gaze along the golden sands of Rhossili beach. Curving in an arc the bay stretches out in front of us for more than three miles. It truly is a place of contrasting beauty. The headland has something to offer all tastes.

For the energetic, there's the long walk out to the promontory where, if you're lucky, and the sea conditions are favourable, you might see and hear the blowhole in action. Reaching Worms Head itself can only be achieved at low tide, with a maximum two-hour window on either side.

For the family, there's the aggressive descent down onto the beach - and an even tougher walk back - where I'm told that with the right conditions, surfing can be very good. For those seeking a more thrilling activity, hang-gliding from way up on Rhossili Down is a must - so I'm told. I like to keep my feet firmly on terra firma. Flying of any sort isn't my idea of fun - I actually despise it!

Mal's little sermon has got me hooked. It's not as if I need convincing further, but dropping Mrs. Williams home - after negotiating a deal on the finances – I decide to explore Gower Peninsula further. Cutting across the middle, through Reynoldston, passing through what I would describe as moorland, I head for The Mumbles. The town itself has a certain charm, but the view out across Swansea bay toward Port Talbot - with its filthy emissions billowing into the sky, polluting the air we breathe, spoils it for me. Clearly, with eyesores like that, selling Wales to the tourist is going to be a tough job.

My faith in Mal is soon restored. Leaving the Gower, heading back home, the rolling hills and mountains inland from Swansea rise spectacularly. Beyond them, are the Brecon Beacons, and Black

Mountains. Today, low cloud and mist obscure the highest peaks, but that doesn't stop me wondering what it would be like to be up there, seeing for myself the views on offer. I've lived in this area for eighteen years and I've not once explored the great outdoors right on my doorstep. Perhaps its time I should?

Heading west, I decide to pay my old mate and mentor, Tom Morgan, a visit. Tom lives near the village of Llanfallteg West, a little out of my way but I haven't seen him or Mother for some time, and it's high time I put that right.

Tom's farm is where it all started. His dairy farm and guesthouse is where I met Linda. At the time, she was Tom's daughter: Maria's, best friend, and worked through the summer holidays on the farm helping out in the bed and breakfast. That was way back in the summer of 1970. I wonder where Linda is now?

Most of the year, the farm works to a fairly rigid routine, and if I time this to perfection I'll make it to the farm in time for tea and one of Mother's wonderful home-cooked meals. In the eighteen years I've lived here in South Wales, I have never come across a better cook, and doubt I ever will.

I have something bothering me, too. In the back of my mind, I have a nagging feeling that Tom knows of Reginald Moss. I can't connect the name to Tom or his farm, but when I think of Reginald Moss, I see Tom's face. That could also explain why Richard recognised Moss's name too.

Tom's old sheep dog, Fang, has long since died, but his direct descendant has that same vicious streak inbred in him. I miss old Fang. He was a wonderful, loyal dog, when he let you get to know him. Buried in a special place in the lower field, he will be remembered with real affection. Once he got used to me being round the farm, Fang made it his business to accompany me wherever I went. He spent many an hour sitting on the riverbank with me while I fished. Outside the immediate family, I was the only person he would tag along with for company. He was my protector against the might of Tom's dairy herd.

The next generation rules the yard today and getting safely from the car to the house depends on surprise and stealth. Arriving by car denies you both, and it boils down to pure good luck as to whether or not you avoid the new kid on the block. He doesn't attack or bite, but by hell, his growling and snapping as he runs around one's ankles is enough to scare the living daylights out of most normal people.

This time of year, because there are no paying guests, the front entrance to the farmhouse is kept locked. One is then left with little choice, and crossing the yard to the back door lessens the chance of avoiding him.

Tom's latest version of the 'beast of Pembrokeshire' lives up to his name. Sniper is his name, and boy, is he good! I gained Fang's trust because I spent a lot of my early years in Wales around the farm, but I spend so little time here now that to Sniper I'm a compete stranger, and where he's concerned I'm legitimate game. Meals on wheels.

Fingers crossed, hoping that Tom has been delayed and is still out in the shed milking the cattle; I drive past the front of the house, through the gate, and across the cattle grid into the yard, parking my car as close as I can to the back door. The milking shed is closed up and the lights are off. Tom has finished his twice-daily chore, on time.

A dull flickering light radiates from the small kitchen window on the side of the house. Tom and Mother are sat in front of the warm kitchen range with the fire door open, relaxing after another hard day - much as they've always done. It's very still and quiet, and beginning to get dark.

This is ridiculous. I can't sit here in my car all night worrying about the bloody dog, so with one last careful look around the yard, quiet as I can, I clamber out of the car. I wait a second or two before I move too far, Sniper may have heard my car door closing. There's nothing to see, but at this point, that's not unusual. Deciding it's safe enough to proceed, I step out into the open to give Sniper his chance - his best shot. He is an intelligent, crafty dog, which is enough to give any God - fearing man the shits! Only when I see Tom appear at the back door - with the dog firmly attached by the scruff of its neck in his huge hands – can I relax.

Over tea - which is of Mother's usual high standard - we catch up on three months' worth of gossip, and in time honoured tradition, once we've eaten, Tom and I retire to the comfortable chairs in front of the range for a smoke, beer, and a chat. I'll only have the one very small glass of beer because I really must get home tonight. Tom rolls a couple of cigarettes and we sit in silence while we enjoy our smoke. He has always maintained that tobacco is way too expensive to waste with idle chat.

The huge, square kitchen we're sat in hasn't changed since the day I first stepped inside room. Older of course, and gazing around the room today, the décor really is showing the eighteen years of neglect. This room holds many memories for me, mostly fond ones, but there are times I'd sooner forget. Tom and Mother have become my adopted grandparents and this kitchen, in their home on their farm, has been a bolthole for me; a safe haven, where over the years I've come for comfort and advice. They love me, and I them. They are good people and great company.

This is the real Wales, where generations of history wait patiently to be told. It should be recorded for posterity while those who can recall the hardships they faced are still here to tell the tales of yesteryear. Tom is one of a dying breed. By today's standards his ways are judged as old hat and uneconomical, but he is the custodian of his heritage and 'best we not forget', for if one forgets one's humble beginnings, one's heritage; one has no future direction. Unfortunately, for me, that doesn't sell books.

Sitting here, smoking Tom's tobacco, sipping his home brew, and reflecting over the day's events, is very, very relaxing. A tradition I fear that will die along with Tom's generation. In the future, I will have no one to share moments like this with - or will I?

Tom's roll-up always lasts longer than mine. When I first noticed the difference, I questioned him on why that was, and concluded I smoked faster. Today, I know the truth; he puts more tobacco in his than he does mine - the tight fisted old git! – and, he'll save the unused tobacco for another day.

'Have you heard the name Reginald Moss, before?' I ask Tom, once he's stubbed out his cigarette.

'Yes, boy,' he responds, without thinking. I have never been absolutely sure if Tom calling me 'boy' is a compliment or not. His response though is what I'd hoped for, but unusually no further information is forthcoming.

'Do you remember where, Tom?' I prompt.

'Not something we talk about around these parts,' he tells me.

Now, he has raised my interest. I cannot understand why, if he knew the name straight away, I don't share the same recognition. I have been part of this farm for the past eighteen years and nothing, as far as I know, has happened here without me knowing.   Why don't I remember?

'What if it's important for me to know about Reginald Moss? Will you talk to me about him then?' I prompt. Throwing a quick look at his wife, Tom begins to open up.

'1981,' he says, which means absolutely nothing to me.

'What about 1981?' I prompt, again.

'You asked about Reginald Moss; that's when it happened.'

'When what happened, Tom?'

'I'm surprised you don't remember, boy,' Tom retorts.

I am too, as it happens, because normally my powers of recollection are very good. It is a helpful attribute in this line of business.

'I thought you would recall with some clarity the day Gavin Thomas's lad, David, was killed? Don't you remember how they were predicting he'd go on and play rugby for his country one day? Young David was a very good player, and if my memory serves me well I'm sure I took you and Richard along once to watch him play.'

Tom's words slowly build a picture in my mind. It was hunt day on the land of one of Tom's neighbour's, and the saboteurs were out in force.

'I remember, Tom. A teenager was hit and killed by a passing train while opening the unmanned level crossing gates on Gavin's land.'

'That teenager was Gavin's son. What a waste of talent,' Tom sighs. 'It was thought David was amongst the saboteurs that day. No one knows why, for sure, because he had no reason to be there, disrupting his own father's hunt. The man leading the hunt saboteurs on that terrible day was Reginald

Moss. There was a rumour going around at the time that Moss ordered the gates to be opened, but it was never proven. Young David was very popular lad and his death was a tragic loss to our community. No one talks about his death, because no one wants to dwell on what might have been. Moss for all his sins got away scot-free.'

Tom gently shakes his head in disgust and exhales loudly. 'Shouldn't have happened, boy, and Moss should pay for what he did,' he angrily adds.

The incident is clear in my mind, now. No charges were ever brought against Moss or anyone else. There were no witnesses, and there wasn't enough evidence to support the claims. If I remember correctly, the coroner's court recorded David's tragic accident as 'death by misadventure'.

'I'd like to get my hands on that bastard, Moss.' Tom angrily states.

'What would that achieve?'

'Revenge; that's what!'

'Perhaps we can, Tom, but my way…if you know what I mean?'

'You and your fancy ways boy! If it was up to me, he'd be tied to the rails and made to suffer the same fate as David.'

'Probably no more than he deserves. Fortunately, for Reginald Moss, we're not allowed to do things like that in our so-called civilised world. What I need you to do; is to keep this conversation within these four walls. If Moss gets wind I'm after him, he'll disappear from sight again and right now, Richard and I have him right where we want him.'

'Do I have a choice, boy?'

'If you really want to see justice done, Tom, no!'

Tuesday, 19 January 1988

One of the plusses of being single is that you can please yourself. Do what you want, when you want and as often as you want. One has no one to answer to and no-one nagging in one's ear, demanding an explanation for one's absence. Last night Tom became upset over this Reginald Moss thing, so I stayed over and sank a few beers with him, to make sure he was all right, you understand. A terrific excuse for sinking a few home brews, and to be honest, reliving those halcyon days.

Staying the night on the farm has never been a problem. I have my own room here, my own toothbrush in the bathroom, and my own seat at the dinner table. The farm is my second home, though stating that publicly might upset Jan.

The range has been stoked and a fresh layer of coal lies on top of yesterday's embers. A bright, warm glow greets the wakening household to the kitchen this cold morning. Sitting on the range, the battered old copper kettle I remember from my first visit here is warming through. Gasping for a cuppa, I check to see if the water is hot enough to make a coffee, before I brave the elements and join Tom, out in the milking shed.

Like sitting, having a smoke and beer after a meal - when I stay here overnight - getting up and helping Tom with the milking is just another one of those traditions we've kept going since day one. Over the years – out there in his milking shed - Tom has helped me make many important decisions while we've worked side by side, and he'll expect me this morning to finish our discussion of last night.

Hanging in the porch, which leads out into the yard, is my boiler suit. In readiness for my next gruelling shift, Mother has washed them since the last time I wore them. Beneath my overalls are my Wellington boots, sat on the cold, stone floor: one black one and one green one. That's a long-standing joke. Quickly, as I squeeze into my overalls, it becomes evident that they have shrunk. The pop fasteners around my waist flatly refuse to meet, and try as I may, breathing in to overcome their stubbornness doesn't cure the problem. They just won't fasten. Mother has used a too hot a wash, I'd guess.

In a relaxed mood, I stride out across the yard in the dark, a cup of hot coffee in one hand and a cigarette in the other. I have completely forgotten about Sniper this morning, that is, until he ambles past me without acknowledging the fact that I'm here - thankfully! I can't work that out. One minute he wants to savage you, the next you don't exist. Perhaps that's because I've come from inside the house and he recognises the familiar scent on my clothing. Whatever his reason is for ignoring me, I sigh with relief and pause briefly to watch him disappear into the dark, murky morning on his early morning round.

Standing for a moment outside the milking shed, I take a long look around at the familiar surroundings. Nothing has changed in eighteen years, nothing at all. It strikes me that perhaps they should have done. If Tom is not keeping abreast of the modern technology available to him, and observing the new regulations being enforced by the Milk Marketing Board, he will encounter huge problems in the future. Maybe he's not aware of the new legislation, or perhaps he doesn't want to know. I know what he's like. As far as he's concerned, there's nothing wrong with the tried and tested methods his ancestors used. I'll need to keep a close eye on the farm, if my life-style allows me to.

Stepping inside the milking shed is like going back in time, not only through the way everything looks and is, but because it holds so many memories for me. It was in this very milking shed, eighteen years ago, when I came back to be with Linda, that Tom admitted he'd befriended me. Tom doesn't have a son, and therefore has no male heir to his farm. He asked me way back then to look after his farm when he'd gone. He knew I loved the place, and he knew then I'd make a good job of doing so. It was here that he told me Linda liked me, but she was already seeing someone and was two-timing me. As I later discovered to my cost, her boyfriend, Adam, was a rugby-playing man-mountain! Not everything we've discussed in here has been doom and gloom in nature; much of what we have talked over has made me what I am today - successful.

Tom glances over his shoulder in my direction as I close the shed door, then turns away to finish off what he's doing while grunting a 'good morning'.

'Morning, Tom,' I reply brightly. 'Hope you don't mind me joining you?'

'You know I don't mind. Staying for breakfast, boy?' he inquires? I hadn't planned to. I really do need to be back in the office early but passing up on one of Mother's wonderful cooked breakfasts is an act of gross stupidity.

'Have you ever known me to refuse?' I reply, joining him by the milking machines and leaning on the low, dividing, brick-wall.

'Not that I can remember boy,' he says, standing upright and slowly stretching his back.

'Are you all right this morning?'

'So, so. You have a habit of digging up names from the past. Where on earth did you hear Reginald Moss's?'

'I went to see a client with Richard, and his name came up in conversation. I knew I'd heard the name before but I couldn't work out where. Since then, I've been asking everyone who I thought might know. Peculiar thing was, driving back from the Gower yesterday; I associated his name with you. I apologise if I've upset you, Tom, raking up the past like that again, but I had to know.'

'I'll get over it, boy, as long as you see that justice is done. Your intuition wasn't wrong, was it? I did know something about Reginald Moss.'

'What I don't understand, is why I had nothing to do with the case, especially as it was on my patch, so to speak.'

'Easily answered, boy. William Marchant.'

I instantly recognise that name. Until a couple of years ago, Marchant was a competitor of mine. Poor health has forced him to retire, and to be truthfully blunt, he wasn't very good at what he did. Marchant talked a good game, he most certainly had the gift of the gab, but when it came down to the nitty-gritty, he didn't cut the mustard. Then, who would; living on the customer side of a bar?

'What about William Marchant?' I ask Tom.

'Gavin Thomas's brother-in-law, and David's uncle. It was common knowledge that you and Marchant didn't get on, and Gavin wasn't likely to ask you to look into the accident, was he? Got to tell you though, boy, I tried to tell him because we all knew what Marchant was like, and he proved it.'

Tom stops what he's doing, rolls a couple of cigarettes, and we sit down on the straw bales neatly stacked against the outer wall. Lighting our smokes, we didn't realise or care about the stupidity of that action; it is just another one of those little things we've done a million times before. If Tom has anything further to add, I'll have to wait until he's finished his smoke.

I expect Jan will be wondering where I am this morning, but she's not my keeper, so what the hell! I'll phone her when I've settled in at the office, check in, and make sure the builders are OK. I'm so thoughtful in these troubled times.

Richard is my target. I have a vested interest in his client and I want to know how his meeting with the lovely Victoria went yesterday, and what he's promised 'my' company will do for her. I've made the decision to go after Moss myself and I don't want him messing things up. He will have to manoeuvre around me. I figure by now that Moss will know we're involved in Victoria's big hunt day, and will be watching Richard's progress closely. If he's got any sense, he will be.

On the way up to Richard's office - ignoring my daily routine, once again - I notice the lack of coats being worn by my staff. The heating must be back on. His door is wide open and although I knock, I walk straight in uninvited.

'So,' I taunt, 'I'm not good enough to meet your clients, then?'

'I didn't think you'd want to tag along. You made it very clear you don't like Victoria,' he answers, in his defence.

'I'm not keen on the barman in our local, but that doesn't stop me going in for a pint. How is the lovely Victoria Jackson, anyway?'

'She's fine, and we've struck a good deal,' he informs me.

'Fantastic! I'm so pleased…for the both of you. And, what have you done about the Moss problem?'

'Nothing yet.'

'Good! I want you to leave him to me.'

'I don't understand?'

'Let's just say I've found a number of interesting things out about our man, Moss, and for the moment it's best for all concerned that word doesn't get out. Something he was involved in a few years ago just doesn't sit comfortably with me, and to get to the bottom of this I don't want him becoming suspicious of us, or our motives.'

'What do I tell Victoria,' he asks?

'Nothing! And if she persists, use your charm. Oh, and we haven't had this conversation, do you understand?'

A little bewildered perhaps, by my involvement, Richard nods in agreement.

Normally, I would trust Richard's judgement implicitly, but for the moment, I have to assume Moss will be monitoring his every move. I don't want him spooked, which perhaps may drive him underground. I don't want Moss becoming suspicious of the depth of Richard's involvement with Victoria Jackson. This is a one-off, and if he thinks Richard is purely working to protect Victoria's interests, he won't see me coming, until I'm ready to let him know.

Tom made me question this. When he told me that he'd spoken to Gavin Thomas after the accident and recommended me, he said Gavin persisted with his brother-in-law's services. Gavin, of all people, must have known what Marchant was like. I recognise that blood is thicker than water, but William Marchant really is a fucking tosser, a loser, and that's a professional opinion.

I first met Marchant seventeen years ago, and he was drunk as a skunk, that day. I stopped him from driving his car in a very inebriated state. Naturally, he thanked me for my concerns, and has held my goodwill against me, ever since. Eighteen years of experience behind me - in the field of detection – raises one question immediately: if Gavin really wanted answers, and he knew Marchant as well as I do, why in God's name did he hire him?

I find myself back down by my car when I remember I haven't phoned Jan. I'll pop home first to check in, take a quick shower while I'm there, and then trot around into Fenby to see Reg Wallace. 'Nicholas' a male voice calls out as I open the driver's door. Apart from my real mum, only one other person addresses me in that fashion…Reg.

He's almost stood right beside me when I look up. In his right hand he holds what appears to be a file.

'I've got something for you,' he says, with a sickly grin on his face. 'Case notes on Reginald Moss. Seems he didn't do much wrong,' he adds, handing across a rather thin police report.

'Apparently not,' I respond.

'You already know? I do hope you've not been wasting my time. I had all manner of people trying to recall his name.'

'Not at all,' I reassure him. 'I know what he was involved in, but not what happened in any great detail. Old Tom Morgan told me.'

'Your old adversary, William Marchant, seems to have been involved in some capacity or other,' Reg continues. 'Or "Wild Bill hic, hic" as he was known down at the factory. Loved a good scotch, did Bill…shame he never drank one. Takes all sorts, I guess. Listen…' Reg says with purpose, 'I'll have to put that back before it's missed, so do what you need to do, and see that I have it back in a couple of days.'

'No problem, thanks.'

'Got to rush, important things to take care of. You know how it is?'

I take his comment to be a dig at my choice of work. Reg has a conveniently short memory when it suits him. His rapid rise to Inspector is as much my doing as his own, and he certainly can be an infuriating man at times. However, with the file in my possession and his comments on the case, duly noted, I know he's read it through for himself. Reg sees no point in pursuing the case further. In his eyes, there's nothing to be gained by doing so. There's no cream to be had and no feathers to put in his cap. That's the way Reg operates.

Chapter five

Wednesday, 20 January 1988

The file Reg gave me yesterday contained little in the way of positive information. The investigating officer, DC Smith, clearly assumed right from the start that this incident was, in fact, a tragic accident and investigated it in that manner. Other than the train driver involved, only one witness gave evidence at the coroner's hearing three months later, and that was a youth called Stephen Jones. His testimony alone cleared Reginald Moss of any wrongdoing. At the time of the accident, Stephen Jones was nineteen years old. A small amount of research informs me that at twenty-six, he's now married and his wife is expecting their first child. I've traced him to an address in Cardiff.

Like all good door-to-door salespersons, I find evenings and weekends most productive when making house calls. Unlike Richard, I've done my homework, and know exactly where I'm headed.

The weather is awful this afternoon, creating very hazardous driving conditions due to the lying water and vehicle spray. My journey to Cardiff is cautious and exceptionally slow going. Luckily, for me, Stephen Jones lives on the northern most fringe of the city, saving the tedium of fighting against the evening rush hour traffic, and his house is relatively easy to find. By the time I reach my destination, it's dark and raining even heavier.

A smart, well-appointed, detached house in a nice part of town greets me. Stephen Jones is doing all right for himself, but the research I've done, so far, contradicts what I see. Stephen works for the local council authority as a plumber, and from what I've found out it's not a particularly well-paid job, certainly not white-collar status. A salary under that potential earning level wouldn't get a mortgage on a place of this size, in this area.

By the time I switch off the car's engine, my mind is in overdrive. No matter what he tells me - or doesn't - I will explore his financial background.

I've separated his statement from the file. With it tucked into my inside jacket pocket, trying to dodge the cold raindrops, I jog energetically up his garden path to the front door. It's lashing down as I press the doorbell while frantically searching my pockets for a business card.

There's a photograph of Stephen in the file. When he eventually opens the door to me, I know I've got the right place. Older and thinner on top, he hasn't changed that much since the photograph was taken. Waving a business card briefly in front of his eyes, but long enough for him to read the details, he speaks first.

'Private Investigator?' he questions me. 'What is it you want with me, Mr Marchant?'

'I'd like to ask you a few questions about David Thomas?' I reply. The look on his face when I mention David's name is worth a thousand answers. I've shocked him with my opening statement. 'Do you mind if we step inside for a moment, I'm getting soaked,' I add, while he stares vacantly past me into space.

'I don't know what you're talking about,' he finally blurts out.

'Oh, I think you do,' I immediately respond. Waving a copy of his statement in front of him, I continue. 'I have the rest of the case notes in my car if you need further proof, Stephen.'

Stephen steps out of the way to let me in. Once he's closed the door I follow him through into his lounge. Inside, what I see in this very neat, tidy, and well-decorated house also contradicts what I've read. A council plumber can't afford quality fixtures and fittings like these. Then again, his wife might be the breadwinner in this partnership. One should never judge a book by its cover, my old mum use to say.

'What do you want to ask me, Mr. Marchant?' Stephen asks, warily.

I knew old William Marchants business cards would come in handy at some point. I had forgotten all about them until his name came up, the other day. A few years ago, I called into the printers to collect some stationery I'd ordered and helped myself to a few of his cards when I saw them lying on the counter in the shop. Things like that are always useful.

'Some new information has come to light and I've reopened the case.' I'm a great believer in telling a small white lie when searching for the truth. 'In your statement,' I add, scanning his statement, pretending to find the relevant place, 'you said that you were with Mr. Moss throughout the entire afternoon of the hunt, and at no time did he order anyone to open the crossing gates.'

'That's correct; I was with Mr. Moss all afternoon,' Stephen says positively as he retires to his expensive three- seater leather settee. 'And he didn't.'

'You're quite sure of that, Stephen?'

'I was there Mr. Marchant; I should know what happened.'

'Of course,' I agree with him. A tactic used to make a person believe they're winning, which allows them to relax. A person with their guard up is hard to break down. 'So if a new witness has come forward, suggesting they'd seen you out on the road by yourself, you'd naturally say that they were lying…wouldn't you?'

Stephen sits back in the settee, his wide, brown eyes stare at me - his mouth gawping. My line of investigation to the very last word is pure fabrication. As far as I know, there are no new witnesses to the accident. Stephen doesn't know that, and my plan, this evening, is to see what he does about it. The point of turning up is to cast doubt in his mind, and see whom he runs to.

'I'd like you to leave, now,' he tells me. While he stands, I hold out one of William Marchant's business cards for him, which he reluctantly takes.

'I'm going to get Reginald Moss, Stephen. Don't let him take you down with him. I'll see myself out.'

Stepping out into the rain, I have no doubt that by the time I've reached my car, Reginald Moss will know I've paid Stephen a visit. What Stephen doesn't know is that I've been followed here tonight by one of my own operatives. If Stephen leaves the house, he will be followed, his every move reported back to me. Richard won't be too pleased when he finds out I've seconded his top investigator. Why should I worry? Who's the boss in this outfit, anyway? What I'm doing will help him too, but it won't stop him moaning.

Thursday, 21 January 1988

William Marchant lives in Narberth, about a fifteen-minute car journey from the office. I'm familiar with the area and I have been to his house before, many years ago – uninvited!

I heard recently that Bill is not a well man. Rumour has it, years of heavy drinking have left him with irreversible liver damage and only his daily dialysis treatment is keeping him alive. I learnt only the other day from a close friend of his wife's that unless Bill has a transplant he'll soon pass from this world. Not an ideal time to be paying him a visit, particularly as we have never seen eye to eye, and seeing me could upset him - as if I really care!

My hope is that Bill has mellowed enough to assist me in the death of his nephew, David. His time on this planet of ours is running out, and if he is remorseful, he may wish to make amends for years of gross negligence. His illness may have affected his ability to remember, and it's possible he may not recall the events of that day in any great detail, but it's worth finding out exactly how much he does remember, and whether he made and kept notes.

It's an advantage having friends in the right place. Aware that Bill attends the hospital for his daily dialysis treatment, I'd used my inside source to find out when that was. I hate wasting my own time, so making quite sure he was at home when I paid him a visit was good detective work.

It's close on two-thirty in the afternoon when I pull up outside his bungalow. There's a notable difference about the place since the last time I was here. Money has been spent on the bungalow, lots of it, mostly towards making life easier for him, like improving the access. A gently graded, concrete ramp runs up to the front door, with a sturdy handrail for holding on to. The furniture on the new double-glazed door is lower than normal and fitted at a sensible, workable height for someone confined to a wheel chair. There's also a ramp fitted over the threshold.

Pat, Bill's wife of thirty years, opens the door. We've met before but her expression tells me she doesn't remember. I introduce myself and ask if I can speak with Bill. Pat tries her best to turn me away, insisting that Bill is tired after his treatment. He may well be, but with a little persuasion from me, and the promise of not taking up too much of their time, she escorts me through the bungalow to a newly constructed conservatory built across the rear of the property. Bill is sat resting in a high-back chair, facing the window; an oxygen mask lies on his chest.

'What do you want Thompson?' he wheezes, angrily, when he sees me. 'Come to gloat have you?' That was the least I expected from him. His appearance shocks me. Gaunt, his grey-coloured face stuns me, and he looks every bit a man who's very ill. The bright red nose he once sported - which had become the butt of everyone's sick humour - has long since disappeared. His red nose was his trademark. His huge conk lit up a room whenever he entered.

I stop in the doorway opposite him. In the past, his fiery nature and fond use of his fists laid out many an opponent. Today, Bill probably isn't capable of inflicting such humiliation on a fellow human being. That said, he might want to die a happy man in the knowledge that he had one last chance to lay me out, and I'm not taking any chances.

'I've not come to gloat, Bill.'

'Then why are you here?' he snaps at me. 'Won't be a social call, that's for sure.'

'I'm hoping you can furnish me with some information.'

'Furnish you,' he wheezes loudly at me, mustering the strength of a crazed and angry man! 'Did you hear that, Pat, my love? The famous Nick Thompson wants my help,' he scoffs. 'You must be bloody joking, Thompson. I think you've wasted your time coming here. I'm not going to help you; not now, not ever. So do us all a favour and piss off!'

To be honest, I had expected this. 'David Thomas,' I say, which stops his ranting and we lock stares. 'What about David?'

'He was your nephew, wasn't he? You investigated his untimely death for your sister and brother-in-law, didn't you?' I say, slowly edging closer to him.

'I have no wish to discuss David with you. Please go?'

'I'm not going to ask you to, Bill. However, if you made notes at the time, I'd like to go over them, if I may?'

Close up, Bill looks worse. Sunk into their sockets, his eyes are a hazy yellow colour. It's hard to look him in the eye without staring and being intrusive.

'No can do, Thompson, even if I wanted to.'

Stubborn as always, I think to myself.

'I'm a little surprised to hear you ask me this. My brother-in-law, Gavin, sacked me a few days after the accident and I naturally assumed he had asked you to carry on the investigation. After all, you were, and still are as far as I know, the blue-eyed boy around here. Gavin thought I was a useless, drunken waste of space and dispensed of my services. Tell me though, why for God's sake, after nearly seven years are you taking a renewed interest in my nephew's death?'

'A name from the past has come up in something we're working on and there may be a connection.' I inform him.

'Reginald Moss,' he sighs.

I nod my head in confirmation.

'I didn't like that man. Something about him makes my skin crawl, even today. I've always felt that he was up to something more than sabotaging the hunt that day. Sadly, I wasn't given the chance to find out. I'd like to help you with this, Thompson, but when Gavin gave me the elbow, he demanded my notes from me. If I didn't give them to him, he wasn't going to pay me for the work I had done. He gave me no choice, sorry.'

I find that strange. Why would Gavin Thomas insist that Bill gave him his notes? Perhaps Bill did a better job than he remembers. Maybe Gavin Thomas has something to hide. Bill thinks his notes were passed onto another private investigator, in this case, me. Having read the transcript of the coroners hearing - excluding Stephen Jones's statement and the drivers – other than the transport police report, and the local police report, no other evidence was submitted; nothing else, not a mention of Bill's findings, or anyone else's. Why?

'Not that he paid me much for my time,' Bill groans. 'Do you know what? I've not spoken to Gavin since.'

'Do you remember anything at all from that day, Bill?'

'Some days I can't remember what I've had for breakfast,' he angrily responds. 'The alcohol abuse has fuddled my brain.'

Bill stops to think for a moment. I'm hoping that today is one of his better days.

'Sorry, it's not clear. I do recall being confused by the events leading up to the accident, but I don't remember why that was. I know people thought I was a bumbling, drunken, useless excuse of a human being, and maybe I was, but David was my nephew, for Christ's sake. Don't you think I wanted answers, too?'

Covering his face with his oxygen mask, Bill closes his eyes. His whole body falls into a state of total relaxation and he's asleep within seconds. Pat suggests that he's had enough for one day and I should go. I agree with her; thank Bill for his help and although he doesn't answer, somehow I know he's heard me.

Heading back to the office, I go over the things Bill has said. There's nothing concrete on Reginald Moss to work with, which is disappointing. Much of what Bill did say needs an explanation and he has raised my suspicions.

Did Gavin Thomas, for instance, bank on his brother-in-law living up to his reputation and old Bill surprised him by pulling out all the stops for his sister's sake? Or was he that predictable that he invited the inevitable? I don't think so, because had he been a total waste of time and money I feel sure Gavin Thomas would have hired someone else to do the job.

For someone in my position, and the way in which my mind works, I think Gavin Thomas has, or had, something to hide - to cover up. Taking Bill's notes would then make sense, and I'll wager they're long since destroyed. There's also the little matter of Stephen Jones; the one person who gave evidence appears to be living well above his means…come to think of it, so is William Marchant!

Jenny breezes out through the main office door nearly taking my outstretched hand off as I reach for the handle. Not the ideal place to meet but living in a small community like ours it's bound to happen on occasions. I am a little surprised to see her here, though, and ask her what she's about.

'You wanted me to drop off a wedding present list; don't you remember?' she growls. 'Unfortunately, your office is the easiest place for me to do that.'

'Course I remember, Jenny!' I snap back. Five seconds, that's all it's taken for her to annoy me. I might deliberately forget to do things; I don't forget things.

'I've told Tony you're not coming and he's asked me to ask you to reconsider. We'd both really like you to be there. At least come to the service,' Jenny adds.

'Why is my being there so important?' I ask as she nervously looks back across the harbour toward the town. Maybe Tony is watching us.

'It would prove to both of us that there are no hard feelings, and that you and me are really over,' she mumbles.

'And you believe that by giving you my blessing will prove that? I know what I would think if I were Tony when I saw me sitting in the church. I'd think that I was there to stop it. Don't flatter yourself Jenny, I won't be there, and that will never happen. Not in this lifetime.'

Jenny turns back to face me, staring hard into my eyes.

'Tony doesn't trust you, does he? And I've got to be honest with you, Jenny; I don't know why you're marrying him. He's not right for you.'

'I'm marrying Tony because I love him, and he loves me. And because we want to spend the rest of our lives together,' she informs me.

I don't believe her and she's not convincing me otherwise. My views on Jenny haven't changed. At twenty-two years old, being left on the shelf bothers her. Who she marries isn't the important factor, the rock on her wedding finger is. Knowing Tony, that's all it'll be - a rock, granite of something. Still, at least she'll be happy - she hopes!

'I'd best get going. Tony will be waiting for me. Please give it some more thought?' Jenny says, taking a glance at her wristwatch.

'Off to the pub, again?'

'As if it's any of your business, but for your information, yes I am.'

'Should you be drinking in your condition, Jenny? I believe it's not advisable when you're pregnant.' I suggest, with good reason.

'I am being careful. I've cut my drinking right down because of the baby,' she says, trying to convince me she cares.

'When's the baby due, Jenny?' I drop in, out of the blue, and she doesn't respond. Her hesitation speaks volumes; because a woman who's pregnant would reel off the expected birth date without a moment's thought. It should roll of the tongue with excitement and joy.

'August,' she splutters. 'August, twentieth.'

Very clever, or so she thinks. Had she said July, twentieth, she knew I'd ask more questions. Her hesitation allowed her to add a month and come up with a safe answer. I'll give her the benefit of the doubt, but I'm not taken in.

'Satisfied?' she adds, trying to prompt a reply from me.

I stroll back to my car, open the passenger door, and remove the contraceptive pills from the glove box.

'No, Jenny, I'm not satisfied,' I tell her when I rejoin her, holding the contraceptives in front of her face.

'I can explain,' she struggles to say.

'This ought to be interesting.'

'Those were making me sick so I went back to the doctors and asked her to prescribe me a different sort.'

A rehearsed answer, I might have guessed.

'I never stopped taking the pill while I was with you. Tony wanted to have a baby straight away so I stopped taking them.'

Now that is clever, because she knows I can't easily prove it. Her doctor won't tell me because it's unethical to divulge another patient's medical history, and she's not about to help me, either. Jenny forgets how resourceful I am, and if there's a way to find out, I will.

'Is the baby mine, Jenny?' I ask. Why not? It's about time I did.

'No, Nick, the baby isn't yours. Tony is the father,' she answers, without hesitation.

'I only have your word for that. Trust me when I say I will find out. Maybe not tomorrow, or the following day, but I will, so pleases don't lie to me.'

'I have no reason to lie to you. I have everything I want, and so do you. A fact you made very clear to me not so long ago…remember?'

There she goes again, challenging my powers of recall. I did indeed tell her I didn't want children, but if by accident I have, I certainly won't ignore the fact. As an expectant parent, one has responsibilities and I would not turn my back on my own flesh and blood. Christ! It's taken me eighteen years to realise that - a little too late, where my own parents are concerned. Things have changed and I'm discovering it's not so pleasant when the boot's firmly on the other foot.

'I hope you and your money live happily ever after, Nick. I know Tony, our baby, and I will.'

The bloody cow! I want to tell her as much. Even now, though, I think she's hankering after just one thing; Jenny wants me to ask her not to marry Tony. She wants me in that registry office, a week from now, to stand up when the registrar asks if anyone knows why she and Tony shouldn't be joined in holy matrimony, and say, I do. If this baby is mine I don't want her to marry Tony, but I can't do that. Bloody hell! What a mess.

'If you're bothered, I gave the wedding present list to Sue,' Jenny informs me, before walking away back toward the town, and yet another session with her intended in the pub.

I watch her for a while, wondering whether I've made the right choice. With my doubts over the parenthood of her baby, should I let her walk away? Do I want her enough to stop her making the biggest mistake of her life so far? Am I making the biggest mistake of my life so far?

Richard appears at my side. He's just returned to the office, probably from yet another visit to the lovely Victoria Jackson.

'Problem?' he asks, looking at me, looking at Jenny as she disappears off into the distance. When I look at him, I can see he has a genuine concern for my wellbeing in his facial expression.

'No,' I reply confidently. 'Jenny dropped off a wedding present list for me to look at.'

'Are you sure that's all it is?' Richard continues, with a line of questioning I'd rather he'd not pursue. 'Is she pestering you for money?'

'Why should she want to do that?' I know where he's trying to lead me and I'm not taking the bait. While growing up under the guidance of Jan, and that's a loose term, the situation we found ourselves in drew us close. We're not in the slightest way related, but we've come think and act like brother's do.

'Because I know what a scheming bitch she can be at times. You're very low at the moment, and I think you'd believe anything she told you, right now.'

His observation of me is worrying. Richard has seen a change in me and I should be concerned by the fact he has noted that change.

'Jenny has got nothing I want, Richard, and no, I'm not jealous, if that's what you're thinking. As I friend, I feel sorry for her, that's all.' I tell him, doing my best to side step his concern, but even as we speak, I'm having second thoughts. Not over my relationship with Jenny, that will never happen. The root concern of my troubles is who the father of her child is. The need to know is fast becoming my number one priority. 'How did your day go?' I ask, quickly changing the subject matter. I need to.

'It was going fine until I found out my top operative is working for someone else.'

'Ah, yes. I intended to talk to you about that, but as you know, things happen so quickly in this line of work, I didn't have time. It's only for a couple of days, you won't miss him, and what he's doing for me will benefit you in the long run.'

'I think I should be the judge of that. You should have asked me, because I've wasted a lot of my time trying to contact him. And I will say, if he's working for you, his wages for this time are not coming out of my budget.'

'Don't worry, they won't,' I reassure him. Richard's budget is safe. My problem is, I don't have a contract for what I'm doing – so therefore I have no budget set aside to cover the costs. I'm breaking all my own rules. We do, as a company, have an emergency fund, but what I'm doing doesn't meet the criteria required to draw money from those funds. Nor do I have the permission of the board, Richard and Graham. Funding my own time isn't a problem. I may, however, end up paying Richard's operative, Ben, out of my own pocket - a last resort, and only to be considered when all other avenues have been explored and exhausted.

This is fast becoming a testing time for me. I'm entering into a period where my personal finances are being stretched unhealthily by the unnecessary extension work on the house. Not dangerously so that it will embarrass me, but this is a time to be careful, and staying fully aware of where the money is being spent is essential.

'I want Ben back on board as soon as possible, I've got important work for him. Just what is he doing for you that is so secretive anyway? Richard demands.

I smile smugly. 'You'll find out in good time. I told him he had a couple of days, and I meant what I said. Once he's reported back to me with his findings, he's all yours, and if he's done a good job, I'll tell you all about it!'

If Richard gets to hear about Ben's work before I do, then Ben won't get paid - or have a job. That would suit me. At eighty pounds a day, which is inclusive of overheads, and not what Ben gets, two days worth of expenses is enough pressure on anyone's wallet. Funny, how the sound and thought of money is nicer and easier to handle, when you're the one asking for it, not the one being asked to cough up!

The house is cold. Sheets of polythene cover numerous holes the builders have left in the brickwork, and the gusting wind is doing its utmost to undo their work. The constant noise of flapping polythene is driving me crazy, and I'm having difficulty concentrating on anything.

When the odds are stacked against you - whether actually, or in one's mind - you search for familiarity. Seeking out those creature comforts that keep you safely cocooned in your own world. I'm lonely, feeling sorry for myself, and I have way too many things going around in my head to cope with, satisfactorily. I'm very unsettled in my own home, tonight, and I can't find my comfort zone.

My old flat, down by the seafront, in town, wasn't like this. I really loved that place. God, what a mistake selling that has turned out to be. For over thirty months, I've lived in this house and it is home, but it's way too isolated for my liking. I miss the comings and goings of my old penthouse flat, with the constant flow of visitors at the door. I was never alone, there. It's times like this, I miss having Jenny around; perhaps that's why I asked her to move in with me in the first place. Stuck up here, on the edge of town, there are no passing visitors dropping in and asking me down the pub for a drink. I can't simply close the door behind me, and walk a few yards along the street to connect with the outside world.

I'm beginning to see and understand how Richard is suggesting that I've changed. There's no fun in my life. Apart from the Friday night drink with the lads – which currently is no more than a release from the stress of daily life - and darts with Reg on a Monday, I do little else to relax and unwind.

There are huge contrasts, too, in my everyday life. During the day, I'm in demand and I make demands. At night, I'm alone and isolated from the world. One could attribute my current mood to post-Christmas depression. Certainly, the hype surrounding the festivities had masked the rapid decline in my social calendar. Halfway through January - where most are scrimping and saving, dreading the end of the month bills hitting the Welcome mat - the problem of 'Johnny no mates' is really hitting home.

'I hope you and your money will be happy together,' Jenny said. Right now, they're not. There's got to be more to life than this.

Checking the old, battery clock still hanging on the wall in the kitchen, I discover it's only twenty minutes past six in the evening. Even for me, that's way too early for the pub, and far too late to drive over to Tom's for dinner. Isn't that depressing? I have a total of two choices of how to enrich my life. Isn't it sad that my social life has come down to this?

Aware that seeing Jenny today has blackened my mood, also serves as a reality check. My decision eighteen years ago to put work before anything else is slowly beginning to backfire on me. I've heard people on the outside look at my life and say, "Oh, look at him, isn't he a lucky man to have all that money". I've heard that said a thousand times. Oh, how little do they know.

Sulking, wallowing in self-pity, I remember that I'd promised Mal I'd phone him and arrange lunch on Saturday. I'm warming to his idea and as long as it's done tastefully, writing a book on my life here in South Wales is becoming more attractive by the minute. He wouldn't want to write about this episode in my life. That would be nothing short of a disaster. A hobby, well not exactly, but occupying my spare time productively might just stop me from going mad. Under the circumstances, it's a good idea. I grab a cold beer from the fridge and head back into the lounge to make that call.

Friday, 22 January 1988

Mal and I spoke at great length last night on the possibilities of this book he wants to write becoming a reality. On the surface, it appears that we are on the same wavelength, and his enthusiasm has cheered me up no end. His publisher and friend, Baz, won't entertain a deal containing cheap trashy material, and after running a few facts and details of my early days here past him, he's more convinced than ever that we are onto a winner. We have a lot to discuss, but we now have a solid platform to work from, and I have an idea for Saturday's meeting that might - if he needs convincing further - settle the decision.

Once my usual morning routine at work is out of the way, I retire to my office with a cup of coffee and phone Jenny's doctor to make an appointment; business, as far as he is concerned. I may not gain anything by the exercise, but if you don't ask, you don't get. I'm sure too, that once her doctor knows what information I'm after, Jenny will be told about my visit. As far as I'm concerned, that's a good thing. Jenny has to know that I meant what I said. I will find out, and if I upset her along the way, then good. Winning is all about applying pressure at the right time, and if she is hiding the truth from me she will always be in a vulnerable position. I will push her until she cracks.

Richard's top man, Ben, is beginning to worry me. He should have been in contact, by now. If only those so-called mobile phones weren't so cumbersome and expensive. Richard hasn't seen or heard from him either, which bothers me, further. Despite Richard's hype of Ben being the best, perhaps he isn't up to the job and he's not cutting the mustard. I suggest that to Richard, in passing, and he throws me out of his office, bleating on about avoiding tactics for not sanctioning his wages. Perish the thought! Money and circumstances aside, I need to talk with Ben before I can move this on. His input is vital to my next move. If my hunch is correct, it will determine it!

Jenny's doctor's surgery is in Fenby, near the railway station. The building is relatively new in what is otherwise an old and forgotten part of town. Pretty much the vision Mal's passionate speech in my office, the other day, had conjured up.

Inside the surgery, it's busy with both young and old, coughing and sneezing in unison. Winter; the time of year when the cold, damp weather wreaks havoc amongst the population, in general.

After booking in, I look around for a spare seat. I'd prefer one next to someone who isn't brandishing a hanky or tissue. A vacant seat would be nice. I get lucky when one of the duty doctors call an elderly lady into their room, and quickly manoeuvre my frame down in her place. There isn't another spare seat to be found in the waiting room, and I fear I could be here a long time. Seems I was lucky to get an appointment today, and I worry that Jenny's doctor will give me a hard time for wasting his valuable time.

Whilst waiting, I go over in my mind what I want to say, and ask. My appointment time comes and goes and with only two other people, apart from myself left waiting, I've had plenty of time to make up my mind.

Eventually, my name is called out over the tannoy system and I push through the first swing door into a long, clinical, ceramic-tiled corridor. I'm looking for the third door on the left…*Dr. S. M. Vaughan.* I knock, enter, and stop in horror. When I heard my name called out, I hadn't connected with the fact that Dr. Vaughan is female. That changes everything.

Dr. Vaughan, I would guess, is over fifty, with short-cut grey hair. Her thick-framed glasses dominate her face, but apart from her glasses, her dress code and appearance are rather plain. She smiles softly and offers me a seat.

'I understand, Mr. Thompson, that you're here on business?' she says, in one of those matter-of-fact, monotone, but caring voices.

'Well, sort of yes,' I splutter. *For god's sake, pull yourself together, old son!*

Confronting a female doctor over matters somewhat delicate has thrown me, and she peers at me over the top of her glasses waiting patiently for me to continue. Her look un-nerves me.

'My ex-girlfriend is pregnant. I…er… Doctor Vaughan, there's some doubt as to who the father is,' I tell her.

'Who's doubt, Mr. Thompson, yours?'

'Yes!'

'Why don't you speak to your ex-girlfriend about this?'

'I already have done.'

'And?' Doctor Vaughan questions me, her voice slightly raised in frustration at my evasive answering.

'She says the baby is her fiancé's.'

'Is she right?'

'With the date she's given me, yes, but I don't believe her.'

'How can I be of help, Mr. Thompson?' She eventually asks and sits back in her high-backed black leather chair.

'Jenny is a patient of yours; I'm hoping you can help me find out.'

'Jenny Anderson?' she asks.

'Yes,' I reply sheepishly.

'I can confirm that Jenny is pregnant, Mr. Thompson, then you already know that. I'm afraid I can't tell you anymore than that. Who the father is, is between you, Jenny, and her fiancé.'

'There's a problem,' I inform her, and she looks inquisitively at me.

'A medical problem, Mr. Thompson? Do you have a genetic disorder that we should test the baby for?'

'No nothing like that!' I exclaim, and I haven't, but as my words drift through the air I realise I might just have scuppered my only chance of discovering the truth. *You bloody idiot Thompson! You'll never have a better chance than that.*

'Then, what is the problem?' Dr. Vaughan asks, looking at her wristwatch. Oh, that's not very subtle. I immediately apologise to her for keeping her from something, but this is important to me.

'When I went to throw Jenny's rubbish out of my house I found three months' worth of unused contraceptive pills in a black bin liner. Jenny told me that she came to see you to change the brand because the ones she was taking were making her sick. I don't believe her because she still had the originals, and as her doctor I'd like you to confirm that.'

She stares at me for a moment, thinking, fiddling with the biro held in her hands. 'May I suggest, Mr. Thompson, that you sit down with Jenny Anderson and have a real heart-to-heart discussion. I can't help you with this, only Jenny can.'

'I know, I know, patient confidentiality. Doctor Vaughan, Jenny is getting married in eight days from now. I can't let her do that if the baby's mine,' I tell her, in a last ditch effort to extract the vital information. She shakes her head at me.

'I can see how distressing this is for you, Mr. Thompson, and I do understand how you feel, but this is between you and Jenny. Take my advice, talk to her again.'

I realise that what I'm attempting is futile. I had to try. Dr. Vaughan is only doing her job, as she should be, and to be honest, she's done it well. Her job is to protect her patient, administer the best treatment available for Jenny and by telling me how it is, she's done just that.

I thank her for her time, stand up and head for the door.

'Do you want Jenny back, Mr. Thompson?' the doctor asks, whilst I open the door.

'No.'

'Then you really do have a problem.'

Despite the fact that the sun is shinning, for the first time in several days since meeting Jenny's doctor, my good mood has taken a huge dip. In such a wonderful part of the world, feeling depressed shouldn't happen. Being surrounded by some of the most wonderful scenery known to mankind should be enough to brighten anyone's day. Not mine, not today. I'm back at square one, and the time to get the answers I want is fast running out. I don't have the time for this, or the inclination with everything else that's going on in my world, but thoughts of Jenny and the baby are beginning to consume me. The conniving cow!

Leaving my car outside the office, in an effort to clear my head I wander down the quayside to where my boat is moored, and take some time out. My expensive hobby is just another thing I've ignored for the past few months. She's a money-draining toy, too much of a waste, sitting there idle.

On the plus, side she's a forty-foot pleasure cruiser. Not top of the range, as motor launches go, but she has four to six births, and she's fitted with all the latest mod cons available. Perfectly adequate for my needs.

This time of year, when the seas are rough and the weather conditions are unpredictable, the wise old heads don't put out to sea all that often, anyway. What those sensible folk do is to haul their prized possessions out of the water into temporary, dry dock and have all the essential repairs done. Every boat owner should undertake preventative maintenance, with pride. January is fast coming to a close, and although you wouldn't know it, spring is just around the corner. I'd best have a word with Ed, the boat builder, about sorting her out for the new season.

The tide is out and she's way down below me, sitting at a slight angle on the sandy bed of the harbour. My boat is a constant reminder of why I came to South Wales in the first place. I named her *Linda*. Now, there's a good story for Mal to write about. I came here for Linda - for love. Nothing's forever, I guess. What powerful words they are.

Eighteen years ago, when I first met Linda, I thought our love was forever. That magical bond wasn't to be. Feelings can be strong, dominating - as mine were for her - and you don't forget, especially the good times, but the feelings one has toward certain individuals change over the years, and therefore they're not lasting, not in the way one once hoped they would be. That's hard to accept, standing here thinking about Jenny and her unborn child.

Out on the quayside, looking back toward the town, the sunlight picks out the array of bright colours painted on the shop fronts and houses, giving a serene and prosperous look to the town. They mask what Mal is promoting: the realities of life behind the picture postcard scene. The mist-covered, grey-green colours of the hillside rising behind them are in stark contrast, mirroring my own dark mood.

The golden-yellow sands of the beach stretch for miles around the bay at low tide, gently sloping down to the tumbling waves. The tide is on the turn, now, creeping in waves toward the landmass, temporarily covering and washing the sand. It will be dark well before high tide, when the cycle starts all over again. For the sea, time has no meaning, it only has highs and lows. I'm envious, I have too many lows and too few highs, and time means everything to me.

Ed's workshop nestles beneath my office. When I bought the building, almost six years ago, I became his landlord. Most of Ed's work is done outside. Strangely, the noise he occasionally makes rarely seems to bother anyone in the office, but there's no doubt it is a cold and wet job at this time of year. Having readily made that assumption I rarely see him working. Work he must, though, because he has a constant flow of different boats sitting outside his workshop, on the quay. Like now, he has five vessels of varying sizes blocked up under repair, none that large, though.

The roller door to his workshop is open and I wait in the entrance calling out his name. A clatter of crockery from the far end – where I know his office is situated - has me peering down through the gloom of the untidy, health-hazard workshop. A man's shadow presses against the grimy window of his rest room-cum-office, and I call out, again. Ed opens the office door and waves a tatty-looking teapot in my direction, before inviting me down.

Inside his office, a three-bar electric fire blazes away unchecked. Closing the door behind me to keep the heat in, I begin to appreciate why he spends so much of his time in here. It's real cosy. Fucking hot, to be accurate.

Ed is in his late forties, although his ruddy complexion and full beard makes him look much older. I've heard some described him as *Captain Birdseye* lookalike, and there is a resemblance, particularly when he sports his tatty sailors cap. Ed is one of the few genuine locals I've met in my time here. Learning his trade in the navy, he came home to make his fortune. Sadly, the recession is affecting him, too. A few years ago, at this time of year, you couldn't move outside with the volume of boats he had in dry dock. Ed is surviving, but only just.

Ed wipes a second cup out with a rag - I'd rather not know where it's been - and proceeds to pour me a cup of tea.

'Not behind with me rent, am I?' he asks in his strong, rich Welsh accent.

'Not that I'm aware of, Ed,' I reply, but it's not unusual for him to be behind. I think he gets a good deal from me, but like any tenant, Ed would disagree.

'Must be your boat, then; saw you out there a while back,' he grunts, handing me the mug of tea, and God knows what other added extras! 'Want it serviced?'

'When you've got time, Ed. There's no rush.' Come to think of it, I've never seen him rush.

'I might be able to squeeze you in next week. Couple of urgents on, you see.'

'Like I said, no rush.' I reiterate, as Ed clears a space for me on the old settee he has in the room.

I should do the same as him and pull on a pair of overalls before I sit down on that mangy-looking thing.

'Want to drop the keys in, so I can take a look at my leisure without disturbing you. I'll probably take her out for a run as you haven't for some time,' he suggests. 'You really ought to turn the engines over regularly; I reckon it's been at least three months since I've heard you fire them up.'

'I've been busy. I forget about her.'

'Maybe you should sign a service contract with me and let me do the remembering for you.'

'Not a bad idea, Ed. Work some figures out, can you?'

'Might work out expensive,' he warns me. 'A user like you will need to consider a service every two or three months. You don't use her enough, and the sea salt plays havoc with the workings. Very corrosive, you see.'

Oh, very clever, I've walked right into this one. Thing is, I can't argue with him, but I'm not stupid. 'Just give me a price, Ed, and if it comes anywhere near your monthly rent payments then you can forget it!' I warn him.

We sit in silence sipping at our hot drinks, warming ourselves in front of the electric fire. Until now, I hadn't realised how cold it is outside.

'Bad news about the rents, isn't it?' Ed says out of the blue.

Quite frankly, I don't have a clue as to what he's talking about.

'Colin, the harbour master reckons the mooring fees will go up by a minimum of twenty percent this year.'

The completion of his announcement makes me choke on my tea, or, I could have swallowed one of those unidentifiable lumps floating on the top. 'You are joking, aren't you,' I splutter?

'Not according to Colin, and you know why that is, don't you?'

'A twenty percent rise in the mooring fees? That's scandalous!'

'Not enough people like you,' Ed adds.

'What exactly, do you mean by that?' I snap at his insinuation.

'Permanent moorings. According to Colin, they've more than halved over the past three years and as yet he hasn't had a single springtime visitor booking. If they want to stay in business and protect their precious jobs, the likes of you and me will bare the brunt of the charges.'

'They can't do that!' I shout at Ed.

Once again, Mal's words enter my thoughts. The decline in visitors and holidaymakers certainly is taking a stranglehold on our very existence. Everywhere you look there are problems.

'Appears they can do what they like, and what he's saying has all sorts of knock-on effects. This time next year, I doubt I'll be sat here talking to you. One or both of us won't survive another year in business,' Ed says solemnly.

His long, deep sigh tells me he's already resigned himself to what's in store for him. It's little wonder he's keen to offer me a service contract.

Incensed by what Ed has just told me, coupled with an unusual daytime appearance of someone in the harbour master's office during the winter months, I storm the short distance across the quayside to have a few timely words. The office door at the top of the stairs, on the first floor, is open and Colin, the harbour master, is sat with his back to me, concentrating on some paperwork. I knock to announce my arrival and without looking, Colin invites me inside.

'How can I help you?' he asks.

'By squashing a nasty rumour, Colin,' I reply, which has Colin spinning around to face me.

'What nasty rumour is that?'

'The one currently circulating, suggesting that you're increasing our mooring fees this year by twenty percent.'

Colin isn't in uniform, but nonetheless he still looks very much the part. Like Ed, he sports a full beard, which, unlike Ed's is well manicured. Colin is a tall, thin man with a thick head of greying hair and a bronzed complexion, a product of many weather-beaten hours working outside.

'No decisions have been made yet,' he tells me.

'But?' I inquire.

'Increases are inevitable; I don't know that twenty percent is correct.'

'Last year, you guys charged me fifteen hundred quid for the pleasure of mooring my boat in your harbour. If my quick mental calculations are correct, a twenty-percent increase will add another three hundred quid to that. That's an unacceptable level of increase, and I hope you're ready to fully justify that sort of price hike?'

'Like I said, nothing has been decided, yet. You'll be informed of any increase by the first of March. That's all I can tell you.'

'Well, so you know in advance, I'm in a position to fight you long and hard if a rise above the current inflation rate is imposed, and I'll want to see the proof as to why.'

'My job, Nick, is to enforce the rules and regulations, not make them.'

'Without a harbour to enforce your rules and regulations over, Colin, you don't have a job. Just think on that!'

Having got that off my chest, and feeling a lot better for doing so, I walk back across the quayside toward the office, fully intending to do some work when I get there. My outburst may have been a little unfair on Colin, but my objection to a massive yearly rise in mooring fees had to be lodged. Personally, I can afford to absorb the increase, but I know of others who aren't in such a fortunate position. The way I see it, the authorities are shooting themselves in the foot by expecting them to. Other local harbours like Fenby already have the edge. With better local facilities, and more to offer as a town, Saundersby has always struggled to compete with that. The more cautious and less adventurous nautical folk prefer the quieter life of Saundersby. In the past, the harbour's position, and protection from the prevailing westerly winds has drawn the less experienced sailors amongst us to its tranquil safety. Until now, that has stood Saundersby in good stead. Money, though, is a major influence, and value for money is a big player when making a committed financial decision.

Value comes on top of most folk's list. Further increases in mooring fees will devastate our ability to compete, and all but sign the death warrant on our wonderful little harbour. The controlling authorities are so short-sighted.

Ben has finally surfaced and I hunt him down like a bloodhound tracking its prey, yelling and snapping until his quarry is caught. Once I have him in my sight, he stands little chance of escaping, and finishing his coffee in peace. Barking out my orders in an authoritarian manner, I march him to my office and close the door.

'Well,' I ask impatiently? 'What have you got for me?'

'I've had two very boring days, Mr. Thompson,' he replies nervously, and not what I want to hear. 'From what you told me I figured I was in for some excitement, see a bit of the countryside you said…'

'For Christ sake, Ben, get on with it will you!' I bellow at him in a state of high impatience.

Ben takes a small notebook out from his back jean pocket and somewhat startled by my outburst, he continues with caution.

'The only place Stephen Jones went to, other than where he went while he was working, Mr. Thompson, was a farm in Llanfallteg West. That's between Whitland and Narberth if you're not sure…'

'I know exactly where Llanfallteg West is, Ben, thank you,' I butt in. 'Have you a name for this farm?' I add, sitting down behind my desk.

Ten-Acre Farm. It's along the road to Clynderwen. That really is the only thing of note I can tell you about. I took some photographs of Stephen leaving the farm,' he adds, looking at his wristwatch. 'They should be ready to collect by five. I'll write up my notes, Mr. Thompson, and leave the report on your desk.'

'And you're absolutely sure he didn't go anywhere else, Ben?'

'Positive, Mr. Thompson,' Ben replies with confidence.

'OK, Ben, thank you. If you haven't already spoken to Richard, I would suggest you let him know you're back. And remember, Ben, Richard doesn't need to know about this for the moment.'

Ben nods his head and goes to walk away, but he stops, turning to face me again. 'I had a little time to do some research before you got back, I found out who owns *Ten-Acre Farm*…'

'It wouldn't happen to be a certain, Gavin Thomas, would it?' I ask, interrupting him.

'Yes sir, it would!'

I'm late, and the lads are well settled into their Friday night session by the time I arrive at our local. Mac, my builder, delayed my progress, and in doing so has given me far too much to think about. The work he's doing on my house is in an advanced state and what he wants from me is something I'd conveniently put to one side. I never did engage the services of an interior designer like I threatened to do, and Mac has reached a stage where the orders for the fixtures and fittings need placing. Orders for such items, like the tiles for the swimming pool; colour for the kitchen unit doors and the work surface. I have a list as long as my arm to wade through.

In a naïve way, I had thought all this had been decided upon at the outset and was furthest from my thoughts. My perception of colour schemes is zero. I have no vision for what is required and I can't imagine what the end product will look like; something frequently commented on because of my dress sense.

I rate myself amongst the worst when it comes to style and colour co-ordination, and with the sort of money involved in the project, I can't afford to get it wrong. That kind of worries me a little. I also don't have the time or inclination for the challenge and quite rightly, Mac has refused to help out. The colour schemes, he says, are my problem, and I don't know what to do about them.

Dodging the unfair comments of 'doing a Reg' because I'm late on duty, I notice our beer appreciation group has swollen by one, this evening. Amongst the usual crowd of reprobates is a new face, a guy called Tim, who I would guess to be around thirty years old. Tim is clean-shaven, has short, black hair, and is smartly attired in a collar and tie. A professional man who is never really off duty and I quickly learn that my initial thoughts are not wrong. What Tim does for a living has more than a passing interest for me. He's a doctor and has recently joined paediatric team at the county hospital. The very hospital, where in seven months' time – or if I'm right, six - Jenny will have her baby. What is it they say? When one door closes, another one opens.

Graham, who's back from Great Malvern for the weekend, introduces us. It turns out that Tim is renting the house next door to him while he looks for a more permanent place. Plenty of time to get to know him. How good is that?

Tim would be horrified to learn that the only reason I'm taking the time to get to know him is because of Jenny and my needs, but I simply can't ignore the opportunity. When Graham informs me he wants to discuss the Great Malvern office, the decision to sit down with them both is easily made. The chance to introduce myself properly to our new social and drinking colleague is one not to be over looked.

Finally, it seems, Graham has some good news to share with me regarding the new office. He confidently informs me that a guy he interviewed for the position of office manager yesterday is right for the job, and he wants me to attend a second interview with the candidate next Wednesday. Eager to move the situation forward, I agree without consulting my diary - never a good move.

Tim listens to our conversation intently. Our line of business fascinates him and he's eager to know more. *All in good time*, I think. What we do is all I've known throughout my working life and think nothing of it. To an outsider like him it must be unusual, after all, it isn't everyday you meet a private detective.

In the early days, especially when I first opened the Saundersby office, the locals stopped us in the street and asked about our line of work. Now, even they have become blasé about our affairs. The fact is, over the years, many have, and still do, work for me. To them it's just a normal everyday business. Truth is, this is far from being a normal business, and very few of my employees are exposed to the worst this line of work can throw up from time to time.

It's not long before tales of past cases are aired in public, and watching Tim I get the impression, the more bizarre they are, the better he likes it. After eighteen years, there are plenty of tales to tell, but not tonight. His new position at the county general maybe an advantage to me in the coming months, and carrot and donkey come quickly to mind.

Listening to both Graham and Richard meander through some of their more successful sorties, it becomes clear that the early days were more locally based. I guess I already knew that, because as the company grew so did our area of operation. I think of what Mal has suggested, and that's not what he wants. Mal has this unmoveable desire to write my life story around Pembrokeshire, that's my understanding, but to be successful he'll need to expand on than that, and to satisfy him, the early days won't provide him with what he needs. I'll find out tomorrow.

Growth is important to any business, diversity and excellence equally so, and the ability to deliver that service, under open-book contract conditions, paramount. Striving to maintain that growth has taken the company further and further afield - hence the office in Great Malvern - and away from our roots. I don't ever want to lose sight of where it all began; my roots are important to me.

'What about you, Nick?' Tim asks, out of the blue. 'What do you consider to be your greatest achievement?'

A good question. What do I consider my greatest achievement?

'You must have quite a few to choose from,' Tim adds.

Leaning forward, resting my elbows on the table, I pick up a soggy beer mat and begin to pull it apart. A distraction while I settle on what, over the years, has given me the most satisfaction.

'At the age of eighteen,' I begin, in front of a captive audience around the table, 'Christmas 1970, as Richard will verify...' I look at him nodding his head, and notice the others looking at him too, for confirmation. 'Almost overnight, I went from a spotty, penniless teenager to a young man with several thousands of pounds in the bank. *How?* You might ask. Well, because I felt passionate enough about the village I then called home, to do something about the problems they were encountering. I took risks, gambled on doing what I thought was right, and reaped the benefits.'

I take a moment, sipping on my pint of beer, with eyes keenly fixed on me waiting for me to continue. To intensify the deceit, I slowly take another long pull on my beer.

'Is that it?' One of the lads pipes up. 'Your greatest achievement is making thousands of pounds over night?'

Carefully placing my pint glass down directly on the table - no decent beer mats, as usual - I pick up my cigarettes, take one out of the packet, and light up.

'Dentist,' Reg shouts from somewhere in the gloom, and furthest point from the bar, no doubt. He is referring, of course, to the fact that I only take one out at a time. I wish I had a pound for every time I've heard him say that.

'As a naïve but quick learning eighteen-year-old, those thousands of pounds could very easily have been squandered. Cars, drink, holidays, you name it, I could have wasted that money on anything I wanted to.'

'Why didn't you?' Tim ask. 'Any normal eighteen-year-old would have done. Not that I'm suggesting you're not normal, you understand,' he adds, as I look him in the eye.

'That's the point I'm making. Maybe, I wasn't a normal eighteen-year-old. I fell in love with this place, and the people I met in that time looked after me when I was down and out. They accepted me with open arms and treated me as one of their own, part of their community. My greatest achievement is being allowed to put something back into that community. By that statement I mean not only employing local people; over the years, I've financially supported a number of local projects and that has given me the greatest of pleasure.'

There's a strange sort of silence while my gathered audience take in what I've told them, probably because it wasn't what they expected me to say. I could have chosen any number of past cases, some with happy endings, and some with tragic consequences, but nothing has given me greater pleasure than repaying those who mean the most to me. There's no doubt that South Wales has treated me well. Eighteen years ago, it was my choice to stay here with the friends I'd made, and I've worked hard to make that life-changing decision work for me, and those around me. I have no regrets.

By the start of 1971, I had a five-figure number in my first, ever, bank account. I could have gone anywhere I liked and done anything I wanted to. I had the world at my feet. I stayed and gave my friends and colleagues a chance in life that perhaps they would never have had. Richard is testament to that, but there are many others.

'You should write your autobiography,' Tim suggests.

I say nothing.

Chapter six

Saturday, 23 January 1988

I read through the case notes Reg had given me, again, last night, when I got home from the pub. He wants them back ASAP and before I return them to him, I want to go over the train driver's statement once more. Something about his statement doesn't sit comfortably with me. That's why I'm here in Llanfallteg West, this morning, in the pouring rain, standing on the unmanned level crossing where the incident took place. The crossing is identical to the one on Tom's land, and only used for moving livestock safely across the railway from field to field - rather ironic when one thinks about it.

I'm on Gavin Thomas's land - *Ten-Acre Farm* - and I've got to be careful. After what Ben told me, Gavin must know by now that if not me, then someone is snooping around. He will know for definite that his brother-in-law, William Marchant, wasn't responsible for knocking on Steven Jones's door, the other day.

I've parked my car at the end of Tom's lane in the entrance to his top field, not entirely out of view from the road, but I don't think anyone will make a connection.

Standing in the middle of the crossing on the track bed, looking both up and down the railway, I cannot understand how on earth David Thomas failed to see or hear the train approaching. Even in these foul conditions, the view both ways is reasonably good. Why the train driver failed to see him and apply the train's brakes is a different matter, and one that must be explored.

The crossing gates open outwards into the fields - not across the track, which is the normal arrangement - and for that reason, there isn't a safety-locking device to prevent them from being opened when a train approaches. Only a phone, linked to the nearest signal box or control centre, stands between safety and potential disaster.

David's failure to reach safety isn't easily explained away, unless he was deaf and had his back to the approaching danger. Apart from the howling gale today, it is very quiet, but stood here, I'm certain I would hear a train coming long before I saw it. Some seven years ago, on the day David died, conditions were very different. I gather from what I've read the weather that day was a damn sight better than it is today - which in my mind, and what I now see, judging it to have been an accident is very unsafe. Granted, there would have been a great deal of noise at the time: hounds barking and yelping, the sound of riders on their horses, and the sound of the master of the hunts bugle. The hunt saboteurs themselves certainly added chaos and mayhem to the proceedings in any way they could to distract the dogs away from the kill. All things considered, none of that affected what the train driver saw and heard.

To the east, the railway line sweeps down under a stone road bridge some half a mile from where I'm standing. Beyond that lies Tom Morgan's land. The murky weather this morning obscures his farmhouse from view, although I can just make out the bare, oak tree silhouettes on the steep bank behind his property.

Looking west, the line climbs away gradually, running alongside a steep embankment rising sharply on the southern side of the track until it eventually sweeps away left and out of sight. The train that hit David came from that direction, downhill, and probably at speed, but I would guess at no more than sixty to seventy miles per hour. How the driver failed to see David on the crossing just doesn't make sense.

Witness statements to the accident are at best, sparse, and those that were taken are extremely vague. Not one witness, however, claims to have heard the train's driver sound the engine's horn as a warning to David. Were they confused perhaps, by the sound of the hunt's bugle? Then why would the sound of the trains warning horn alert them to a problem? According to the statements, no one knew where David was, or what he was doing.

On the evidence available at the time, and the poor work done by those charged with collecting the said evidence, a verdict of accidental death, or death by misadventure, was inevitable. Seven years on, it may be difficult to prove otherwise.

To prove my point on the driver's part in this, and to put my mind at rest, I want to walk up the track and look back at the view he had of the crossing that day. I'm cold and wet, and I'm due at Mal's in half an hour. My walk along the railway will have to wait, and I've certainly picked the wrong day to show Mal around.

Since the conversation in the pub last night, I have given a lot of thought to Mal and this book he wants to write. My first six months here in South Wales has just about everything a good book needs. Love at first sight, heartache, friendship, hardship, and most importantly, humour. With that in mind, I plan this morning not only to discuss its potential, but to also take Mal on a guided tour so he can get a feel of the places most significant to those early days; a sort of visual storybook.

Baz is at Mal's place when I arrive. Apparently, he's coming with us. My original arrangement with Mal was for lunch, and it's not because Baz is tagging along and I'm tight, but our first port of call is Tom's farm. I know Mal and Baz won't be disappointed by one of Mother's superb lunches, and if I know her, she'll go the extra mile to impress. I didn't plan this. When I phoned earlier to make sure it was all right to call in, Mother insisted we stayed for lunch. That's the sort of people they are, generous to a fault.

Their farm played a major role in those 'never to be forgotten' autumn and winter months of 1970. I can't leave the farm out of the tour I'm about to inflict on Mal and Baz, because without the farm there is no story.

Tom is in his element. He's a terrific storyteller when he has a captive audience and he has the ability to turn a funny story into something hilarious - a real rib cracker. A tour of the farm in Tom's old Land Rover - God knows how he's kept it going all these years – with an airing of stories of our fishing expeditions, and discussing my drunken state when the harvesting was done; we retire to the farmhouse for lunch. By the time we sit down around Tom's table, I can gauge that both Mal and Baz are hooked by what they've seen, and they want to see and know more. All at my expense, of course, but at least it shows I'm human. Perhaps I should have invited Jenny along for the tour, there's a side to me that she knows nothing about, and one I had long forgotten existed.

Our schedule isn't critical, however, there are a number of other places I'd like to show them both before it gets dark, like the old post office in the village. Tom has taken to them readily, as they have to him, and it's not long before the home brew starts to flow. Not what I wanted to happen. From personal experience, neither Mal nor Baz need any encouragement to drink, as I discovered to my cost last weekend. I ask – no, plead - with Tom to stop the drinking and to let me get on with their tour while Mal and Baz can still stand. His response takes me by surprise.

'You've got something weighing heavily on your mind, boy,' he says. 'Do you want to talk to me about it?' He adds, topping up three glasses of home brew. Tom isn't listening to my pleading, but he's certainly got my attention. I have got something weighing heavily on my mind - Jenny. How does he know? I've not said a word to anyone, apart from Jenny. Richard might speculate over her pregnancy; Jan too, but no one knows for sure - not even me!

I look up at the old clock, hanging on the wall above the Welsh dresser, whilst Tom staggers back across the room to the table with a couple of fresh beers for Mal and Baz. This tour isn't going to be concluded today so I may as well join them. I'll stay here again tonight, and when the two old sods are ready to go home, I'll phone my old mate, Dan, the taxi driver, and get him to drop them off. It won't cost me, either. I've known Dan since day one, when he worked for a large local cab company. Dan now has his own business and we, as a company, have an account with him. Not to be used for personal reasons naturally, but what the fuck - I'm the boss! Pouring myself a beer, Tom returns to my side and hovers.

'What makes you think I've got something on my mind, Tom?' I ask him.

'You should know me by now, boy. I can see it in your face, and I can hear it in your voice.'

'No,' I reply. 'I'm not having that. Besides, you've got it wrong this time.'

'Have I?'

'Absolutely! I'm as happy as a sand boy and full of the joys of spring,' I tell him.

'I wish I could believe you, boy,' Tom barks at me. 'I know you've lots going on at the moment, but I sense there's something deep inside making you hurt. When you're ready, you'll tell me.'

As always, at times like this, Tom produces a roll-up. Holding it out in front of him for me to take, he looks down at my full glass of beer. 'Decided to stay overnight again, have we?'

Tom's observation worries me because he's not the first to notice a change. 'You'll tell me in the end, boy, you know you will. Just don't leave it until it's too late,' he adds, walking away to rejoin Mal and Baz sitting at the table.

He sees it in my face, and he can hear it in my voice. What am I doing and saying that's different to any other time we've spoken? I concede he's not wrong, and whatever it is, I am doing and saying, Tom has clearly seen a difference. Tom has often said that he knows me better than I know myself. I'm beginning to believe him.

Sunday, 24 January 1988

Staying the night at the farm gives me the opportunity to enact my wish and walk the railway line earlier than planned. I'm up at first light, dressed and out of the house by seven thirty. Tom will be upset by my absence in the milking shed. Today that age-old routine will go by the by, and for the record there's the added bonus of it being Sunday. The train services are, at best, infrequent on a Sunday, if not almost non-existent. Much safer to do what I have in mind. Before I leave on my expedition, I let Mother know where I'm going - always a good idea - just in case something goes wrong.

Reaching the point of impact, I head west, striding from sleeper to sleeper, stopping on every hundredth one to look back toward the crossing. A distance I guess to be approximately, in multiples of hundred yards, give or take. After several stops, tiredness takes over. The distance between the sleepers is far greater than my natural stride pattern and the abnormal stretching hurts my calf muscles. Losing count of how many times I've counted out one hundred sleepers comes early in the exercise. Too many beers again last night. The exact distance from the crossing isn't important, so when my thigh muscles come out in sympathy with my calves I decide to call it a day. I'm satisfied, though. I must be somewhere between half a mile and a mile from where I started - to the point where I've decided to call it a day - and the crossing is clearly visible.

The train driver would have been sat some five or six foot above my eye line, making his overall vision far superior to that of mine. With his route knowledge, he should be aware of the crossing's existence and been looking for it. He would also be aware, through his training, how important the dangers of unmanned crossings are, and the potential hazards they can create. If my understanding is correct, he had a duty to sound the train warning regardless of the situation.

I hold the opinion that the driver's statement is total bollocks, because if someone were to use the crossing right now I would see them with no trouble at all! Why didn't the driver, on that fateful day seven years ago? Satisfying my curiosity with what I see, it's clear to me that he either lied through his teeth to protect himself, or his attention was focussed elsewhere.

In his statement, he claims he didn't see David until the last seconds, and that David appeared from nowhere as if he were playing chicken. I know from what I've read that the gates were open and secured back, if David had opened them alone that would have taken him several minutes to achieve. That alone puts David in a position of safety, because the gates open out into the fields. If by chance he were crossing back over the lines, having completed his task, his all-round vision would have been good, and David would have seen the train bearing down upon him.

I'm nowhere near the point at which the crossing first came into view for the driver. I would estimate that he had between two and three minutes in which to apply the train's brakes, make enough fuss with the engine warning horn to wake the dead, and, even if he couldn't stop the train in time, he had the chance to make a great deal of noise while he gave it a go. According to the statements, he didn't do any of those things.

There is a risk here of overlooking the fact that David might have committed suicide. He may have lain on the ground close to the crossing and at the last minute stepped out in front of the train. That would verify the driver's story and exonerate him of any wrongdoing. It is a possibility, and one that opens a new line of inquiry, but why would a young man who had everything going for him commit suicide? In the same vein, why would David want to sabotage his own father's hunt?

Reginald Moss was here at the time of the accident and I feel sure he knows the truth behind the events of that day. Whether or not Moss is responsible for David's death isn't so clear. A few days ago, I would have bet my shirt on it, but Stephen Jones' visit here to see Gavin Thomas and not Reginald Moss has changed my view. My gut feeling tells me there's something much deeper, and far more sinister going on, and William Marchant's apparent willingness to help upholds that gut feeling.

Linda was the reason I came to Pembrokeshire in the first place - although 'returned' would be more accurate. My first memories of this beautiful place are two weeks B&B holiday on Tom Morgan's farm with my parents. That's where I met Linda, and for me it was love at first sight. For two glorious weeks we were almost inseparable.

When that wonderful holiday came to an end, I believed that I couldn't live without her. By saving every penny I earned, after a few weeks I had enough money for the train fare and returned to Pembrokeshire to be with her. I very quickly discovered that I'd made a huge mistake. Linda didn't love me the way I loved her, and she already had a steady boyfriend. Not knowing what to do, or where to go, I chose to stay here, because I believed I couldn't correct the mistakes I'd made with my parents. I'd convinced myself that going home wasn't an option open to me.

For another four months, Linda played a big part in my life. The connection with Tom's farm and her friendship with Jan saw to that. Until Linda went off to Bristol University, our paths often crossed. After that, our involvement was not so intense. It is for that reason the first stop on today's tour continuation with Mal and Baz is to show them where Linda lived.

The stop is brief. Even now the memories of that first day are painful. There is no place in my heart for her today, and that hurt remains buried deep within me. Maybe that's how Tom knows - he's seen it before.

Next stop is the village, and I'm surprised to learn that neither Mal nor Baz have ever set foot here before. Parking the car right on the seafront - near the old phone box - I suggest that we take a stroll along the promenade while I fill in the details.

I'm automatically drawn to the old post office, my home for just over thirty months. It lies empty and unused. A sign of the times, which Mal is quick to pick up on. I have vivid memories of life in the old place, some good and some not so good, nothing really bad, but they were testing times. The months spent living, working with Jan and Richard in the shop, and the problems they had, taught me a lot about life. It's where I can honestly say, with hand on heart, that I grew up. This is the place where I became the person I am today. The independence and the strong character that emerged during my time here moulded me into a successful businessman.

I want Mal and Baz to see where I live now. After a brief visit to my first abode in Saundersby, via my office in the harbour, I take them up to the builder's yard on top of the hill. To understand my humble beginnings, and why I chose to stay here, they need to see what I've achieved through hard work - and a little luck along the way, and how this green and pleasant land, with its friendly people inspired me. If I'm right, that's exactly the sort of thing Mal wants to hear.

Mal takes his time trawling through my personal effects. I get the impression he's looking for the little things that say more about me than I care to divulge; a tough job to undertake given the state of my house. A good biographer will want to be accurate, take care, and get to know his subject before putting pen to paper. The understanding and knowledge of me that he will posses by the end of this venture is frightening. It's not something I feel at all comfortable with!

'I'd like to get started on this as soon as possible,' Mal says quietly, pulling me aside. 'A rough draft first to see how it works out.'

'Do you think it will then,' I ask?

'There's potential, definitely. When can we get together again?'

'I'm genuinely quite busy at the moment, Mal. Let me check my diary in the morning and I'll give you a call,' I tell him.

'Sure, and until I've done the rough draft I'd prefer it if Baz didn't know. He has this annoying habit of trying to influence the storyline. I find that terribly distracting,' Mal informs me.

'I tell you what, I'll try and find my diaries. I know they're here somewhere and they may be of use to you,' I inform Mal.

'You've kept diaries!' Mal says excitedly.

'From about the age of ten, yeah. I'll ask my old mum to send me the ones from her place.'

'Will that be necessary? I mean, how far do we need to go back?'

'There's one very important one. When I came back here, I forgot to bring the diary of 1970 with me. In it are all my thoughts and dreams of life with Linda, and the time we spent together on Tom's farm. Going over my own scribbling is not something I personally want to do, but to really understand why I came back you'd need to read through them and ask me questions.'

'Ok, then, why don't we wait until you've got the lot together?' Mal suggests.

'Might be better for me anyway. I'll give her a call now before we go for a pint. I assume you fancy a liquid lunch?' I stupidly ask.

Monday, 25 January 1988

My top employee – agent, as he prefers to call himself – is a young man called James. His parents are to blame for his arrogant attitude. For the past twenty-six years, James has lived with the surname of Bond. Now a mature adult and a rising star in the world of private investigation, he uses his name to great effect. His coolness and suave manner match his good looks and dark complexion. James has the office girls and clients alike clambering for his attentive bedside manner. I find it all rather sickening, but James is good at his job - very good. He's a bright young man, clever, thorough, and diligent; a perfectionist, with sneaky, slimy, underhand methods for getting results. All the attributes required to go a long, long way in this business.

I keep James focussed and busy, dictate to him what he does and where he goes, and with good reason. Someone with the talent James has at his disposal could easily survive out in the big wide world on his own. If James decided to take that route and really put his mind to it, he could become a serious threat to my organisation.

I ask James to join me once I've done the morning rounds. He never sits down in my office - it's too dirty for him in his Armani suit. I can't help but feel that James is overdressed for this job. Jeans and a tee shirt are perfectly adequate, and I've said as much to him on many an occasion. Our line of work isn't glamorous, not in the way the public perceives it - quite the opposite, to be honest. James though, is dressed to kill, or thrill, depending on one's gender.

'Morning boss!' he says, swaggering into my office. I hate that, *boss*.

'What are you doing for me today, James?'

'The Mason affair, but if you've something more urgent boss,' he chirps.

That's another annoying habit of his. Every job to James is an affair. The young man standing in front of me really has found his true vocation in life. James walks the walk, and talks the talk.

'Two actually, James.' I inform him, and hand him a slip of paper.

'David Reece,' he repeats, reading it back out, aloud.

'I want you to find out where he is and what he's doing.'

'What do we know about him, boss?'

'David Reece was the train driver involved in a fatal accident near Llanfallteg back in 1981. Originally from Swansea, he was living in Fishguard at the time of the accident.'

'I gather he no longer lives in Fishguard, boss?'

'Not sure, James, that's what I want you to find out. And when you've done that, I've got something much bigger for you get your teeth into.'

'Consider it done. Is there anything else I should know about Mr. Reece?'

'Only that it's highly unlikely he still works for British rail, but you never know, James.'

'Ok boss,' he adds and he's gone.

James will be back within the hour with all the information I need on David Reece. James is that reliable.

A commotion outside my office door breaks my concentration. I hear raised voices, one I recognise to be Sue's, and she's shouting at someone to stop. Jumping up out of my leather chair, I negotiate a passage through my rubbish and head for the door to investigate. My office door flies open before I reach it as Jenny bursts in without knocking. She looks a touch agitated.

'What the bloody hell are you up to, Nick?' Jenny screams at me, wagging her right index finger accusingly in my direction.

'Sorry, Nick,' Sue says, appearing behind Jenny. 'She just walked straight in. I couldn't stop her.'

'It's all right Sue,' I reassure her. 'I've been expecting this to happen. Go and get yourself a cup of tea. I'll deal with Jenny.'

As Sue turns to walk back down the corridor, I gently close my office door for some privacy. Jenny is sat on the windowsill when I turn back to face into the room. Her face is like thunder. 'What's rattled your cage, Jenny?'

'As if you didn't know?' she questions me.

Keeping my distance, I lean back against the closed office door until she's calmed down. Jenny has a tendency to lash out when she's angry.

'If you're referring to my visit to your doctor, then let me inform you that I have the right to know the truth,' I tell her, and she laughs at me.

'You're obsessed. You already know the truth, but just in case you didn't hear me right the first time,' she says, being very animated and cock sure of herself, pointing with both hands at her stomach. 'This baby is Tony's and nothing to do with you. Not yours…Tony's. Have you got that?' she finishes with, raising her voice to me.

'Then prove it,' I respond, challenging her confidence.

Jenny remains silent as I walk back to my desk, pausing a moment before sitting down. 'Let me assure you, I won't rest until you do.'

'There's nothing to prove. I know who the father is and it's not you.' Jenny slowly and deliberately walks from her position on the windowsill and stands facing me across the desk. 'Leave me alone. Let me get on with my life the way I want to. This baby is Tony's. I have no reason to lie to you and absolutely no need to prove to you who the father is.'

Staring at Jenny for a moment or two, trying to gauge the sincerity on her face first, I pull out my chair and sit down at my desk. I have a little advice for her before she leaves.

'Remember this, Jenny, won't you? Once Tony's name goes on the birth certificate, you release me from any financial obligation for the child. If that is your choice, then so be it. I will not take a paternity test in the future to suit you. Your one opportunity to sting me for child maintenance is now. That, my love, is your decision, but it doesn't mean that I'll stop looking for the truth. If it takes me the rest of my life, I will find out. Now if you don't mind, I'm busy. Close the door behind you on your way out.'

Dangling the golden egg in front of Jenny might be a desperate move, but I know what she likes, and that's all things that glitter. The idea is to give her something to think about before she takes her wedding vows. Greed is a powerful emotion, and the temptation may be too great for her.

'You bastard,' she whispers.

'I'm busy,' I reply quickly. I'm not going to conclude this with her now. Jenny needs time to digest the implications of her actions. 'If you don't mind, I'd like to crack on with my work.' I tell her, looking at the office door.

'That's typical of you. You think your money can buy you anything…'

'Goodbye, Jenny,' I snap, stopping her in full flow. I know I've touched a raw nerve, because I know Jenny likes money, and I know she loves spending it! The extension work currently being undertaken on my house is proof of that.

I wish I'd thought of this when I first learnt that she was pregnant. Her wedding is five days from now and there may not be time to cast enough doubt in her mind to call it off.

Jenny slams the door behind her. I shouldn't, but I feel good knowing that I've got to her. Time alone will tell how strong her devotion to Tony is, and how sure she is that the baby she's carrying is his.

James does a lot of background work for me. Three years ago that's why I originally employed him. James quickly showed his worth and has his own workload to keep him occupied, he still likes to please the boss. He has come up trumps on the train driver. David Reece still lives in Fishguard and works as a barman in a public house in town.

It's a pretty dingy place and not my cup of tea. Tucked along back street in the centre of town I would say that it's a local's pub where all sorts go on. The interior décor is rather tatty, not dirty, but cries out for a lick of paint to cover the nicotine stains on the paintwork. Fortunately, I arrive before the lunchtime rush – if the place has one – and the bar is relatively quiet.

My trip out to Fishguard isn't on a whim, but I have taken the chance on David working. In the file Wallace produced, there was an old photograph of him and I believe I've struck lucky. In his own sweet time the guy ambles down the servery to where I'm waiting and gives me an old fashioned look when I ask for an orange juice and lemonade. He's in no hurry to return with my drink; his mate at the other end of the bar is far more interesting – for the moment.

'That'll be one pound and five pence, mate,' he rudely says, placing my drink on the bar.

'You're David Reece, aren't you?' My question takes him by surprise and he stares menacingly at me. I've been here a number of times before.

'Whose asking?' he responds, his hand outstretched, waiting for me to hand over the money.

'My name's Nick Thompson. I'm a private detective.' I inform him, placing the money on the counter beneath his hand. 'I'd like to ask you a few questions.'

'No.'

Shaking his head, he eventually replies. 'David isn't on until tonight,' he adds.

'Ready for another when you've got a minute, Dave,' his mate shouts, from the other end of the bar.

'Must be very confusing, Mr Reece, I say. 'Having all these Dave's working behind the bar.'

'What do you want,' he mumbles, leaning over the bar?

'Accident near Llanfallteg, 1981.'

'What about it?'

'I'd like to ask you a few questions about the accident.'

'I'm working mate,' David says, dismissing my request.

'So am I, mate.'

David stares at me through his large, piercing, blue eyes, trying to warn me off. Been there, done that, and got the tee shirt. His threatening posture and mannerism doesn't bother me. I simply stare back at him, letting him know that I'm not going anywhere.

'Take a seat; I'll be with you in a minute,' David responds, backing down. He was never going to win that battle. I can stare for England – so I'm told.

There's a little more urgency about him as he goes about serving his mate, and I'm not kept waiting very long. Sitting himself down opposite me - so his back is toward his friend – David is keen to point out his innocence.

'I was cleared of any wrong doing,' he opens with. 'I told the police everything at the time; it's all in my statement.'

'I've read your statement, Mr. Reece.' I thought I should tell him that. 'The thing is, new evidence has come to light very recently which brings your statement into question.'

'Bollocks!' he shouts.

'I thought that when I read your statement.'

'I told the truth. That lad came from nowhere. There was nothing I could do.'

'I don't believe you,' I say, and I don't, but he insists, and turns nasty on me.

'Do you know how much I've been through? Years of counselling, that's what. Because I couldn't cope with life, I had to give up my job with the railway, and I lost my house as a result of not working. All you're interested in is laying the blame at someone's door.' David stands, flicking a beer mat at me he continues, 'Well, it isn't going to be me.'

'Sit down, Mr. Reece. Please?'

'Sod off. I'm not going to made a scapegoat of, just because you fellas can't do you're jobs properly.'

An interesting comment; what makes him think I'm looking for a scapegoat?

'Please sit down and hear me out, Mr. Reece,' I repeat.

'Give me one good reason why I should?'

'Because you can help me stop history from repeating itself. I'm not out to get you, Mr. Reece; I'm after someone else. That someone else is still out there going about business the same way he was seven years ago, and there's a very good chance he'll be the cause of another death.'

'What makes you so sure I can help you?' David asks slowly sitting down. He appears much calmer now, and that's because I've suggested he may not be in trouble. He still might be, for all I know.

'I walked the track yesterday,' I tell him, changing tact. 'I got about a mile away from the crossing before my legs decided they'd had enough. I'm puzzled by what you said in your statement. What was it? Oh yes, you thought that young David was playing chicken.'

'That's the way it looked to me. The lad appeared from nowhere, right in front of me.' David tells me, sticking firmly to his original story.

'Mr. Reece, I laid my black coat on the ground, beside the crossing, before I tramped along the line, and I could clearly see it from where I stopped, which means, Mr. Reece, that David had to be hidden in the bushes further back so you couldn't see him. I paced that out, thirty-five of my strides, about thirty yards I'd guess. Three to four seconds of running is a fair assessment of time across that uneven ground before he reached the crossing. Three to four seconds in which you had time to see him and apply the brakes.' I didn't do any of those things, but I know David is lying and I want the truth from him. If he feels cornered - found out, hopefully, he will sing.

'This is not my fault. I didn't see the lad until it was too late.'

'I don't doubt that. The question is, why didn't you apply the brakes until you hit him, and not before? If David did run out from behind the bushes in front of your train, I would agree that you didn't have time to stop, but had he done so, you would have seen him, had time to apply your brakes and sound your warning horn. You didn't do any of that. Why?'

David sits back in his chair and lets out a long, loud sigh of resignation. I guess he's fallen into the fact he knows I know he's lying, and he's going to have to tell me exactly what did happen that day.

'I'm in trouble, aren't I?' he whispers.

I shrug my shoulders. 'That's not for me to decide.' I suggest, removing a small Dictaphone from my jacket pocket and placing it on the table in front of him. 'Want to tell me about it, David?'

'They'll throw the bloody book at me,' he insists.

If he's proven to be negligent, they may well do.

'I wouldn't normally have been there at that time,' he says, beginning his account of that day.

I press down the record button on the Dictaphone to the *on* position.

'The trains were all to cock. Some problem in the Cardiff area, the day before, meant trains were being cancelled because the rolling stock was in the wrong place. I was given the job that morning of taking an empty stock train to Swansea to balance the shortages. I had no second man and there was no guard. With only six coaches on and a good *class 47* under my control, I stupidly decided to see what I could get out of her down the gradient. I'd got her up to about ninety, half way down the gradient, when a dip in the track bounced my full cup of coffee off the control module into my lap. It landed in a very delicate spot and scalded me. I was trying to sort myself out when I heard a bump. I knew I'd hit something and applied the brakes. I hoped that it was an animal of some description.'

'So you didn't actually see anything?' I suggest, butting in.

'I hit the brakes the moment I felt the bump. By the time I looked up, the over bridge was looming. I knew then that whatever I hit was on the crossing, and that could have been anything. What a mess,' David confesses.

'Then what happened?' I ask, prompting him to complete the chain of events.

'I brought the loco to a stop as safely as I could and jumped out to survey the damage. That's when I saw what I'd hit, and it wasn't a very pleasant sight. I puked up violently several times, Mr Thompson.' David buries his head in his hands, and pauses for a moment, gathering his composure. 'There was no doubt in my mind what I'd hit. I had to deal with the situation and my training took over. I walked on down the line to the next signal and called in to control. I was told to stay put and wait for help. It was at that point I realised I could be in serious trouble and covered my tracks. I cleaned the cab and myself, and thought up my story while I waited for help to arrive. I didn't know it was a lad of seventeen…I'm so sorry.'

I switch off the recorder.

David looks questioningly at me. 'Is that it, Mr. Thompson?'

'There's just one thing, so it's clear in my mind. From what you're telling me, you're admitting that your concentration was elsewhere, and you didn't see the events as they unfolded in front of you. Is that what you're saying?'

'Yes,' he whispers. 'What are you going to do now?'

His spoken word has fear in every syllable. There's no doubt his statement changes the outcome of previous findings. David is in big trouble and I should take this to Reg Wallace immediately, but as always, I'm going to wait, and see what James comes up with.

'David,' I continue. 'You used the word 'scapegoat' earlier and that puzzles me a little. It sort of makes me think that you know more. If there's something you're not telling me, now would be a good time to come clean.'

David remains tight-lipped, staring at the licking flames of the log fire a few feet away. It needs attending to

'A few days after the accident, a man calling himself Afon Lewis contacted me. I had no idea who he was, but he wanted to know what I'd told the police. At first, I wouldn't tell him but he became very insistent, saying it was important. Eventually I gave in and told him what was in my statement. This Afon Lewis seemed quite pleased with what I told him, then his mood changed and he threatened me with life - changing violence if I changed my story. As you now know, I couldn't, even if I wanted to. That was the last I heard from him. I'm scared, Mr Thompson, because no matter who's at fault here, I will get the blame. I killed that lad through my negligence and if they want someone to blame, I'm in the hot seat. That's what I meant by "scapegoat".'

'And Afon Lewis, did he say why he wanted to know?'

'No, and to be honest I didn't want to know. I was mightily relieved he believed me, and he left a happy man, with the content of my statement, but I've often wondered, since that phone call, if something funny was going on there, because nothing further came of our conversation. Of course, I've never questioned it, because if I had, I might have got myself into big trouble. Like now.'

'Don't disappear on me, David.' Standing up, I place the recorder back into my jacket pocket. 'It maybe necessary to talk to you again, and if I can't find you, you'll leave me with little choice in the matter. For what it's worth, I think you're right. I too believe that something funny was going on back then. David, I want to make it clear to you that this will stay between us if you keep quiet about this meeting. Do I make myself clear?'

'Perfectly,' David adds, with a sigh of relief.

David's taped confession proves he was negligent. His lack of concentration killed David Thomas, but until I find out why David was on that crossing, and why he was there that day, it will be hard to prove whose fault it was. Moss, David's father - Gavin, Stephen Jones, and I believe, Marchant, too, are all suspects. They all know something of what went on that day - if not all - and I know who's the most likely to break down first.

Working regular hours in a regular job creates habitual people. Clock off at four-thirty, home by five o'clock, dinner on the table for six. Isn't that crap? Stephen falls neatly into that category, and as long as the slow-moving traffic improves, I can be sat outside his house waiting when he arrives home. It's time to renew our acquaintance, and time to start turning up the heat. I'm in Stephen's face the moment he climbs from his works' van. He's a little surprised to see me.

'I told you last time that I've got nothing to say to you,' Stephen says, slamming shut the driver's door of his van.

'Why did you go to see Gavin Thomas, Stephen?'

'I don't know what you're talking about, Mr…'

Stopping in mid-sentence, pretending he's forgotten my name, tells me he knows exactly who I am. From the inside pocket of my jacket, I pull out a copy of one of the photographs Ben had taken of Stephen leaving *Ten Acre Farm* - one where he's clearly recognisable – and wave it under his nose.

I notice that Stephen's hand is shaking when he takes the photograph from me. He stares at it, long and hard, before trying to put it back into my pocket. I resist his feeble attempt and it flutters unceremoniously down onto the pavement. He has little chance of denying this. Ben had made quite sure the farm's name board was clearly visible when he took the picture.

'I've got nothing to say,' Stephen repeats, and starts to walk away.

'Shall I come back tomorrow and tell you what else I know?' I shout after him.

Stephen stops, turns and walks back to where I'm stood. 'Mr. Thompson…' he says. Realising his error he stops himself.

The last time I was here, I introduced myself as William Marchant. I even gave him a business card with Marchant's name on. Bending down, I pick up the dropped photograph, write my phone number on the back, and hand it back to Stephen.

'I'm ready to listen when you're ready to talk,' I tell him. 'And the next time I pay you a visit, I won't be on my own, if you get my drift. I'm closing in, Stephen, and it's only a matter of time.'

I'm not, but I love playing mind games.

Chapter seven

Tuesday, 26 January 1988

A few months ago, I expressed my worries, and my doubts, to the builder, Mac, that I thought he wouldn't complete the extension to schedule. I gave him the chance to re-evaluate the contract we signed and he declined. This morning, I'm leaving the house early to avoid him. I know Mac will throw a barrage of questions at me if we meet face to face because I haven't done as he's asked, which will allow him to proceed. Mac is well ahead of schedule and he's looking to complete three to four weeks early. It now appears I will be the one holding him up, and my penalty clause for his work running over time won't be worth the paper it's written on.

Jan hasn't arrived by the time I walk out through my front door, which means I've gone without my usual cooked breakfast. Jan isn't late; I can't afford to hang around for her this morning and run the risk of bumping into Mac. I'm hungry all the same, and decide to call in at *Jay's Café* in town for a fry-up to satisfy my hunger pangs. Moving stuff, clearing rooms, and choosing the interior décor for Mac will have to wait another day.

Many thought-provoking moments occur when one least expects them to. Sitting down at a vacant table in the café, having first ordered my 'full Monty' breakfast at the counter, I start to question why I'm here. Hiding behind my work, saying I'm too busy to take care of the little things, is becoming my stock excuse for avoiding them - much as I'm doing this morning.

Work is my passion. I enjoy dealing with other people's problems – not my own. Results drive me, winning has become a need, and I love nothing better than getting my teeth into a good case. Those little everyday things, like the décor, are just as important, and really should be granted the same degree of importance. I've had too many easy years where, with a click of my fingers and an open chequebook attitude, things have got done without too much effort on my part. Maybe I've become lazy in my old age, or maybe I find it easier to pay someone else to do the mundane things for me. One thing is for certain: the constant pressure I'm under is getting to me.

Trying to fit Jenny into my life didn't work because of the way I am. While working I'm single-minded, blinkered. There's little room in my life for anything else, that's because there's always something more important to attend to, and money to earn.

But what if this baby is mine, what then? How would – could - I fit a baby into my hectic lifestyle? Do I let Jenny marry Tony on Saturday, and together leave them to do my job for me? Let Tony Morris bring up a child of mine? I don't think so. Do I ask Jenny to come back, live with me in my house and together, as the loving couple, bring the child up? That certainly would command a lot of my time, time I can't give because I don't know how to. Why, then, do I really need to know who the father of Jenny's baby is?

If I can't, or won't change, do I reach for my chequebook once more to make me feel better? Doing just that has been my answer to many problems along the way. It takes no more than ten seconds to write a cheque. It takes a lifetime to raise a child. Which of those is more convenient to me? But how will I know if any money I give to Jenny will be spent on the baby, and not over the bar, by Tony?

There are too many 'ifs' and 'buts', to settle this situation in a way that will keep everyone happy. The time I personally have left to satisfy my involvement in this - to an amicable conclusion - is fast running out, and I may well end up being the loser. Things certainly look that way. Yesterday, in a last ditch effort to salvage the situation, I dangled the carrot in front of Jenny, and I haven't heard from her. Could that be because I've been wrong all along? Then, why do I want so much to be right? Is that because I know I am? And, I wonder what I'd actually do if Jenny told me the baby is mine?

'Mind if I join you, Nick?' a male voice asks, bringing me back to reality with a jolt. In my daydream world, I was staring out of the window across at the harbour, watching this everyday morning slowly come to life. Very little of what I've seen has sunk in; none of it has any great importance to me. The person standing next to me - holding a cup of coffee in one hand and cutlery in the other - does.

'Taken to following me have you?' I snap, seeing the guy I met at football a couple of Saturdays ago; Brad, if I remember correctly.

'May I?' he asks again, gesturing with his full hands toward the table.

'Please yourself,' I mumble back.

'I thought I might have heard from you, by now,' Brad asks, sitting down opposite me and making himself comfortable.

'What part of 'I'm not interested' didn't you understand?'

'You're interested,' Brad suggests.

'So why are you following me?'

'I'm not following you. Not in the way you think I am.'

'What way should I be thinking?'

'I need to talk to you. I have a business proposition to run past you that even you will find attractive,' he informs me. 'It's tough, risky, but financially rewarding. Time is critical, and I need to know if you want in; can't say anymore than that, here.'

'Brad, I'm up to my bollocks in work. I haven't got the time to take on more.'

'Hundred grand each,' he whispers, leaning across the table.

Typically, as always, my eyes light up when I'm offered a chance to earn big money. Once again, the little things in life pale into insignificance.

'And if you're worried about the taxman finding out,' Brad continues 'don't be. I can have a Swiss bank account opened in your name by this time tomorrow.'

Having given me the good news, I wait patiently for the bad. There has to be a catch.

'How do I know you're for real? And how do I know I can trust you?' A couple of very important questions, I think. A hundred grand is a lot of money in anyone's books. This has to be a bogus offer to set me up, and quite naturally, I'm suspicious of Brad and his amazing offer. My thirst for money is common knowledge; even the village idiot has the capabilities to work that out for himself. I am a real sucker when it comes to hard cash, and I guess that makes me an easy target for anyone wishing to get his, or her, own back.

'Give me a chance to prove to you that this is a genuine offer,' Brad says. 'Meet me and let me show you.'

The activity going on inside my tiny, driven brain is giving me a headache while I try to decide if the risk is worth taking. Risk-taking is part of my everyday life. It makes what I do, exciting, exhilarating. It's my job. It's why I do what I do. The thrill of the next challenge is so moreish that you can't live without it! An addiction for which there is no cure. Unlike smoking, it's an addiction that pays very well, and my driving force for doing whatever it takes to succeed. In my case, money is the root of all evil, but can I trust him? Brad the mystery man.

'Where and when?' I ask.

James wheels his own chair into my office for our meeting this morning. I've asked Richard to join us so he can share the information James has gathered on Gavin Thomas. There might some points of interest for him to consider.

Sue brings in a tray of coffee before we start and I hastily clear a space on my busy desk for her to sit it down carefully. I want a quiet word with Sue before she disappears and follow her to the door.

'Sue, no calls or visitors until we're finished, unless Jenny calls; she and I have some unfinished business to take care of.'

'Nick,' Sue whispers, taking hold of my forearm. 'I know it isn't my place to tell you how to run your life, but let Jenny go. Take a good look at yourself, and you'll see what she's doing to you. I'm telling you this as a friend, because I'm concerned for your wellbeing. I've known you long enough to know when you're troubled, and that woman will be the death of you. For you own sake, you have to let her go.'

I take on board what I'm hearing from Sue, and say nothing. She is the third person close to me who has publicly expressed their concerns on the state of my health. Tom, Richard and now Sue, and they can't all be wrong.

I can't tell any of them my thoughts, and fears, about the baby. I don't want them to know because they'll only interfere in my personal business, and going public may push Jenny further away from me. I'm doing a pretty good job of that myself, without their help. The most worrying thing for me is that I can't let it go, and what will that do to me in the end? Kill me?

Once Richard joins us, we get down to the business of the day. James settles himself in opposite me and rests his file across his lap, propping it up against his left leg, which is folded across his right. I nod at James to start.

'Gavin Thomas, owner farmer of *Ten-Acre Farm.* Slightly misleading by name, his farm is almost five-hundred acres in size and prime dairy farming land. Currently, Mr Thomas has approximately one hundred and fifty dairy cattle, but that fluctuates throughout the year. *Ten-Acre Farm* is managed by a gentleman called Afon Lewis.'

'That makes sense.' I say, interrupting James. 'That name came up in a conversation I had yesterday.'

'This is where my investigation becomes very complex boss.'

Jesus! I detest that.

'From the work I've so far done, it appears that Mr Thomas has his grubby little fingers in lots of pies. The income from his dairy and beef herd is enough to support his current lifestyle, but he has further incomes coming in from many other varied sources, making him a very rich man, on paper. Other businesses, so remote and obscure, that they are hard to trace, and difficult to prove that he's in some way connected.'

'What sort of businesses, James?' I ask.

'I'm still working on that, boss. The four I've found to date, which Mr Thomas has almost certainly got some involvement in, are hard to confirm. He, or someone close to him, knows all the tricks of the trade and they're shifting money all over the place. There does seem to one common denominator, which I'm hoping you might be able to help me with.' James says, frantically flicking through his paperwork. 'I ran a check on a name that appears as a director on all four of the companies I've currently found, and I've drawn a blank. Now, I'm not one to brag, because this type of work is bread and butter to me and I don't usually encounter this sort of problem, but this has stumped me.'

James places a sheet of A4 paper on the top of his open file and sighs. 'Here we are. Do either of you know, or have you heard of, a man by the name of Max Walker?'

The name means nothing to me, and as I look across at Richard to see his reaction he shakes his head.

'Sorry, James, we don't have the answer to that. What's the significances of this Max Walker?' I ask James.

'Well, I'm not entirely sure yet what the significance is. Let me explain why,' James continues. 'On the twenty-eighth day of every month, money is withdrawn from the accounts of every business and transferred into a Swiss bank account. It's done in such a way that it looks like invoice payments, but again that's proving hard to confirm.'

I don't believe that! Twice now, within the past hour, I've heard those same three words: 'Swiss bank account'. Am I the only one not taking advantage of their services?

'Seven days later,' James continues, 'money from a different Swiss bank account comes back the other way and is paid into numerous accounts here in mainland Britain. The form of those payments is interest paid out on savings accounts. Every recipient is a director of one or more of those same companies. Max

Walker is one of those directors. His account here in Wales is in Haverfordwest. As far as I can ascertain, he does not exist.'

'Max Walker could be Gavin Thomas, James, and the whole thing could be an elaborate way for not paying British taxes,' I suggest to him.

'That's what I thought, boss, only Gavin has an account at the same bank, and I feel sure someone there would question that. If I'm right, and Max Walker doesn't exist, how can he open a bank account without an address?'

'James, I'm puzzled.' Richard butts in. 'I know you like to keep certain things to yourself, but how have you found all this out so quickly?'

The question makes James smile. 'Lets just say I have a very good friend working in the city of London, and company details are not that difficult to come by, this day and age. It's slightly more difficult when it comes to peoples personal details, but I'm working on that.'

'So you know who these four companies are, and what they do?' Richard asks, continuing with his questioning of James.

'I do,' James replies, positively.

'Would you like to share that information with us, James?' Richard prompts him.

I watch as James flicks through his paperwork once more. I'm impressed. In less than twenty-four hours, James has compiled a file larger than the one Reg passed onto me covering the original investigation. There's no doubt that James has far more gumption about him than ten of Reg's people put together. He truly is an asset to this company. An asset I know I've got to keep, and an asset that's going to cost me financially.

'Right,' James says, sitting up straight. 'One is a night-club in Swansea called "Mad Maxx"; the second one is a small but profitable chain of garden centres with five commercial outlets. The third is a domestic and commercial appliance repairs company, and the fourth, a security firm specialising in event, home, and personal security. I'm pretty certain there are more.'

'What's the name of the security firm, James?' a concerned-sounding Richard asks.

'Sandfords,' James replies.

'I don't believe this!' Richard shouts. 'Fucking Sandfords. Are you sure you've got this right, James?'

'No question. Their head office is in Neath, and the managing directors name is -'

'I know. I know. Rob Williams,' Richard butts in. 'You'll both be pleased to hear that I've recently contracted them to cover the security at Victoria Jackson's little bash. Now what the fuck am I going to do, Nick?'

Hard fucking luck is my first reaction. I really couldn't give a toss as to what happens to the lovely Victoria Jackson and her bash for the elite snobs. Then common sense takes a grip and I realise that my company's reputation is also at stake here.

'My suggestion is, Richard, that you do nothing.'

'What?' he questions me. 'How can I have a company we're investigating, protect a client of mine? And a hunt meeting, to boot!'

'Think about what you've just said, Richard. Surely, from our point of view it's better to know what Sandfords are doing. While you're working with them you have a foot in the door, and you have access to their managerial structure. Believe me, when I say that in any office environment there's always someone prepared to say more than they should. That could work to our advantage, and we've time to do something about it if we need to. Take that away, under the current circumstances, and you'll close that door forever. Can I suggest something to you, if you're still worried? Ask Sandfords for the full list of employees they plan to use on the day, and tell them it's because you want to run a security check on everyone involved in the hunt-day security. It's a high-profile bash, Richard; no one will question your reasons. And James,' I continue, turning to face him, 'I want a full list of directors' names from you, and I want a near as damn it estimate on how much the directors have made since the payments began – and more importantly, when they began.'

James has taken longer than I expected to find the information I asked for. The three of us reconvene two hours later. In that time, I've sat alone in my office and done some research of my own, compiling a list of names that I hope to see on James's list of directors.

Without a fuss, James hands both Richard and myself a copy of his list, and stands in silence waiting for us to comment. Two names jump out at me straight away, but there's no mention of Reginald Moss. Then, he could be the one using the name, Max Walker.

'None of these names ring any bells with me,' Richard informs us.

'Is this the complete list, James,' I ask, for confirmation?

'So far, boss, yes,' he responds.

I thank James for his effort and ask him to carry on with the good work. This groundwork he's doing is a thankless task, and very time consuming. What James needs - what the company needs - is the information at our fingertips. At the next board meeting, I've got to press for the finances to be made available for a new computer system.

James's list has answered a couple of questions for me, and given me the ammunition I needed to press on with. He's on the right track and it's only a matter of time before we can make a definite connection between Moss and the death of David Thomas. What we have, so far, will only see the directors of his companies investigated for tax evasion. As tempting as that prospect is, it's not enough for me.

Richard won't have picked up anything positive from James' list, and I wouldn't have done had I not done my research.

'Do I gather, Nick, that there is some thing of interest here for you?' Richard asks me, waving James' list around in the air.

'Not sure, yet, Richard. I'll need some time to run through these names before I can answer that,' I tell him, and I'm lying. Two of the names hold a great deal of interest for me.

The Severn Road Bridge disappears slowly from view in my rear view mirror. I'm back in England, my home for the first seventeen years of my life. Being in England these days is not unusual. Fact is, I deliberately stayed away for a number of years, but more recently I've become a regular visitor to the country of shires. The new office in Great Malvern and Graham's shortcomings, have seen to that! What hits home on this particular journey is in road I'm on, and where it would eventually take me. In this case, the M4, and the Home Counties. Even now, after eighteen years - as an ex-pat I suppose one would describe me - I can still feel the strings of home pulling on my heart. That tug weakens as each day, week, and year drift by, but the curiosity of how the old homestead is coping without me remains deep-rooted.

My childhood had been a reasonably happy one and I have many fond, loving memories of those halcyon days spent with friends and family. I didn't leave England because I was forced to, or had to, I wanted to. Pembrokeshire is my home now. I have made a success of my life there and I have no real desire to return to my roots, other than to be nosy. I'm not anti my roots, far from it, but after eighteen years of living away there's nothing left there for me to return to. When I pull back my bedroom curtains in the morning, I'm reminded of why I made that decision all those years ago. From my bedroom window, I have the most beautiful view of Carmarthen bay. Why should I want to return to the traffic jams and over-crowding of the Hampshire borders?

The family home isn't on my agenda today. The Home Counties will have to wait a little longer before the prodigal son returns. This afternoon, I'm turning north, heading for Gloucester. Even so, the signs for London are hard to ignore.

Nearing my destination I begin questioning myself again on why I'm here doing this. All of a sudden, it doesn't seem to be such a good idea. A meeting with Brad - at a *Little Chef* in the middle of nowhere - isn't one of the best decisions I've made recently. Mind you, several others run it close.

I rarely bother with insurance – like bringing along a colleague, or having one follow me – but because of the Jenny situation, I have taken a little extra care on this sortie. When Brad insisted that our meeting today remained a secret, I took the necessary personal precautions. I've kept my side of the bargain by coming alone, and in return, he's promised to explain his reasons for the secrecy if I turn up. Well, here I am, and I don't know why. Further more, I don't trust Brad, and for that very reason, I decided before I left home to do something very alien to my beliefs.

The need to carry a gun disgusts me and I detest what they stand for, but I do own one. I hate what the ultimate weapon can – in a split second - do to ordinary people's lives. I'm a firm believer that, if someone chooses to carry one, they fully intend to use it! That's why my handgun is generally locked away in my safe, but occasionally one has to challenge one's own principles, for the sake of one's own survival. Today is one of those days when I've made an exception to the rule. I've tucked my snub nose *Smith and Wesson* away in the boot of my car - just in case.

Stretching my legs after the long drive, I scan the *Little Chef* car park for anything unusual or suspicious. Standing out in the open, I feel isolated and vulnerable, and as it's the middle of bloody winter, it's also cold and miserable. There's no sign of Brad, not that I can see, but I know he's here. I can sense his presence and I'm not usually wrong when I experience these feelings, especially when the hairs on the back of my neck stand up. Nicholas doesn't like feeling vulnerable. I guess that's a control thing.

I head inside the *Little Chef* to warm myself up, and for a cup of something hot to drink while I wait. The restaurant is virtually empty, however, I do as the sign asks and wait to be seated. Aren't we British fucking stupid? Or, is it because we actually like queuing? Or, is it because we like moaning about queuing?

'My coffee is far superior to this crap, and the service is better,' a familiar voice from behind me announces. 'My place is ten minutes' drive from here, Nick,' Brad adds. 'I'd like to show you around before it gets dark.'

Even at this stage - with the uncertainties I carry - I could back out, but mystery, intrigue and money - as always - clouds my ability to think straight, and together we walk back toward my car.

'I walked here, Nick, I'll jump - '

'No!' I butt in. 'Sorry, Brad, if that really is your name. I've changed my mind. There's something not right about you, and what you're up to. I'm not letting you get into my car.'

Brad sits himself down on the boot lid of my car, takes a cigarette out of a packet, offers me one and before replacing the packet in his coat pocket he lights our smokes. In silence, we both take a couple of long draws, exhaling the smoke into the cold, winter air.

'Why did you come this far to change your mind?' Brad asks, taking another pull on his cigarette.

'I wasn't sure, until a few moments ago, that is, what I wanted out of this and I've decided its nothing. Despite your offer of untold riches, this isn't going to work.'

'I understand your concerns. Believe me, this is hard for me, too, and I share the same concerns.'

'Yeah right,' I scoff. 'What possible concerns can you have about me? I'll wager that you know all there is to know about me. I know jack shit about you, and you expect me to let you jump into my car and drive off in to the countryside in to God knows what kind of situation. I may look stupid, but I'm not.'

'I know you're not, that's why I approached you in the first place. You see, there's only one person in this country who knows who I am, really knows who I am, and he's bound by the official secrets act to never reveal my true identity. I was prepared to share as much of that information with you as I reasonably could.'

'Oh, this is good, really good! You'll be telling me next that you write novels for a living, and your real name is Ian Fleming. What sort of idiot do you take me for?'

'What sort of idiot do you want to be taken for? One that walked away before finding out the truth, or one that stayed and became very, very rich.'

Brad takes another long pull on his cigarette before he continues. 'The things I've seen and done would make any best selling author of thriller stories look like Enid Blyton.'

I smile visibly at his suggestion, because who the hell does he want me to think he is?

'Don't take the piss; I'm doing my best to explain here,' Brad responds.

'I'm listening.' '

You don't trust me, do you?'

'No, and you haven't given me one reason why I should. You appear in my life from out of nowhere, offer me one hundred grand to do a dangerous job with you, and then tell me you don't really exist. I think you may see my point.'

'Trust is a big thing for me too, and if this partnership is going to work, I must have complete trust in you,' Brad warns.

'Partnership? At what point in our short association did we discuss the formation of a partnership?'

'That's the only way it'll work.'

'Then it doesn't. I've been my own boss for a long time, and no one tells me what to do, or when I should be doing it! I like things that way, and I plan to keep them that way.'

'I'm disappointed in you,' Brad says, standing up and treading on his cigarette to put it out. 'I thought I could trust you, and I was prepared to tell you as much as I could about my past. Looks like I misjudged you. You're not the person I thought you were, and you're not the person I want to work with,' he adds, and pushes past me, knocking my left shoulder with some force as he does.

'You're research on me is incomplete?' I reply, as he walks away. 'Because, if you had been thorough, you would know exactly what sort of person I am.'

Brad stops, and slowly walks back toward me. He pauses right behind me. I can hear him breathing close to my left ear.

'For the past five years, I've been sat twiddling my thumbs, waiting for the dust to settle so I can get on with my life. I can't do that alone because as far as the world is concerned I perished in unknown circumstances five years ago. I don't exist, not as the person I was. Imagine how many doors I can open because I don't exist. I'm ready for some action. I just need a partner; a legitimate front man.'

'Why me?' I ask, and turn to face Brad.

'Why you? You're good. I do know pretty much all there is to know about you, but until you meet the man, you don't know him! I know that you're well respected amongst your peers and you get results. No one could ever question your success. That makes you the perfect foil.'

'Why not on your own?' I enquire. 'If you can open doors without people knowing, you don't need someone like me.'

'Wrong, because like you are now, I was very successful in my line of work, but my methods were somewhat unorthodox and frowned upon by those in high places. I got the results they wanted, however, and they turned a blind eye to my belligerence. My problem is, because I was given free license to do things my way they became habitual, easily recognisable by those in the know, and if I was found to be operating again they'd come after me. Immobilised, Nick. Terminated.'

Brad lights himself another cigarette and blows the smoke out over my head.

'And you're right, my real name isn't Brad, and that's the one thing you'll never learn from me. For your own safety, that is part of my life I cannot discuss or disclose, so please don't ever expect me to. You do realise…' he continues, taking another pull on his cigarette, 'that now I've told this much, you leave yourself, and me, with only two choices. Either I terminate you here and now, or we go into partnership. And if you choose the latter, which I recommend you do, I'll teach you all I know.'

'Does that include my colleague hiding in the boot of my car,' I answer flippantly to his remark.

'You stupid bastard!' he shouts, and lunges at me. 'Give me your fucking keys.'

I calmly remove my car keys from my jean pocket and hand them to Brad, watching as he frantically inserts the key into the lock, flipping the boot lid open. Expletives pour from his mouth when he discovers that the boot space is empty, except of course for my handgun, which is tucked safely away in a secret compartment.

'I didn't know if you were joking or not, but remember one thing: you are one, and I am many. You may well be number one in this arrangement, but I am numbers two to two hundred,' I tell him, closing the boot lid. 'I'm in no doubt that your training is vastly superior to that of mine, and you will out-class me in almost every field, but I too am not to be messed with. I don't take kindly to being threatened, and I will fight my corner, regardless of the odds. Any partnership I enter into will be on equal terms of mutual respect, and total trust. Nothing else is up for discussion.'

We lock stares and enter into a Mexican stand-off. I'd like to know what he's thinking, until that is, he offers me his hand. It appears Brad is ready to commit to this working partnership. Am I? A voice inside my head tells me to give it a go.

'I'll need to know more,' I insist, whilst we shake on the deal.

'Then do what you came out here to do, and let me introduce you to my world.'

Brad's estimate of a ten-minute drive is spot on, and so is his house. Knowing the little I do, about Brad, it's difficult to associate him with a thatched-roofed, nineteenth century, Cotswold stone cottage. It's real picture-postcard stuff, with climbing roses over the front porch, and ivy growing up the front of the house. The only thing that's missing on this winter's day is a covering of snow, and a Robin redbreast foraging for food in the garden. This is a place dreams are made of, and one that invokes memories of bye-gone days.

I pause for a moment, watching the trail of wispy smoke rising from the chimney into the darkening sky. The serene picture takes me back to my early childhood, to a time when every household had an open fireplace, and life wasn't so complicated. A time when all I had to worry about, was not getting my clean clothes dirty, or what time I was going to be sent to bed. A time when I was questioned about whether I had done my homework, and if I hadn't, why? Arguably they were the good old days. I'm not so sure, because thirty years from now I'll probably look back on this time and think the same. As far as I can tell, only one thing has changed in that time, and that's something Mal has spoken of - community spirit. Progress has changed that.

Thirty years ago, you could go out for the day and leave your house unlocked. If I were to do that now, I'd return home to either a house full of squatters, or my worldly possessions missing. I remember well, the time when the youth who stole an apple from the farmer's orchard wasn't labelled a criminal; he was merely described as a young scallywag. There's no doubt that one looks back on one's childhood through rose-tinted glasses, with great affection, but were those days really better? Were they really the good old days?

Inside, the cottage is just as impressive. Following Brad into the lounge, the striking, open, stone fireplace forms a magnetic centrepiece. Low, oak-beamed ceilings, small doors, and windows create a sense of cosy, tranquil harmony, and the room hugs you with its warmth. The decoration adds to the ambience - comfy and not cluttered. The blend of old and new is tastefully achieved. Brad's television and video recorder compliment the décor. They are brand new, but they could quite easily be one hundred years old. Not possible of course, but they don't jump out at you screaming '1988'.

While I take all this in, something strikes me as being a little odd. There are no personal effects, no pictures, or photographs of any description. No trophies or trinkets giving away clues to Brad's mysterious past, and like Richard's office, it's unusually clean and tidy. Clinical, I believe is the best description. Men aren't supposed to do housework, or is my perception?

'What can I get you?' Brad asks, pouring himself a large 12-year-old malt whiskey into a cut glass crystal tumbler. I'm over a hundred miles from home and really do need to get back tonight. I decline his offer of an alcoholic drink, and ask him for that cup of coffee he promised me.

'So what do you think of the place? Not what you expected to see, I'll wager?'

'With every twist and turn we're making on this journey, you haven't failed to surprise. I'm learning not to expect anything, but expect everything.'

'Are you sure I can't tempt you?' he asks, waving his tumbler under my nose.

'No thanks. I've got another long drive from home to Great Malvern tomorrow morning. Interviews with Graham at the new office.'

'Great Malvern's a hop and a skip from here. You're welcome to crash out here for the night. There's plenty of room.'

'Bloody hell, Brad! You must be desperate for company. I'd hardly describe us as friends yet, and already you're asking me to stay for a sleep over.'

'Yeah, well, if you play your cards right, once I've shown you around I'll rustle us up a nice candle lit dinner.'

'Fuck off!' I respond.

Brad is the perfect host. Unlike me, he is totally at ease with his domestic situation and in no time at all, with little apparent effort, he's knocked up a tasty spaghetti bolognese. Over dinner, Brad talks about his exploits while renovating the cottage, and the cost to him in achieving this excellence. Our conversation is lubricated by a continual flow of expensive red wines - on his side of the table. I watch as he opens a third bottle, inhales the bouquet - almost drinking the fumes - and pours us both a glass of his latest choice. Brad clearly likes the finer things in life, a connoisseur of just about everything.

'Ireland,' he says out of the blue. 'Ever been there?'

'No,' I reply, shaking my head.

'The Emerald Isle they call it. Well don't believe everything you read.'

Emptying the contents of his glass in one swallow, Brad nervously refills it before sitting himself down opposite me.

'I first went there in '77' on a six-month tour of duty. Parachute regiment.'

As he continues, I detect a change in his mood. He has detached himself from today's reality, taking himself back some ten years as if we were in real time.

'Belfast, God-forsaken place back then. Well it was if you're a serving soldier in the British army. Made the time I spent in Germany more like a Butlins holiday camp.'

A packet of cigarettes appears in front of me, Brad gestures for me to take one.

'You don't have to do this.' I tell him, watching him struggle, and seeing how agitated he's become.

'Surprisingly, yes I do have to do this,' he snaps at my suggestion. 'Firstly, because you have the right to know where I am, and secondly, for myself. Apart from a very short-lived debriefing, I've never talked to anyone about my time in Northern Ireland, and I need to get this crap out of my system.'

That's all I need, someone else unloading their stress on me. It must be my face, or my charming and pleasant nature, inviting the tale of woe.

'When I got back to old Blighty, on leave, after six months of absolute terror I should tell you, I hoped and prayed that I wouldn't be sent back on another tour of duty. Well I wasn't, for a while anyway. You see, top of the class, I was selected as a SAS recruit and was sent… I can't tell you that', he adds shaking his head. 'What I can tell you is, that that is why I joined the army. Becoming an SAS soldier was a boyhood dream of mine. It's all I ever wanted to be. I knew why they wanted me, and I knew I would be going back to Ireland if I succeeded. I could have messed up the training, pretended not to be up to the task, but I'm a perfectionist and I can't abide failure; least of all in myself.'

Brad meanders through his second and third tour of duty in Northern Ireland, graphically describing every single detail. With every gory sentence, he empties his wineglass and lights another cigarette. Sickening, gruesome, blow-by-blow accounts of what he did, and what he saw. No man should ever be subjected to such vile and evil atrocities, and left alone to deal with the mental trauma. I actually feel sorry for him as he rambles on, and I fear the worst is yet to come.

'I was sent back to Northern Ireland alone in the spring of 1981.' Brad continues, popping the cork on another bottle of red wine. 'My brief was simple. Join the IRA. Become one of them. Nine months, nine bloody months of lying my way into their trust with absolutely no contact with civilisation. Kneecappings, shootings, car bombings, you name it - I was part of it! All this so that intelligence could sort the chaff from the wheat, identify the men at the top so the top brass could rip the heart out of the IRA. When all the fucking time, it was me committing the crimes.'

Brad takes a breather. Swallowing the contents of his glass, he refreshes it imediately. 'The IRA's intelligence was as good as ours, if not better, and they became suspicious of me. I laid low for several weeks while they checked me out. I feared for my life and I wanted out, but my orders were to stay put and complete the job. You see, and no one will ever admit to this, but as a SAS soldier, you are expendable. A soldier volunteers for the job and he's trained to survive. It's your job to take risks for the cause. To cut the crap, I was summoned to a meeting with my IRA cell leader and put to the test. I was going back into front-line action for them. My orders were to blow up an army patrol vehicle.'

Brad empties and replenishes his wineglass once more. He's pretty drunk now.

'Six good SAS men dead with one gentle squeeze of a detonator button. I knew every single one of them. They were my mates for Christ sake. Drinking buddies, and good, solid blokes. Some test they set me, hey?'

I watch Brad, closely. The anger the bitterness he has for those involved in this act of violence shows in his voice and body language. Who the resentment is aimed at isn't clear, but his moving account of that day is visibly disturbing for him.

'I hated myself for doing what I did. At the end of the day though, I thought my role was more important and as a person, I had to survive. I was only carrying out orders, from both sides of the Irish Sea. That's what you do when you're in the army, right or wrong, you carry out your orders. I can tell you I was very, very scared, and I was in way too deep. My SAS training meant nothing to me. I lost the ability to think straight and I was living off instinct. Like a coward, I ran for deep cover to regroup. That fear quickly changed to anger. I wanted to revenge my mates' deaths. Nothing else seemed to matter. I shot and killed the IRA cell leader and two of his henchmen, but that wasn't enough to satisfy my revenge. I wanted to kill the man who'd sent me out there, the person who, in effect, killed my SAS colleagues. Luckily for him, I didn't get the chance,' Brad says, bringing his left hand down heavily on the table.

I become concerned over Brad's state of mind, as he pours his heart out in my company, and what his excessive drinking, under these conditions, might mean to me. He is telling me that he is a highly trained, killing machine, and in his current state of mind, he's undoubtedly capable of doing anything. Should I suggest to him that he stops, and risk an angry drunken outburst from him? Or do I let him carry on and get this episode off his chest. Clearly, he has a need too. Fortunately, Brad makes the decision for me; his mood changes to a more sombre one in the time it takes to click a finger. He becomes far more relaxed and controlled.

'I went AWOL,' he says, calmly. 'Lived off the land and stole food whenever the opportunity arose. I knew the IRA were out to get me so there became a need to be very careful in what I did, who I spoke to and where I went. I decided to head south, travelling at night by any form of transport available to me. Mostly, that meant I walked, and I ended up in County Cork trying to jump a boat. That was when I discovered I was also top of the British authorities' wanted list. They too were keen to know of my where abouts. I was, by now, a wanted man on both sides of the Irish Sea. Somehow, what I'd done had got out, and even the army - my own unit - had turned their backs on me. Going home wasn't a decision I really wanted to make because I knew if the SAS caught up with me, I would be a dead man. Despite those conflicting thoughts, English soil was the safer of the two options open to me.'

Brad pours himself another drink and sits the wine bottle down on the table in front of me. For a change, I take the opportunity to top my glass up. I'm rather pleased I haven't attempted to keep up with him, because I still have my wits about me, and he'd be talking to himself by now. I certainly couldn't handle the amount of alcohol he's drunk tonight.

'The moment I stepped off the car ferry at Fishguard I was surrounded by suits and bundled into a waiting car. Stupid move I guess, thinking that I was safe and would walk away scot-free. I knew the authorities would be watching the ports and airports, but I also knew I had to get out of Ireland and took the chance. I thought that that was it, and resigned myself to believing that daylight, good food, and alcohol, were all but things of the past. The suits drove me straight to London. The next thing I knew, I was in a plush office in a government building beside the Thames. I can't expand on that, for obvious reasons. I was told that, as far as the world was concerned I had been killed while on active duty and that I no longer existed. Two days later, with a totally new identity, a family history to match and a more than generous golden handshake, I was dropped at Heathrow airport and given strict orders not to come back. Well I didn't, because I never got on a plane to come back from anywhere, and here I am. Although I don't actually exist, someone has the power and knowledge to come and get me if I step out of line. I haven't been idle in that time. I've set up contacts around the world and there's work to do. That's why I need you.'

Brad sits back in his chair, cigarette in one hand and his glass of wine in the other. I wait for him to continue; he doesn't. Seems that for the moment he's finished.

'I don't understand you,' I tell him. 'If I had gone through all that and had enough money to survive on, the last thing I'd want to do is go back into the business. You're either mad, or the money's running out?'

'I'm not coming to you with cap in hand, if that's what you're thinking. For your information, I dabble a little on the stock market and I'm doing very nicely, thank you,' he responds, seemingly annoyed by my suggestion.

'Sorry. It's just that, had I been in your shoes, I would have got on that plane, travelled the world, and left my troubles behind me.'

'Yeah, well I couldn't do that; I've got unfinished business, and being in the army, I'd already seen the world. I did travel the length and breadth of Britain looking for my ideal home. When I came across this place, it was love at first sight. Finally, I had somewhere to put down my roots. My problem is, I'm a man of action, always have been, and I can't sit still for very long. I miss the thrill, the buzz of the challenge. I'm sure you can relate to that. Once the renovations were complete, I started looking for something to do. That's where I'm at, and I'm eager to get on.'

I can relate to what he's saying, but there comes a point in one's life when you've seen and done everything - in Brad's case, far more than he bargained for – and for your own peace of mind it's better to walk away. The next job could be your last. I lean forward, resting my elbows on the table, my mind full of questions to ask Brad.

'I know I've asked you this,' I say, 'but why have you singled me out?'

'Like I said, you're good and you get results. Eighteen months ago, when I made the decision to get back into the business, my first task was to plan everything down to the last detail; what I wanted to achieve, how I was going to achieve it and with whom. You see, because I can't run the risk of being traced, the first consideration I had to engage was to find a person whose work ethic is similar to mine. It soon became obvious to me that to achieve what was required would mean working alongside a like-minded person, someone with a military background; a total non-starter as far as I was concerned, because I couldn't trust anyone with a military background, so I had to change tact. I'll be honest with you, at first, a private dick, like you, wasn't a consideration; I didn't see them as serious candidates. Present company excepted, but in general, they're a bunch of wankers. Frustrated by the lack of quality in other areas, I was forced to make a list of you guys and drew up a shortlist. Your name, of course, was on my list, and one thing made you stand out from all the rest: the growth of your business. Whatever you were doing, you were doing it right, and for six months I conducted my own survey on you.'

'You've been spying on me for six months,' I butt in, feeling violated. 'I'm not entirely happy with that. Some parts of my life are very private, and I wish to keep them that way.'

'Like it or not, you are a very public person. I'm only interested in your working practice, not your private life. Seeing as though this is a time set-aside for confessions, and having studied you at work, I've got to confess I don't know how you do it?'

'What's that supposed to mean?' I snap at him.

'You flit from job to job; there's no pattern to how you work and you're not consistent or predictable. My conclusion was that you're either very lucky, or you have a good brain capable of logging, sifting, and retaining vital information. I personally don't believe its luck.'

'That's big of you,' I reply, thinking he's a condescending big-headed, has-been, who, despite his gripping life story, has yet to prove he is who he claims to be. 'So if you don't like the way I work, what's this all about?'

'That's the very point, I do like the way you work. You're unpredictable; confident style fits nicely into my plans.'

I stare at him long and hard, once again he's suggesting 'his plans'. This constant reminder of it being his plan, and not a partnership on equal terms doesn't sit easily with me. It's not why I came here, tonight. To play second fiddle to a man I hardly know - when my own business keeps me fully occupied and financially sound - isn't going to happen. I thought I had made that very clear from the outset, and maybe this is a good time to remind him of that.

'Brad, so far, this has been all about you and what you want. Sorry to disappoint you, but I'm doing very nicely without you, and I don't need, or want, this extra work. I've told you this once, but in case you missed it the first time, I don't work for anyone except myself. And having sat listening to you going on for most of the evening, I'd say that you need me more than I need you.'

'Doesn't the money interest you?' he asks, leaning forward. 'That is why you came here, isn't it?'

'I love everything about earning money, just not on the terms you seem hell bent on achieving,' I reply.

'A big mistake,' Brad warns me.

'I don't think so!'

'I could make life very difficult for you.' he threatens me in return.

'And if your little stories are true, so could I for you.'

There's an unpleasant silence between us while Brad pours himself yet another drink. He stares at me for a moment before sitting back in his chair.

'Shall we start again,' he suggests?

'I'll not back down, regardless of what you want, or offer. A partnership with joint decisions, and full consultations on everything we do, is the only way I will consider working with you.'

'And that's it,' he asks with some surprise?

'And an equal share of the spoils,' I add to my original demand. I too relax back into my chair with just one thing troubling me: quite how I'm going to fit all this extra work into my already hectic schedule beats the shit out of me.

Chapter eight

Wednesday, 27 January 1988

Brad lives on the outskirts of a village near Stroud, in Gloucestershire. His assessment of Great Malvern only being a hop and skip from his place wasn't entirely accurate, but it's certainly a lot easier than trekking all the way up from Saundersby.

Arriving at our new office in good time, I park near the main door, next to a white Escort van. Despite the light drizzle that's falling, I stop for a moment or two before going inside, absorbing the stunning view of the Malvern Hills from the car park. North Hill is closest, and towers above us. The taller Worcestershire Beacon stands majestically behind it. This morning, the fast-moving, low cloud occasionally shrouds the upper reaches from view, adding an air of mystery to the breathtaking scenery. Despite the problems we've encountered during setting up the office, views like this are worth every penny spent. It's not difficult to understand how the Malvern hills inspired Edward Elgar to write his music.

The white Escort van I've parked next to shouldn't mean anything to me, but I have seen this particular plumber's vehicle before, and lo and behold, the keys are in the ignition. Don't know why I have the compulsion to do this, but I open the driver's door and remove them. Old habits die hard I guess.

The new, pretty, young receptionist stops me from walking straight in. Aware of the fact that she's only doing her job as instructed, I am a little miffed by the fact she doesn't recognise me. I decide to play along while she writes down my details and phones through to Graham's temporary office.

'You have a Mr. Thompson here to see you,' I hear her say. After a second's pause, she turns to look at me. 'He'll be right with you,' she adds, seemingly none the wiser.

'I'm just going out to the van, love, I won't be a minute,' the plumber shouts across to the young receptionist as he walks past me. Like the young receptionist, he doesn't recognise me, until he stops for a second look when I shake his van keys at him.

'You really should be more careful where you leave these; I could be half way to Birmingham by now in your van,' I inform him, jingling his keys in my outstretched hand.

'You!' he bellows, snatching his keys from my grip. 'Have you got a problem with keys, or something?'

'Not with keys I haven't; dodgy plumbers I have,' I reply.

'Oh, that's nice. Just because my boss sent me to the wrong place, you think I'm dodgy. I'll have you know I'm a highly qualified and respectable plumber, not some cowboy as you're suggesting.'

'I'll find that out when you send me your bill, won't I? That's presuming you'll finish the job before we have a need to move into bigger offices,' I suggest to him.

As the plumber slopes off outside to the comfort and safety of his mobile office, I catch the young receptionist looking in my direction. Her face has a lovely, healthy, red glow about it. The penny has finally dropped.

'I'm so sorry, Mr. Thompson, I didn't recognise you,' she mutters rather sheepishly.

'Easily done,' I assure her. 'I'm reliably informed that I have a readily forgettable face.'

Graham breezes into the reception seemingly full of the joys of spring. That's worrying, because from where I'm standing, he has little to be pleased about, with the mess he's made over the set-up of this office.

'Nick!' he beams. 'You're bright and early. Did you stay over somewhere last night?'

'No? I drove up here this morning. Why?'

'I phoned you a number of times last night, but all I got was your answering machine,' he explains.

'Oh not again! Mac's blokes have been messing about with the wiring recently. I bet they've done something to the phone line again. I can't be without my phone, I'll attend to that when I get home.'

I'm lying, convincingly I hope, and as far as I'm aware, there's nothing wrong with my phone, or line. Brad and I agreed last night that if our working alliance is going to be successful, then no one should know about it! That includes Graham and Richard. In fact, their names came out top of my list.

It has to be that way, and this is not just what Brad wants. Anything linking us together will compromise the alliance. That could spell disaster, and possibly threaten our very existence. If the money rolls in like he's intimating it will, then I'm all for keeping it hush-hush.

'No matter, you're here now.' Graham continues, and turns to confront the unfortunate receptionist. 'Don't you ever listen, Maxine? I specifically told you that Mr. Thompson was coming this morning. Incidentally, if you don't already know, he owns the company we work for. It's not good enough, Maxine, not good enough by a long way.'

'It's all right, Graham,' I butt in, to save the poor girls embarrassment. 'There's no harm done. Maxine's right to stop people walking straight in. We can't have every Tom, Dick, and dodgy plumber coming and going as they please.'

'I know that, but this isn't the first time Maxine has messed up,' Graham responds.

'I'm sorry, Graham, it won't happen again. I promise!' she begs, attempting to defend her actions.

'Maxine, I take my coffee white with two sugars. Could you bring it through to Graham's office?' I butt in, again, fearing for the young girl's job. Graham is going well over the top on such a small and easy misunderstanding. There's probably more to it than I know. However, I won't allow him take advantage of the situation to impress me.

'I'll speak to you later, Maxine,' Graham utters, turning on the poor girl and threatening her.

'No you won't, Graham. This ends here and now,' I insist.

'Nick, you're undermining my authority here. This is between myself and Maxine, and I'd prefer it if you left the staffing matters to me.'

'Remind me, why am I here this morning?'

Graham turns on me, not saying anything, just staring hard with a look of disgust on his face. 'May I also take this opportunity to remind you that it will be the beginning of February in a few days from now? Do I need to say more?'

I don't, not to Graham. He knows he's a month behind with our programme and to make matters worse, we've gone well over budget on this project. His non-productive hours are accounting for a large portion of the deficit. Company profits are down too, and what he needs to be is back behind his desk in Saundersby earning money.

We shouldn't air our personal and company differences in front of the staff, but he's being totally unreasonable over something that really doesn't matter, and it's obvious to me now why he's having problems. He wants to get everything one-hundred per cent right. Graham doesn't want to fail and he is using me as his benchmark. A noble gesture, but even I know that perfection is rarely achievable. I would surmise from what I've just witnessed, that he's having second thoughts over his choice of office manager, and that is affecting his normal behaviour pattern. Graham is shitting himself over what he thinks I might have to say on the matter.

Driving is an activity one either loves or hates. I fall into a minority category somewhere in the middle, because I don't mind driving. It has become a necessary function of the work I do - a valuable tool. I also don't mind driving for pleasure. Like driving over to Haverfordwest to watch the football, though watching the Bluebirds isn't always pleasurable. The time I spend behind the wheel has another upside for me: it gives me time to think, time to weigh up potential problems and come up with a satisfactory conclusion. - like now, as I'm nearing home.

I shouldn't have had words with Graham in front of Maxine. I will apologise to him. I was in the wrong. I have the utmost respect for Graham, and showing my disapproval of his work in public like that serves no useful purpose. That bothers me too, because it's not my style. It's not the way I've done things in the past.

Turning into the harbour at Saundersby those thoughts vanish - like Reg Wallace does when it's his round – and yet another problem is pushed to one side. I call into to see Colin, the harbour master, on the way through, to discuss a business matter, and drive on down to the NTI office.

My absence has caused some concern around the office, exaggerated by Graham's continual calls yesterday and earlier today. It's not an uncommon occurrence. Frequently, my methods and lack of communication have given rise for concern. This new alliance - the business venture with Brad - will only heighten my sudden and sometimes prolonged absences, raising their level of awareness to the fact that something is going on. They'll get used to it. That's not the correct attitude for a person in my position to have, but its one I'll have to adopt if I wish to maintain the secrecy. A good plausible excuse might come in handy. Throw in a little white lie every now and then to throw them off the scent. Talking of scent, I wonder how James is getting on?

Flopping down into my leather, desk chair, and stretching my aching limbs, I realise that the past twenty-four hours have finally caught up with me. I'm shattered. I tell myself that it's the driving, when in reality, the late-night drinking session with Brad is the more probable cause. I wouldn't tolerate, nor do I have any sympathy toward an employee of mine in this state. Double standards, I believe one would call that. Don't do as I do; do as I say.

The mess on my desk looks a hundred times worse this evening. Perhaps that has something to do with the order I've seen in Brad's life. On top of the jumbled mass of paperwork, right under my nose, James has left the list of directors I'd asked him to compile. Yesterday, I recognised two of the names James had unearthed. His latest list reveals something new. One name appears on the board of every single company: *Amoss Grindle*. A strange name, but one I immediately recognise

A sudden, and un-controllable urge to yawn has me frantically grabbing at my cigarette, trying to stop the disastrous affect it might have on the reams of paper on my desk. Ash falls readily from the burning end down onto James's list, obscuring the "A" in Amoss. What I see confirms my initial thoughts. Shouting aloud, I ask James to join me in my office.

James is at my door within seconds, closely followed by Richard. Asking them to step inside, I'm off and running before they've had time to catch their breath.

'Max Walker, Gavin Thomas; any connection yet, James?'

'No, boss, my source hasn't got back to me yet.'

'What about the name Amoss Grindle on your list?' I continue?

'Nothing boss,' James responds. 'Bit odd if you ask me.'

'What if we were to rearrange the lettering?'

'I'm not with you, boss,' James muses?

'For God's sake, James!' I groan, and pass him his list. 'An anagram. Hold your finger over the letter "A" and tell me what you see.'

Doing as I've suggested, James covers the part of *Amoss Grindle* I'd asked him to, and comes up with the same conclusion.

'Moss,' he whispers. 'Reginald Moss.'

'How the hell did you work that out?' Richard asks me.

'It was obvious, Richard.' I reply confidently.

This is good work, because if I'm right, we now have the link between Gavin Thomas and Reginald Moss we were looking for. The question is: what were they up to, back then?

'What have you done about Sandfords?' I ask Richard, whilst James hurries off back to his desk, armed with the new information.

'Nothing as yet. I'm holding on until you tell me otherwise. In the meantime, I've sourced another company in Cardiff to take over if required, and they're cheaper. Oh, by the way,' he says, stopping in the doorway on his way out, 'Ed called into see you. Apparently, the batteries on your boat have gone flat and won't recharge. He asked me to tell you that he took the liberty and ordered new ones. He's been promised they'll be here by Monday, and when he's fitted them he'll take your boat out for a spin.'

Not what I wanted to hear. Thanking Richard for passing on the information, I decide to pop in and see Ed before I go home. I trust him, but not that much!

Ed is a creature of habit, and that will be his downfall in the end. For years, everything he's needed to survive has been right here on his doorstep; he hasn't had the worry of looking for work. We've already spoken about the decline in the industry. That decline has changed Ed's requirements and I'm not sure he has the gumption or the know-how he needs to continue in business.

Ed stops work at half past four in the afternoon, makes himself a cup of tea, and then sweeps up. Spot on five o'clock he locks up and strolls across the harbour to the pub for a swift pint or three. Then, somewhere between eight and nine o'clock, he staggers home and sleeps off his over indulgence. The following morning, he clocks on at eight o'clock, and his daily routine starts all over again. I've often wondered whose life style is wrong: Ed's, with his boring repetitive daily grind, or mine where I dash from pillar to post in a random, chaotic pattern.

I time my unannounced visit when I know Ed will be at his least receptive, just as he's locking up and thinking of his first pint. Poking my head around the open main door, I catch him closing his office door and switching off the workshop lights.

'Just a second, Ed,' I call out. 'Have you got my spare keys handy? I want to get something off the boat.'

He's not in the least pleased with my timing. I can see him muttering under his breath as I walk towards him. Opening the office door, he steps back inside and picks the keys up off his desk.

Nice security, I think. Anyone could walk into his workshop and make off with the keys to my boat. I'd lay odds that Ed is related to the plumber allegedly working at the Great Malvern office.

'Richard tells me the batteries have had their day,' I say, continuing with the one-sided conversation.

A pair of large batteries lay on the floor outside his office, next to the door. Ed gives them a swift kick with his right foot as he shuts the office door, bringing them to my attention.

'Knackered,' he says. 'Tried to charge them up last night but they weren't having it. Plates must be fucked.'

I guess that's a technical term.

'I've ordered some new ones and they will be here first thing Monday,' he informs me while I take a close look at the old ones. I don't see anything wrong with them.

Ed hovers impatiently at my right shoulder, blatantly looking at his wristwatch, 'If you don't mind, I've an appointment to keep.'

Thursday, 28 January 1988

I didn't sleep very well last night; too many things going on inside my head for my mind to settle. I tried desperately to get my head down for a while, but I got up again around midnight and occupied myself into the wee hours doing the jobs Mac had asked me too. The rooms he wanted me to clear are done, I've settled on the colour scheme for the pool tiles, and the design for fire place my heart desires settled on. The charming Victoria Jackson inspired me to go for a real, open fireplace, and Mac has agreed to undertake the extra work.

My night of hard work brings with it a renewed air of confidence this morning. Once I'd set my mind on the task, I achieved far more than I thought I was capable of. I'm chuffed by the amount of Mac-related problems I solved, albeit a tad tired from the late night. In the end, I did manage to grab a couple of hour's sleep, and with that in mind, I'm not going into the office this morning. Richard will have to cope without me. I'm going to spend my day chilling out at home, sorting out any problems Mac may have as a result of my decision-making. I also have a few private matters to take care of. I'm conscious that this feeling of calm is false, because the next few days are likely to be manic, with a very uncertain outcome.

Emerging from the privacy of my sanctuary - my office, which not even Jan is allowed to enter, and the door is kept permanently double-locked - I head for the kitchen to have lunch with Jan. My office here in the house is the one place in my world where calm and order prevail.

Prompted and spurred into action by Brad's warnings of high risk, I've seen sense and taken this much-needed, time out to put my personal affairs in order. Over the next few days, I will be busy, and my time will be at a premium. There were certain requirements I needed to take care of, in order to move this Moss and Thomas case forward the way I wanted, and I've used the time productively.

By design, the phone line in my office is separate to the main house system, and has a number that no one has knowledge of, except for *British Telecom*, that is, and they only know because they insisted they had to have somewhere to send the bill. I view the second line as secure, and unless someone taps into it deliberately - or accidentally on purpose – no one can overhear my private conversations.

My office-cum-study isn't a big room, but it contains more of my life history than anywhere else. That's why it's out of bounds to everyone, and kept locked by keys only I have access to, which reminds me: Mum hasn't sent the diaries I asked her for. Those missing diaries, literally, are all that's required to complete my life history, so far.

My itinerary for the next couple of days is clearly mapped. Two nights ago - in his drunken stupor - Brad pointed out just how chaotic my life is. I listened and took on board what he had to say. Personal discipline is sadly lacking in my life, and to prove to myself I have what it takes to move comfortably within Brad's world, I've set myself targets. Not a, to the minute, must do agenda; just a simple list of tasks to stop me deviating from my objectives.

Before Jan arrived this morning, I packed an overnight bag and safely stowed it in the boot of my car, away from her prying eyes. Not all of my planned movements are secret. However, some are, and to conclude my program satisfactorily, nothing can interfere with, or distract me from, my schedule. If that means being secretive, not including Jan and those at the office in what I'm doing and where I'm going, then so be it. I've dealt with all the minor irritants around the house, like Mac's wish list, and I'm ready to hit the road once I've had lunch.

Jan does her best to deflate my good mood. She insists I look ill, and I should take this opportunity to relax and spend the rest of the day in bed. I feel pretty good as it happens, and rather excited by the challenge of what lies ahead, and I can honestly say the adrenaline is already flowing in anticipation.

'I'm away as soon as I've finished lunch,' I inform her whilst sitting down at the new breakfast bar. 'If there's anything you want to know, I'll be at the Great Malvern office for a short time after about eleven o'clock tomorrow morning.'

Jan is engrossed in her magazine, a *Woman's Own*, or something, and it appears from her expression that I'm interrupting a gripping article. She puts the magazine down, sits her elbows on the breakfast bar, cups her hands together and rests her chin on them. 'Expecting something to go wrong?' she asks me.

'No. Why?'

'Because you don't usually bother telling me what's going on.'

'That's the only window you'll have if you do need to speak to me?'

'Important, this work you're doing?'

'None of your business.'

'Sorry I asked. I gather you're not going to take my advice, then?'

'What advice is that?'

'That you need to slow down. All this running around isn't doing you an ounce of good. I can see it in your eyes. You'll end up having a heart attack, or a stroke, if you're not careful.'

'Well, aren't you the life and soul of the party,' I snort at her.

'I'm worried about you. You're pushing yourself too hard at the moment.'

'It's nice to know that someone cares, but I'm fine, Jan, really, and once I've got to the bottom of this case I'm working on, I'll take a few days off. OK?'

'Not really, but I'm wise enough to know I won't change your mind.'

Swansea is my first port of call. I have a little trick up my sleeve for Messrs Moss, Jones and Marchant - a trick I've used before with positive results. A printer friend of mine is doing me a favour. It just so happens that he prints the bills for the tax office, and several company directors are about to receive a nasty little shock: a massive tax demand, going back seven years.

The friendly door-to-door salesman touch I've tried isn't working. What's more, they will be armed and ready for me the next time I knock. They'll be hard pressed to connect me to this ruse. It's what they all do about it that interests me, and I will be monitoring the situation carefully.

The idea is to send the chosen few a rather large, but realistic, tax demand. My aim is to throw them into a blind panic – particularly Stephen Jones - and send them running to Gavin Thomas for help and advice. If I achieve that, then the connection will be proved. I'm banking on one detail being overlooked: the bills are as authentic as they are bogus, but will any of the recipients take the time to find out? Doubtless, they'll make the effort at some stage, pleading poverty and innocence when they do, and probably asking for a reassessment because there's some sort of mistake.

To combat an immediate fix to their problem my intention is to post the letters tomorrow, so they won't land at their intended destinations until Saturday morning. With the tax office closed until Monday morning, that will give them forty-eight hours to sweat over their misfortune. Seeing what I've seen, and knowing what I know, it's fair to assume that both Stephen Jones and William Marchant rely on the income they receive from Gavin Thomas. The shock of receiving a tax demand of un-payable proportions might just soften them up. They may also believe that someone in an official capacity is aware of their connection to Gavin Thomas. That, in turn, could open a can of worms for them.

I'm as confident as I can be, now, over the connection, because apart from the lucky break finding the name Amoss Grindle, two other names jumped out from the list James drew up. First was *P. Thomas*, Pat Thomas, née Pat Marchant, William's wife and Gavin's sister. The second one was *L. Lewis*, Lesley Lewis, nee Lesley Jones, Stephen's wife. All three will be recipients of a bogus tax demand designed to act as a laxative.

I let myself in when I arrive at Brad's. On the surface, he appears to trust me implicitly; I'm not sure I'm ready to reciprocate. Checking around the empty house, accompanied by a few shouts of 'are you here', I make my way through to the kitchen, at the back of the house, and put the kettle on. Brad may be very trusting, but he's also a very cautious man and I'd lay odds on him watching me arrive. When he strolls into the kitchen through the back door, unperturbed by my presence, I know he has.

For an hour or so, we sit drinking coffee, talking over the plans for Saturday, ironing out the finer details. During the course of our conversation, Brad informs me that Saturday will only be a dummy run, because he hasn't received the expected confirmation. I'm not convinced, and my faith in him wanes by the hour.

We go on to discuss how we'll operate and what the future holds for this alliance, this most unlikely of partnerships. As we discuss the work, it becomes clear that if this alliance does become a reality, I may be forced in to making changes to my everyday work schedule, and my lifestyle.

One of the ideas I'm currently giving a great deal of consideration to is making Graham and Richard full partners in the business. Sadly, I have reservations. Graham's recent performance up country in Great Malvern plays a huge part in that doubt. He makes heavy weather of responsibility and decision-making, and I don't think he's ready to lead the team.

Richard is only twenty-seven, a young twenty-seven as it happens, and knowing him as well as I do, I don't believe he's ready to take on the extra responsibilities. The decision to make them both full partners is a hard one to call, and one that I'll take my time over. One way or the other, I need to be absolutely sure in my own mind that any decision I make is right for all concerned. Fortunately, I'm in a position to watch their performances closely, and I can take my time to make the necessary informed decision. My doubts may be unfounded, and they could take to the task like a duck to water. Who knows?

Brad is running around doing his own thing. Abandoned, I retire to the comfort of his lounge and put on one of his Queen tapes, *Night at the Opera*. We have at least one thing in common: a good taste in music.

It's rather comforting to know that up until now Brad has lain off the booze - a little hypocritical, sat here tapping my right hand on the arm of his settee in time to the music, holding a bottle of his lager in my left.

'I see you've made yourself quite at home,' he says, bursting in to the room and flopping down into the armchair opposite me. 'I sourced what you wanted and I've put them into the boot of your car.'

Knowing that my car keys are in my pocket, I immediately become concerned over the damage he may have done. I didn't leave my car unlocked, I never do. Brad has broken in.

'Don't panic,' he assures me. 'There isn't a car around that I can't get into. Well not one that I've come across yet, anyway.'

'That BMW is my pride and joy, I hope you haven't damaged it?' When he lets my comment pass without recourse I want to jump straight out of my seat and take a look. When I ordered that car, I had it fitted with all the latest locking and alarm devices available on the market, and Brad appears to have broken in without any trouble. What a waste of money that was!

'Everything ready your end?' he asks.

'You haven't damaged my car, have you?' I ask again.

'Nick, the systems they install on cars like yours are just cheap electronic security gadgets. All I had to do was find the right frequency, and hey presto! I was in! So no, I haven't damaged your car. May I suggest, if you're that worried about having your car broken in to, when we've got time we'll install a proper alarm system. Now can we get on? There's something I want to run past you?'

'Oh, yeah?'

'Before I do, are you ready for Saturday?'

'Once I get home,' I sigh, 'and take care of business, everything we've discussed will be ready for the task.'

'Good! I'm looking forward to this,' Brad says excitedly. 'It should be fun!'

'So what is it you want to run past me, Brad?'

'We need a HQ to work from,' he says, leaning forward. 'Somewhere private; a place that can't be traced back to us.'

'Aren't you jumping the gun here? What if this so called partnership doesn't work out?'

'Why shouldn't it?'

'I'm not saying it won't, but I do think it's way too early to be suggesting we set up an operational base. Let's take this one step at a time and see what happens.'

'Does that mean we're going to use your place, then? Because we're sure as hell not using mine. I cannot have this place linked to anything we do. You know that!'

Sitting back in my chair, I take a swig of my beer. Brad's zest and enthusiasm is hard to ignore and I'm sure that if I were of an impressionable nature, I would be well and truly caught up in his dream by now. Thankfully, I'm not that way inclined, but he does have a valid point. This should be kept out of our everyday lives. I understand his reasons for objecting to the use of his place as a headquarters, and like him, I don't want my place becoming the centre of attention. In theory, it's a sound idea, but I have one slight problem.

'I can't take this on right now. My personal finances are not by any means desperate, but they are most definitely stretched, what with the building work and other things. I don't have the spare cash to spend on another property, not right now. The pot's not empty, but I can see the bottom of the jar, if you get my meaning.'

'Then I'll make you a proposition -'

'I will not borrow money off you,' I butt in. 'I'm not going down that road!'

'Just listen for a minute,' Brad says. 'I told you I dabbled on the stock market. That, according to my new CV is what I do for a living these days, and how I made my fortune. Seeing as it's on my CV, I thought it would be prudent, and in my best interests, to find out how it all worked. Much to my delight I found it very easy to make money, and I also discovered that, when the risks are high, so are the returns.'

'Your point is?' I impatiently ask, with no desire to hear another shaggy-dog saga.

'The money we earn from this job, when it comes up. I have one or two very reliable contacts on the inside and I guarantee I will double your money within a week. With the profits, and maybe some of the original stake, we can buy a place and run our business in total privacy, and you'll still have a tidy sum left in your pocket to pay off your debts, guaranteed. What do you think?'

I stare at Brad for a few moments. What he's suggesting needs a great deal of thought. Sitting here in his lounge, drinking his beer and having a friendly conversation with him, is one thing. Giving him my share of the spoils so he can invest it on some risky stock market deal is a big gamble, and not one I'm sure I'm ready to take. I don't know that I can trust him that much. He could do a runner with the lot. One hundred grand is a lot of money, and to be honest, money I could do with, right now.

Brad seems very confident that it's a done deal. From what I know about the stock market, which I admit is rather limited, there are no such guarantees, unless, as he's hinting, one is privy to insider dealing. That is highly unlikely, given the circumstances.

I feel a little stupid. Normally, I would have done my homework on someone like Brad, checked him out. I haven't this time because I'm preoccupied by my own woes and I've left myself wide open. He's openly stated that Brad isn't his real name and it could take weeks, months even, just to find out what it really is. If he is who he says he is, then there will be nothing to find, anyway, but I don't know that, and that bothers me. I must stall him, without raising his suspicions.

'The timing's not right, I'm going to have to say no to you,' I tell him.

'You really don't trust me, do you?'

'No I don't!' I reply, being as honest and up front with him as I can be.

'I understand where you're coming from, and I respect your honesty,' he says, slapping his thighs before standing up. 'I see now that I need to earn your trust. Can I get you another beer?'

'Getting me drunk won't help your cause.'

'I'm trying to be the perfect host,' he responds. 'Listen, I know it looks as if I'm rushing this, but my life has been on hold for the past five years and I'm eager to move on. I'd like you to understand that.'

'Rome wasn't built in a day,' I suggest, while handing him my empty bottle of beer. 'Look at me; it's taken me eighteen years to get where I am. During that time, I've matured and grown into the experience. That has been very important, not just for me personally, for all those around me too.'

Brad slowly sits himself back down. By the look on his face, for the first time he's really listening to me.

'Can you imagine sitting a sixteen-year-old down in my office and telling him or her to get on with it? They wouldn't cope, would they? They wouldn't know where to start, or what to do next. Granted, this is a totally different set of circumstances. For a start, we're both vastly experienced people in our line of work, but what we're trying to achieve here, is a combination of both our skills, and we don't know if it'll work. We should view this as a new beginning, in the same way I did, eighteen years ago. Experience it, grow with it, mature with it, and adapt to make it work. This can work if both protagonists want it to, but you're pushing me too hard and too fast, and if you continue in the same vein I will walk away.'

Brad sits looking at me in silence, nodding his head in agreement. Clearly, he's listening to my impromptu words of wisdom. Whether they'll make any difference remains to be seen, and I haven't quite finished.

'We both have a lot to learn about each other. We can also teach one another the tricks of our trades. That will take time, nothing like eighteen years I hope, but working and thinking as one, as you have suggested we'll need to do, doesn't happen overnight. The way I see it, you have a problem with that, because I don't know enough about you as a person to think like you do. You have got to open up and tell me more about yourself, or this won't work.'

Brad leans forward and offers me a cigarette from his packet of twenty *Benson and Hedges*. We light up as he ponders over my meanderings.

'You're right,' he says nervously. 'Absolutely right. What I have told you so far, is the God's honest truth. There is a lot more you'll need to know, and I will tell you, but I need more time to sort my head out first.'

'I understand, and as far as I'm concerned nothing has changed where this first job is concerned,' I inform Brad, hoping to put his mind at rest. 'Once it's done, we'll regroup and take it from there. What do you say?'

'Sounds good,' he says, standing up again, still clutching my empty bottle of beer. 'It's a pity you won't commit to buying a place. I've come across the most beautiful property in the country. It's perfect for our needs.'

'Where?' I ask as a matter of interest.

'Not far from where you live: East of Carmarthen and right on the River Tywi. Very secluded and private, and the place comes with five acres of land,' Brad informs me.

'How much?'

'It's up for auction next month. Needs a bit of work, but I reckon I can get it for around three hundred and fifty thousand. That includes the fees.'

'I thought we wanted an office, not a bloody mansion!'

'It is a mansion, but think about it. Who it their right mind would think of looking for the likes of you and me in a place like that,' he scoffs. 'Give it some thought. Go and take a look for yourself and you'll see what I mean. Mark my words; you'll change your mind once you've seen it.'

'No I won't. And what makes you think I'll want to see it?'

'You will, you can't resist a challenge,' he replies.

Friday, 29 January 1988

A detour on the way home to post the tax bills in Bristol is taking me longer than I'd planned. I've hit the beginning of the heavy, out-of-city, Friday evening rush hour, which is going to delay my return by some considerable time. I was rather hoping to get back to the office before everyone disappeared for the weekend, collar James, and catch up with today's progress on Gavin Thomas. I'm at least two hours out and with both Cardiff and Swansea to negotiate on the busy M4, one can easily add two hours to the journey.

I have some urgent prep work for tomorrow's little jaunt with Brad to attend to, and it's beer night with the lads. It's sacrilege to miss that. I really don't want to be wasting my time in traffic!

Brad knew I'd swing in here on my way home. He may have deliberately planted the thought in my mind, yesterday, to make quite certain I did. Now I'm here I can see exactly what he was enthusing over and I have to admit, I like what I'm seeing. This is a dream of mine, and to take a good look around now, drooling over the one thing I've always hankered after, will mean being late home. What the hell does that matter? This is today, this is real, and there's no one at home to give me a rollicking for being late. James can wait until Monday, and I can handle being called 'Reg' for the evening when I finally get to the pub. It's the prep work for tomorrow, which I must deal with tonight that concerns me the most.

The cattle grid doesn't sound too healthy - that will want looking at in the very near future, to make sure it is safe to drive across. The discomfort of negotiating the narrow, overgrown driveway, peppered with deep, water-filled potholes pales into insignificance when I reach the end.

A Victorian manor house of some distinction stands boarded up and empty in front of me, and in Brad's words 'needs a bit of work'. None the less, even in its current dilapidated condition, it is a very impressive sight. Constructed in red brick and locally-quarried stone, the regimented box shaped façade stands as proud today in this fading light as it has done for well over a hundred years. I absolutely adore the place! I'm smitten. Standing face on to the building, taking in the grandeur, one can imagine the Lord of the manor strutting around, presiding over his land. Head held high with a stiff upper lip, barking his commands at the overworked and underpaid servants. This is what made Britain great.

The River Tywi flows past the manor house beyond the long rear garden, which sadly lies in a neglected state today, but once upon a time, I guess, with unrecorded hours of tender loving care, it would have looked magnificent. The whole place is unbelievably serene, and so very relaxing.

I could stand in this spot forever, just looking, soaking up the splendour, but it's nearly dark now, and wanting to take in as much as I can while I'm here, I continue my walk around the grounds of the house.

Around the back, one or two of the windows have had the boarding removed, presumably by vandals, maybe vagabonds, giving me a chance to peer inside. From what I can ascertain of the interior it doesn't look that bad, but I don't profess to be an expert in building work, as Mac will testify. I'm so impressed, I am beginning to wish I had taken the time to collect a key from the auctioneers, to allow me to view the interior properly. The upper floors will remain a mystery until I do.

On the left hand side of the main house - viewing from the front - stands a large stable block. To the rear of that stands a small, brick-built dwelling, which was probably once the residence of the estate manager and his family. Fabulous! I'm sold on the idea. This is so me. This is where I see myself in the future; my dream, living in a mansion, lording over the land and peasants. I fear, though, that Brad's estimate of three hundred and fifty grand is going to be well shy of what it will sell for under the hammer at auction.

Sitting on the bonnet of my car, having a smoke before I leave, I stare at this fabulous building in front of me, taking mental pictures for future reference. I can see myself living here. Owning a place like this - in a part of the country I know well - is a once in a lifetime opportunity, and I don't want to miss out. That gives me a problem because I lied to Brad, and he may well distrust me for that. I do have the funds, tucked safely away on my accountant's recommendation, to avoid the taxman. I see no reason to alert him. I have some serious thinking to do.

Chapter nine

Saturday, 30 January 1988

In an hour and a half from now, my life will change forever. Jenny and Tony are taking their wedding vows at eleven o'clock this morning. I'm not going to the registry service, and I never intended to. The only thing that has surprised me is Jenny's decision to choose Tony over the financial security for her unborn child that she could have had with me.

My mind is elsewhere. This morning I'm finding life distracting, and I slip, frantically wrestling for a handhold on the ladder while climbing aboard my boat. I'm going fishing as soon as the incoming tide is high enough to leave the harbour safely, and that would have been difficult to achieve had I dropped the bait when I slipped. I'm not with it and that's dangerous.

Diligently, I checked the high and low tide times with Colin on Thursday, and I haven't long to wait. A huge plume of thick, black smoke rises into the air from the exhaust as the engines wind up into action. The distinctive, toxic smell of diesel fumes drifts across my nostrils.

The twin 350hp Volvo engines burst into life and settle down into that beautiful deep throbbing tick-over rhythm, which starts the sequence of on board pre-checks I routinely carry out before setting off. With everything working, I check the height of the tide on the markers at the entrance to the harbour.

When the rising tide hits the three-metre height mark, I untie the aft and bow ropes, push the boat away from the quay by hand and climb into the covered cockpit. Setting the throttle to five knots, I gently ease her out through the harbour entrance. Maintaining that speed until I reach the outer marker buoys, I open her up gradually to full throttle - a little over thirty knots – and she sits up and powers out into the bay. When I estimate I'm about a mile offshore, I stamp my right foot three times on the cockpit floor. Immediately, the cabin door below me swings open and a rather dishevelled looking Brad climbs the short, chrome ladder from the lower deck up to the cockpit.

'Any problems?' he asks, straight away.

'Only in fitting the new batteries last night in the dark. That was hard work on my own, getting them from my car down into the engine room,' I reply. 'I think I've pulled something.'

'You're not fit, that's your problem,' Brad delightfully reminds me.

Leaning over to look at the instruments, he asks me if I've set the course. I haven't, because I don't know where we're headed and reluctantly I let him take over the controls.

'Did you?' I ask in return to his first question.

'None, and as long as your mate, Ed, doesn't call into his workshop, we won't have.'

'He won't, not on a Saturday,' I inform him. 'What time did you arrive,' I add

'About 3am,' he tells me as the boat swings to port, heading towards The Mumbles. 'I stuck my motorbike right down the back of the workshop and covered it over with a tarpaulin, just in case. Tell me something,' he asks, turning to look at me. 'How did you get the keys off him without him knowing?'

'Timing. When you asked me for a set of keys to the boat, I'd recently given the spare set to Ed, so he could carry out a full service at his leisure. Ed has a history of losing keys. What he does to combat his forgetfulness is to put the set belonging to the boat he's working on with his spare workshop keys. That way, he claims, he won't lose them. Richard told me that Ed had been down to look at my boat and mentioned the batteries, so I played the laws of average. The trick was to catch him as he locked up and gasping for his first pint. Plus, of course, I wanted to see what type of batteries I needed. I called on him just as he was leaving, and he handed a full set of keys over without checking.'

'Smart. They do say a little local knowledge goes a long way,' Brad says. 'Talking of local knowledge, did you take a look at the house on your way home yesterday?'

I turn and walk away without answering, climbing down the short, chrome ladder to the aft deck. I had told Colin I was going fishing if the weather held fair, so I'd best set the rods up.

'You did, didn't you?' Brad calls out. 'What did you think of the place?'

Lifting the cushioning on the bench seat, set around the edge of the aft deck, I pull out two fishing rods. Both are set up. Easily stored, there's no need to dismantle them after use, but I always give them a quick once over. I ignore Brad's question while I check over the rods because I have no wish to prove him right. Pretending I can't hear him over the noise of the engines I rejoin him in the cockpit when I'm done.

'What are you doing?' he asks.

'I'm supposed to be on a fishing trip, remember? I can hardly return without something to show for my efforts.'

'We won't have the time to "go fishing" when we do this for real.'

'Then we'd better make time in our planning. It would be unusual, but Colin, the harbour master, might just check up on me. We leave nothing to chance,' I inform him.

For the majority of the year, Colin gives me a wide berth, mainly because I ask too many questions and cause him a lot of grief. However, every now and again *Customs and Excise* have a purge, checking every single incoming and outgoing vessel. Today could be that day, and it's not worth taking the risk. Brad wants this to be a professional operation, so we will do this right.

With him sat at the helm, I slide into the seat beside him, taking note of our course, and checking the weather conditions. The forecast for the next few hours is good for late January. A little cold and overcast but the seas are reasonably calm inshore.

'How long have we got?' Brad asks, as a packet of *Benson and Hedges* land in front of me.

'I've got one of the more accessible berths in the harbour, which gives us around six hours max. When planning, I'd allow five to be on the safe side, and if the weather's bad we won't get out so be prepared to abort at short notice,' I inform him.

'When would we know that?' Brad inquires.

'That's something we'd need to gauge when we're ready to sail. A lot depends on the wind direction, and the height of the swell in bad weather. The troughs between the waves can be much lower than its safe to sail in and there's a real danger of running aground. If that was the case we would run the risk of being smashed against the harbour walls by the force of the breakers.'

'Meaning?'

'If we run aground, there's a risk being capsized by the next wave, in fact I'd say that is a certainty. Alternatively, we could be picked up by a huge wave and thrown against the harbour wall. The results of that aren't worth thinking about.'

'Could we get out at all under those conditions?'

'If we we're desperate enough we could try, and if we were successful, that could give us an hour maybe, either side of high tide. That's all!'

'Not enough,' Brad snaps.

'Brad, only someone stupid, or someone desperate would attempt to set sail in conditions like that, and that, my friend, brings attention upon oneself. Not something we want, is it?' I suggest.

'Options?' he quickly responds.

'Options,' I mumble, taking a few seconds to think. 'There aren't too many of those. We could sail and ride out the storm until the next high tide, or if we managed to clear the harbour, we could find a deep-water harbour to berth in. Neither of those options appeal to me.'

I get the impression Brad doesn't like what he's hearing. To the inexperienced sailor, putting out to sea sounds like child's play, and on a clear, relatively calm day like today, one is drawn into making that rather foolish conclusion. I'm far from being an expert where sea conditions are concerned, but I'm aware of my limitations, and I am deeply respectful of the sea's power.

Before I left home, I checked the forecast. I double-checked my interpretation with the people who really know – the local fishermen. Conditions similar to those we have today are rare at this time of year, and many of the local fishermen themselves are putting out to earn some much-needed cash. They confirmed what I had understood of the forecast. Sea conditions will be no more than slight, today. In this western corner of Wales, the weather can be very harsh and changeable. It would be suicidal not to check the conditions for the duration of one's trip. Our beautiful, rugged coastline is frequently battered by violent, heavy storms, sometimes with little warning - especially at this time of year. Five hours of sailing can catch out even the most experienced sailors amongst the seafaring fraternity – and it has.

'We'll need to know if we're aborting, at least three hours before we sail,' Brad informs me. 'What's your knowledge of the shipping forecast like?'

'Reasonable,' I reply, with confidence, after my conversation with the trawler skippers. 'You have to remember that shipping forecasts are general and not local. Conditions inshore can be very different to those out in open seas. The land mass protects certain areas depending on the wind direction, and that can change with a blink of the eye.'

'Christ,' Brad shouts, slamming his fist down hard onto my delicate control module. 'Can't you give me anything positive to work with?'

'Bollocks to you!' I shout back. 'This is not like a Sunday afternoon car drive in the country. The sea is not something to play with. Like the film suggests: it's cruel. It's unforgiving, unpredictable, and extremely dangerous to anyone who under estimates her awesome power.'

'What are you saying? You want out before we've begun? Not got the stomach for a little excitement?' Brad goads. He turns to face me, staring hard through those threatening eyes of his.

'Oh, you've no need to worry on that front; I've got the stomach for it. I'd like to live long enough to spend the money you seem so keen to risk our lives for. I've seen first-hand what the sea can do to a man. Not in hours, Brad, minutes; seconds, that's all it takes. And that's to experienced sailors.'

Standing up, I lean across the control module to check for any damage. Brad's violent reaction to my warning was unnecessary in my opinion. His outburst worries me, because I don't know how he'll react under real pressure. Fortunately, the control module appears to be in good working order, and thankfully unscathed.

'I realise how frustrating this is, but what would you rather have me do? Lie to you and let us sail into trouble, or be up front and honest over what might lay ahead? What would you say to me if I said nothing, let us put out to sea and risk our lives, probably failing in our mission? You'd go fucking ballistic, wouldn't you?'

Brad doesn't respond. His gaze is now straight ahead, concentrating on our course.

'It might help me if I knew exactly what it is we're up too?'

Still he says nothing. I stand, leaving him alone to think it through for a while. 'I'm going below to make us a coffee,' I tell him. 'I'll say one thing before I do. My guess is that we're being paid to either pick something, or someone up. Heavy seas will make that virtually impossible.'

Down below, one first passes through the lounge area - which doubles up as the second bedroom – to reach the galley in the middle of the craft. Beyond the galley, in the bow of the boat, is the main en-suite double bedroom. The living quarters are compact, but well designed and modern. There's ample room for four people to eat and sleep in comfort.

As I switch on the kettle, the boat suddenly begins to roll on the swell. Our speed reduces sharply as Brad throttles back the engines because, as predicted, we've encountered the rougher open sea. Just what I've warned him about, and without looking, I'd guess we've emerged from the protection of the landmass. Probably, St. Cuthbert's island off Fenby, or the point further around the coastline. Perhaps now, he'll understand a little more of what I've been trying to explain to him. Conditions can change very quickly out here, and once you're out in open sea there is no protection. You can run, but you can't hide.

Everything on board is designed with safety in mind, but not compulsory. Like the life jacket I have, and not wearing. The cups have proper screw-on, anti spill lids, not the push on sort BR claim to be the real deal. That epitomises just how important safety is while out at sea. If there is a risk, one should take the necessary precautions to reduce that risk.

I love my boat. I can, on a whim, set sail and be alone with my thoughts. Something I should do more often. One day, once I've retired and I'm ready to see the world I'll buy something a touch bigger - no, a lot bigger; state of the art, an all-singing and dancing ocean-going cruiser. John Paul Getty, watch out. Monte

Carlo, here I come. The bubble bursts, and the coffee's going cold. In the mood I left Brad, he may have shot himself by now – with any luck. What we're undertaking here has got to be a mistake.

Back up in the cockpit, I place Brad's coffee down in front of him and take up the pose, standing quite still while staring directly ahead. Brad has said nothing. Not even the expected 'thank you' for making the coffee.

His lack of sea faring experience has surprised me. His knowledge of navigation isn't in question, but I would have thought the so-called elite soldier would know everything there is to know. Then again, the SAS are only glorified paratroopers who, in my opinion, rather stupidly jump out of aeroplanes with sheets of cotton strapped to their backs, hoping that when they pull a piece of string the cotton will unfurl so they can float safely down to terra firma. I won't suggest that to him, but what a bizarre way to make a living.

I wonder what is going through his mind right now. I'd guess he thinks I'm a pampered softy who knows nothing about how the real world works. That's an interesting thought. Which one of us does live in the real world? Is that me because I'm in touch with real everyday folk, or is it Brad because his training gives him control of the real world we all live in? That's what makes this working partnership so challenging, and the prospects of its development exciting. Our backgrounds are so very different. We are miles apart, and yet, somewhere in the middle, is the perfect solution. Compromise, is the key word here.

Brad's high level of concentration, his vigilance in watching the horizon and the instrument panel, has me questioning our being out here today.

'What going on?' I ask.

'I'm not with you,' he replies, finally deciding to communicate with me.

'All that shit just now; you're testing me aren't you? And this isn't a dummy run, is it?' I suggest.

'If you like, yes, I am testing you. And you're quite right; no, this isn't a dummy run. Today's the real deal,' he says.

'So much for trusting one another.'

'You earn trust.'

'I'll bear that in mind next time - if there is a next time,' I tell him. Disgusted by his attitude and lying, I pick up my coffee and turn to leave the cockpit.

'There you go again,' Brad scoffs. 'Walking away when things aren't going your way.'

'I'm not walking away, and in case you haven't noticed I can't go all that far.'

'You've got a history of walking away from situations you can't deal with, Nick,' invoking an angry response from me.

His statement also suggests that he has an intimate knowledge of my private life. I have never walked away from a work-related problem, so he must be referring to my private life. That's not what he told me a few days ago.

'Just what is that supposed to mean?' I snap, leaning on the control module, right next to him.

Brad looks at his wristwatch, making quite sure I can see the time. His deliberate and exaggerated movement suggests that he knows about today's joyous happening in Saundersby.

It's 10.51am. We've been out for just over an hour. In nine minutes from now, Jenny will marry Tony, and there's no going back. I stand up again and look directly ahead, out through the cockpit window. What I feel and think about today is not up for discussion.

'In the here and now it maybe of little comfort to you,' Brad says softly, 'but you've impressed me, this morning. Not only because of your local knowledge, but because you got into this boat knowing what's taking place at eleven o'clock, today. I think I know what that all means to you.'

I turn to face him, desperately trying to work out how he knows. If he was aware of my personal circumstances, why didn't he help? Surely, helping me sort that particular problem would be to the benefit of us both. I wouldn't be so pre-occupied, and Brad would have my undivided attention. Perhaps he doesn't want to involve himself in my private life. Knowing about Jenny does involve him; maybe that's why he chose today to do this. Out here, I can't change my mind and do something I'll regret in the long run.

Perhaps Brad has been very selfish for the sake of this partnership, and made that decision for me. The right answer to that may take years to find out.

'In our line of business, there is no room for sentiment. Our private lives take second place. You committed yourself to the future, today, because knowing that by coming out here on your boat, other matters - important personal matters were no longer under your ultimate control. I'd say that was commitment,' he reassuringly adds.

Am I committed? Or is the fact that I am here, proof that I have walked away from yet another personal problem? Whatever my reasons are for being out here today, and I'm really not sure what they are, after eleven o'clock today one fact will be indisputable: the surname of Jenny's baby will be Morris. She's made that decision for both of us.

'You can do a bit of fishing in about ten minutes,' Brad announces.

Obviously, we're close to our destination. 'Won't need too. I bought half a dozen off one of the fishing boats last night. They're in the bait box, on ice,' I inform him rather smugly.

'You knew this wasn't a dummy run?'

'Not really, no,' I reply to his question. 'I couldn't make up my mind about today. We'd gone to a lot of effort just to prove that we can do it, so I covered all the bases. It appears that I was right to question your motives.'

I light up a cigarette and turn to look back toward the shoreline, Saundersby, Jenny, and the wedding, deeply imbedded in my thoughts. Against the backdrop of red-faced cliffs, it's difficult to see the town from this far out. I know where it is, I know what's happening there right now and I know I've made the right decision today.

My fight with Jenny isn't over, because the need to know hasn't gone away. One day, maybe when she's forgotten about us, and dropped her guard, I will catch her out. I will uncover the truth about her, as yet, unborn child. My hope is that she doesn't give the baby some silly, nonsensical name, like Tinkerbell, or Brad! That would be an insult.

'So!' I say turning to face Brad. 'Are you going to tell me what the hell we're out here to do?'

'You'd better sit down; there's something I need to explain to you,' he replies sheepishly, which I don't like the sound of.

Right from the off, I've thought there was something amiss with this episode. Two hundred grand, for a few hours' work, isn't a normal return for a job well done. His tone of voice casts even more doubt. This has got to be dodgy and not entirely above board.

'This had better be good,' I inform him sitting down next to him.

'"Good" isn't a word I'd use,' he replies and pauses for moment. 'Sometimes, we all have to do things we're not comfortable with.'

I cut in on him; I've had quite enough of his lectures for one day. 'Get to the point, Brad!'

He swallows hard before continuing, scratching his chin nervously. 'There's a flight due into Swansea airport at twelve o'clock, a delivery of a new aircraft from France. Our task is to wait under their approach path and pick up a package they drop into the sea.'

Brad stares directly at me. 'I know what you're thinking, and I can only tell you what I've been told.'

I butt in again. 'Turn the boat around, I'll not have anything to do with drug trafficking,' I reply angrily, making my feelings very clear to him. I had feared, with the sort of money on offer that it would turn out to be something like this.

'I can't,' he mumbles in reply.

His statement prompts me to do something I've done a lot of recently. I lean forward and quickly switch off the engine, removing, at haste, the keys from the ignition. Brad's look cuts me in half and I brace myself for a heavy right hook to land on my chin. He doesn't lash out as I had expected, just stands staring menacingly at me, in total silence. The only noise to be heard is from the sea, lapping against the side of my drifting boat.

'Give me the keys,' Brad says calmly, his arm outstretched toward me, the palm of his hand open.

'Sorry, I can't do that. I'm not that desperate to earn money, and never will be where drugs are concerned.'

'We don't have a choice,' he responds.

'I do,' I tell him while sliding off my seat away from him, and I certainly do have a choice.

'No we don't! I've had half of the money up front. The rest is payable on delivery. You're in on this, Nick, whether you like it or not. Now give me the keys, please.'

Words fail me. How many more surprises is he going to spring on me today?

Brad pulls my spare set of keys from his jean pocket, spinning them around in front of me on his right index finger. Bollocks, I'd forgotten I'd given him those on Thursday night so he could get onto the boat without me being there. 'Are you really that desperate to earn some cash, because if you are I'll give you a hundred grand?' I tell him, trying to defuse a potential disaster.

'You haven't got a hundred grand to give me, so you've told me!'

'Fortunately for me, you're not as good as you like to believe you are, or I'm better than you've given me credit for. The price of that house you liked; a drop in the ocean. You see, I don't need you, or this shit you're involving me in. So do us both a favour, if you won't give me the spare set of keys then at least use them to take us back to Saundersby harbour.'

Over Brad's left shoulder, I catch glimpse of a large motor launch heading at speed directly toward us.

'We've got company,' I tell Brad while reaching for a pair of binoculars resting on top of the control module. Focussing quickly on the vessel, my first observation of the boat tells me nothing. The vessel is head on to us and any identification it may have is hidden from view. Brad restarts the engine, and with the boat bearing down on us at a high rate of knots, I don't question him.

'Can you make it out?' he asks with a high degree of panic in his voice. 'Talk to me.'

'Two men; possibly a third. Can't see any markings, but it's not the normal type of boat the coast guard use. I don't recognise the type at all.'

'Navy?' he asks.

'No, definitely not.'

Brad powers up the boat and turns toward them. Readjusting my position, I continue to scan the horizon, checking for further activity. Seeing nothing suspicious, I turn back and concentrate on the fast approaching vessel.

'Is there anything else you haven't told me about?' I ask as a matter of interest, because who knows what he's got us in to!

'No,' he snaps unconvincingly.

My head tells me he's lying. My heart wants to believe him.

'Keep talking to me.'

'Definitely three men. They're watching me watching them.' I notice Brad's behaviour. His head is in constant motion, scanning the horizon, straining to see what other dangers are lurking out there. He's looking up too, watching the cloud-covered sky for his alleged contact. Then it dawns on me. What the hell are we panicking for? We haven't actually done anything wrong! 'Shut the engines down, I'm going fishing,' I tell him.

Brad glances questioningly in my direction. He's probably not sure that he's heard me right. To make my point known, I put the binoculars down on the control module, descend to the lower deck and start to bait up the readied fishing lines with diced razor fish. Mackerel fishing is good in these waters and usually productive, although I've never fished quite this far out, or at this time of year.

When I look back, Brad has one hand on the helm and the binoculars held up to eyes with the other. We're still steaming full speed ahead toward the advancing motor cruiser, which is ideal when you're fishing for marlin off Miami, but the mackerel in Carmarthen Bay aren't as fast.

'For God's sake, cut the bloody engines will you,' I shout at him in frustration. 'And get yourself down here.'

There's no finesse about the way Brad throttles back the boat. The sudden and violent change in speed unbalances me and I fall backwards, rather luckily, on to the cushioned bench seat. With the boat now idling, and once again drifting dangerously on the tide, he slides down the ladder to join me on the aft deck. He's clearly nervous, agitated by what is happening, and paces around the deck keeping a watchful eye on the approaching boat. I cast out the first line, reel in the slack, place the rod into the rest, and pick up the second fishing rod. Brad's random movements as he paces the deck makes the casting of the second line rather complicated. I don't want to hook him, but the thought of inflicting pain on him has crossed my mind several times in past few minutes.

I carefully cast out the second line, place the rod into its rest and sit down on the bench seat. I'm strangely relaxed considering the situation we're in, which is more than can be said for Brad. For all I know, the approaching boat could be crewed by Colombian drug barons out to wreak havoc on our green and pleasant land. Brad's behaviour bothers me, because something tells me - watching him pace around the deck in circles - that there's more to come. As things stand, I've had more surprises today than Christmas morning usually brings.

The throbbing of engines grows louder. Before Brad leans over the side to see where the boat is, he tells me to leave things to him. I wasn't planning to interfere in his business, and make myself comfortable, sitting down on the opposite edge of the boat, in readiness for a swift backward exit.

The large motor cruiser glides in alongside my tiny excuse of a boat - several millions of pounds worth, I shouldn't wonder - and two white males appear on deck high above us. A third man keeps an eagle eye on Brad and myself from inside the bridge. I'm not sure which one to keep my eyes glued to.

'*Monsieur Brad?*' the smaller, plumper of the two men ask.

'Who wants to know?' Brad replies.

Hardly original, I think, and the man repeats himself, because he hasn't understood Brad's reply.

'What do you want?' Brad adds.

The two men look at each other, shrug their shoulders numerous times, and wave their arms at each other, while holding a private conversation. The whole thing amuses me. Why come all this way to rendezvous with someone when you can't speak fucking English! Basic stuff.

'*Oui Monsieur,*' I say, speaking out to speed up the proceedings, while nodding my head and pointing a finger at Brad.

'I said leave this to me. I know what I'm doing here.'

'Clearly you do. You're right on top of the situation; I can see that!'

The taller, but equally plump man, who, according to aggressive advertising, believes that wearing sunglasses on an overcast day makes him look cool, beckons toward the cabin area. A huge - and I mean huge – stocky, black man of African origin appears on deck beside the two Frenchmen. I can't help but notice the look of shock and horror on Brad's face when he sees him. He wasn't expecting this.

Is this my cue to fall backwards over the side of the boat into the cold sea? This is the sort of situation you see every night on TV, in one of those crass 'cops and robbers' series they show: a situation where a sub-machine gun appears from nowhere, spewing out round after round of hot lead in a very unforgiving fashion, ripping everything in its wake to shreds. I try to convince myself that I have an over active imagination, and this isn't as bad as it looks, but this is Brad's world, and I guess anything is possible.

When the black guy picks up a holdall, I feel my body tense up, and start slowly leaning backwards over the side of the boat. You read and hear about all sorts of things going on in the world these days, and perhaps my imagination isn't so overactive. Lifting the holdall over the handrail, he drops it down to Brad, who makes an absolute pig's ear of catching the thing. To my amazement, the big guy climbs over the safety rail and lowers himself down onto my boat. The moment he's safely aboard, the engines on our visitors' boat roar into action, and without too much care, they speed off into the sunset, clipping the side of my boat at least twice. Bloody French drivers!

Ignoring my presence, Brad ushers the guy below deck into the cabin, closing the door behind them. Well, that was certainly different. As I sit and contemplate what I've just witnessed, I'd say that the minimum Brad owes me is an explanation. This working together is a touch one-sided. So far, all Brad has done is use me for what I know, and what I have.

Once again, we're drifting dangerously on the tide, without power on, or the anchor lowered; despite the extra ballast we're now carrying. My pride and joy is comfortably a four berth. Looking at the physical size of Brad's friend, I'd say we're now full to capacity, and I'm not going to hang around for the next boat of illegal immigrants to turn up. For me, at least, it's time to head back to Saundersby. I assume that'll be the plan, anyway. One can never be sure where Brad is concerned, and, in his own time, I'm sure he'll eventually tell me what's going on - if I question him enough.

A quick check along the starboard side of my boat reveals a couple of minor scrapes. Fortunately, I note there's no serious damage, and return to the bridge. The necessary repairs will give Ed the opportunity to inflate his bill. I wasn't impressed one bit by the way they took off; seems they were in a hurry to unload their human cargo. I'm curious to know who the guy is.

I listen in, briefly, by the cabin door on my way up, but I couldn't hear a damn thing over the idling engine noise and gain nothing from my action. That makes me angry. The not knowing, being used like this, and taken for granted is beginning to wind me up.

Bollocks! Once seated in the bridge, I remember the fishing rods and return to the aft deck to reel the lines in. Luckily, I haven't caught anything. I quickly return to the cockpit; the vessel drifting on the tide is a concern. Worm's Head on the Gower Peninsula is perilously close, and explaining away the presence of our visitor on board to the coastguard, should we run aground, will be challenging. Gently easing the throttle forward, I turn hard to starboard and set our heading, back toward Saundersby.

'What the fuck are you doing?' Brad shouts up at me from the aft deck.

'That's rich coming from you,' I shout back angrily, stamping my feet like a spoilt brat. 'It's about time you told me what's really going on here. And, for your information, I'm going home.'

'Give me five minutes, please?'

I'm not listening; I've had enough. I slam the throttle forward to maximum speed. The sudden surge of power throws Brad tumbling back inside the cabin. I'd like to think that the bang I hear is his head hitting something solid, but it's more likely to be the cabin door slamming closed. To annoy him even more, I keep the throttle wide open. The choppy seas will make the ride below pretty uncomfortable for Brad and his guest.

Being childish like this isn't something I'd normally advocate, but occasionally one needs to air one's feelings in public and this type of behaviour becomes a necessary evil to express one's displeasure. I'm not thinking about the consequences of mooring in Saundersby - with what appears to be an illegal immigrant on board – I just want to get away from here before we become associated.

When Brad returns to the cockpit, alone, he's a lot calmer than I expected him to be. Hovering at my shoulder, he lowers his hand until it's inches away from the throttle lever.

Common sense prevails. I've calmed down too, and I know we must discuss this before we reach harbour. There's nothing to be gained by charging around like a bull in a china shop. I nod my head and Brad slowly pulls back the throttle lever until the engines return to idling mode, and once again, we're drifting on the tide.

'Cards on the table this time, Brad. No more fucking me around,' I tell him. 'I'm not joking. My life is complicated enough without this shit. I want to know why I'm here. I want to know why you've talked me into this, and I want to know who the fuck that guy is in my cabin?'

'You don't need to know who he is,' he replies, without acknowledging me.

'If you don't mind, I'll be the judge of that!'

'Believe me, for your own sake, you don't want to know.'

My frustration gets the better of me. Switching off the engines I remove the spare keys from the ignition and launch them out into the sea. The original set is in my pocket. If he wants them, he knows what he has to do to get them.

'I'll fucking ask him myself,' I inform Brad and turn to climb down the cockpit ladder. As I grab hold of the top handle, Brad offers up a little information.

'He's a political refugee, but I swear to you, I didn't know we were out here to pick him up.'

'And?' I ask, spinning around to face him.

'He needs to get into Britain.'

'Why?'

'To help his people by raising the world's awareness to the atrocities going on in his homeland. He has powerful allies in Britain who can help him do that. No one, though, will go on record and publicly support him.'

'What the fuck's wrong with using Heathrow airport?'

'The guy's been dodging bullets for years because he's prepared to stand up and speak the truth. He was smuggled out of his country by sympathisers. If his government had got wind of his plans, they'd have done anything to stop him. They're ruthless people, who rule by fear. Like you with your private life, they'll do whatever's necessary to protect what they have.'

'Don't bring me into this and make it sound as if I care, because I don't.'

'You might not, but millions of his countrymen's lives depend on him staying alive.'

'My heart goes out to them, it really does, but we're breaking the law by taking him ashore. And whatever political advantages there are for keeping him alive, I'm not comfortable with what we're doing.'

'Just stick to the agreed plan, and everything will be fine. Trust me.'

I have little confidence in Brad as it is. Having him ask me to trust him, with what he's put me through today, is a big call. Cornered, I know I have no choice, stuck out here with them both on my boat. His plan has to work, or we're all in big trouble.

'Who are we working for, Brad? And don't even think about telling me I don't need to know, because I do.'

I take myself back to the swivel seat at the helm and sit down, keeping the one set of keys we now own safely in my pocket. We're not going anywhere until he coughs up the truth.

'You see, I think you knew all along that this was going to happen, and had you told me at the outset you knew damn well I would have said no. Tell me I'm wrong?' I ask, watching him closely for a reaction. 'Your face was a picture when that black guy appeared. I could tell by your look that you were shocked to see him, but not surprised, and you readily accepted the fact that he was coming aboard my boat, ushering him below deck without once questioning him. That, Brad, told me you knew about him. I'll give you the benefit of doubt and maybe you weren't expecting him today, but you were expecting him, so no more lies. Just who are we working for?'

Brad remains silent as he offers me a cigarette. I don't really want one, but it could be my last under the present circumstances. 'This isn't right,' I say. 'You're still in the army, aren't you?'

'No,' comes a very assertive answer.

'Working for the government then, as some sort of secret agent?'

'Not exactly.'

'I thought so,' I reply, letting out a sigh in frustration. 'How not exactly?'

'I've signed the official secrets act; I can't tell you that.'

'But it's OK to involve me and risk my life? Is that how it works? By putting a well-known face into the frame, the government's spy can sneak away undetected?'

'Of course not,' he mumbles, unconvincingly. 'I'm freelance, and this is a genuine attempt to set up a working partnership.'

'Why don't I believe you?' I ask him, shaking my head in disgust.

'For Christ sake! I'm working for the man who gave me my new identity. It was part of the deal. I have no say in the matter. When he snaps his grubby, soiled little fingers, I jump. Satisfied?'

'Am I fuck, satisfied? How long does this deal you've made last?'

'Until I resolve it,' he responds, staring at me through those piecing, menacing eyes of his.

Throttling back the engines to five knots at the outer marker buoys, I take a quick glance at the height markers before concentrating on the movements within the harbour. The tall sea-facing harbour wall acts as a breakwater, running parallel with the mainland, restricting my view. On the southern-most side, the land forms a natural barrier from the elements, while on the northern side a second wall projects directly out into the bay from the beach, completing the small harbour at Saundersby.

The path into the harbour takes you first due west, heading directly toward the town and beach. As you draw level with the pier head, you turn hard to port and into the protected harbour. The local shore-based fishing fraternity love to cast their lines from the pier head into the running waters, moaning and shouting at you as you pass slowly below them, cutting across their lines. I've never come to terms with their attitude, because they've seen that you're either coming in or going out, and as a boat owner, you have no choice. They do and it's so simple to remedy.

Once between the pier heads and safely in the harbour, I can see much, much more, and scan the horizon for activity. The weather, as predicted, has held fine and it appears that a number of locals are making good use of the dry interlude, taking the opportunity to work on their prized possessions. There are certainly more people around than I had expected.

Slowly, I ease my boat into my mooring, feeling a little more relaxed about the situation. With nothing out of the ordinary going on in the harbour to worry me, I tie off the fore and aft ropes. The bottom falls out of my world. Shutting down the engines and locking up, it dawns on me that I've made a huge error. I have messed up, big time. In a moment of uncontrolled anger, I launched the spare set of keys that Brad needs, out into waters of Carmarthen Bay. On that spare set - lying a hundred feet or more below on the ocean floor - are the keys to Ed's workshop. Not only can't Brad get off my boat if I lock up, he can't get his motorbike out of Ed's workshop. Shit!

In a state of confusion, I race back up into the bridge and shut the boat down. Deep in thought over my next move, I notice through the window that the main doors to Ed's workshop are open. I'm not sure if that's a good or bad omen. Ed never works on the weekend. Something has happened.

I should inform Brad that we have a problem, but I find myself, head down, walking at speed along the quayside towards the boatyard. Peering gingerly around the door, in the general direction of Ed's office, I can't see - or hear for that matter - a damn thing through the gloom. Then, an almighty crash, and the sound of china smashing, followed by a tirade of expletives, echoes around the quiet workshop. I recognise Ed's voice. He's angry, and by the sound of things, he's very drunk.

Ed is kneeling on the floor in front of his safe, when I knock on the office door. He beckons me inside, clearing the floor space of broken china mugs. Ed is pissed out of his tiny mind. Through his almost incomprehensible slurred speech, he informs me that he can't open his safe. His hand to eye co-ordination is severely hampered through his over-indulgence, and he's having a great deal of trouble focussing on the small numbers on the combination lock. Between us, we manage to open the safe and Ed reaches inside to grab a handful of notes.

'That should do,' he slurs, stuffing the notes into his trouser pocket, and while Ed struggles to his feet I close the safe for him and lock it.

'You look as though you've already had enough, Ed,' I tell him.

'Been invited to some do in the pub. Ran out of money,' he tells me, resting his right hand on my shoulder to steady himself. 'Why don't you join me lad? It's a good do. A wedding reception, I think.'

I decline his offer. I know whose wedding reception it is and I'm not setting foot inside the place.

'Do me a favour then,' Ed continues. 'Lock up for me while I crack on with the business of getting drunk.'

Rather relieved at the arrangement, I readily agree to his request. How lucky is this?

Guiding Ed down through the workshop to the door, I point him in the direction of the pub and set him on his way. I realise as I watch him zig zag across the car park that his house keys are on the ring, and he will need them back before the night's out. I have no wish to see Jenny in her wedding dress, but it seems I might have to.

Other than the boat keys, Brad only needs the main workshop key. Leaving him and his mate with what they need, and instructions on where to deposit the keys when he departs, I jump into my car and drive across the harbour to the pub. If I'm quick, I can be in and out of *The Harbour Lights* public house without being seen. Ed shouldn't be too hard to find. He'll either be propping up the bar or lying horizontal on the floor close by.

I pause outside. The noise coming from inside drowns out all other sounds. The *thump-thump* of music – allegedly – from the disco competes with howls of laughter and raised voices. I didn't know Jenny and Tony had so many friends! *Meow.*

This is one of my locals and yet I don't want to step inside just now, but plucking up the courage, I open the bar door, and walk in. My hunch about Ed propping up the bar proves correct and I make a beeline for him, ignoring everything else going on around me.

'Nick, lad,' he bellows when he sees me! 'Let me get you that drink I promised you.'

Again, I decline his offer and drop his keys on the bar beside him. Ed becomes agitated by my refusal and insists I oblige him. Turning away to save creating a scene, I walk straight into Jenny.

'Jenny! You look radiant,' I blurt out, without taking in how she actually looks.

'You don't look so bad yourself,' she giggles, drunkenly, placing her hand on my cheek.

'You're a married woman now; you shouldn't be saying things like that. And Jenny you're drunk, not a good idea when you're pregnant.'

Oh, Nicholas, I think. *Why, why, why can't you, just for a change, keep your bloody mouth shut?*

'What I do, darling,' she slurs while fiddling with my collar, 'is none of your bloody business, and,' she continues, raising her voice and poking me in the chest, 'I don't bloody care what you think. You had your chance, lover boy, and you blew it.'

'I think I made the right choice, Jenny. Don't you?'

Trading insults with Jenny isn't the reason I came in here. Excusing myself, I hurriedly leave before Tony appears on the scene, doing his 'knight in shining armour' thing for the maiden in distress.

Collapsing in front of the TV into my favourite armchair I kick off my shoes, put my feet up on the coffee table, and attempt to relax. I release the ring-pull on a can of John Smiths bitter, and take a well-deserved swig of beer. I am shattered, both mentally and physically.

It's a relief to be home after a long, strange, and intense day. That's the first time in ages that thought has crossed my mind. My day hasn't finished, and I know I won't relax properly until Brad and his African buddy are safely off my boat. That won't be until the wee hours of the morning when there's no one around, so if by chance I do fall asleep here in my chair, it won't matter.

I wish I could nod off, but my mind is already going over my trip to Cardiff in the morning. There is no peace for the wicked. In his post this morning Stephen Jones should have received the mammoth tax bill I sent him. Personally, I hope he's spending his evening shitting himself. By now, he knows that his days of living the good life - at someone else's expense - are numbered. He knows someone's on to him, and through my letter, he believes it is the taxman. My sadistic streak wants to see him squirm and suffer first before I finally wreck his future.

Stephen is the weakest link in the chain and has the most to lose. I figure that if I can offer him a way out, he might break rank and turn against Gavin Thomas, and Reginald Moss, to save his own skin. They're a tight-knit group; tough to penetrate, but there's always a weak link in the chain. It's all I have to work with, right now. The evidence we've so far gathered isn't strong enough to go public with. It's enough, perhaps, to rekindle Reg Wallace's interest, but most of what we have is circumstantial and won't hold water. I need more time to confirm what we've uncovered. In the interim, to achieve my goal, I must push Stephen to his breaking point, and if that doesn't work, hope that James comes up with something more factual. What I really need at this point is a confession from Stephen Jones.

I have one confession, from the train driver David Reece. I don't trust him, though. I think, that when push comes to shove, he'll claim that he made it under duress, and that I manipulated the situation. Apart from my recording, I haven't a witness to say otherwise. In the grand scheme of things, his statement doesn't count for that much anyway - other than proving he was negligent.

Flicking through the TV channels, trying to find something other than a re-run of *Dempsey and Makepeace*, or *Taggart*, my thoughts turn to Jenny. I had accepted my part in her decision to marry Tony Morris. I wouldn't say that I was comfortable with it, but I wasn't desperate enough to challenge her decision. Seeing her, earlier this evening, in her wedding dress, with a ring on her finger, highlighted our problem – my problem. Seeing her drinking heavily while she's pregnant compounded my problem.

I won't rest until I know the truth, and now that she's married, proving who is the father of her unborn child is, will be more difficult. Tony has rights. He is a difficult person to handle at the best of times, and I know Tony well enough to know that he will defend his territory fiercely. I wouldn't hold that against him if he did. I think I would react in the same vein.

To avoid trouble in the future, anything I do to satisfy my own needs on that score will have to be legally transparent, or so sly and devious that no one, except me, will know.

Viewing the TV, I decide that the programs on offer aren't to my liking. Grasping my can of beer, I rise from the sofa and wander around the house checking over Mac's progress. He's doing a good job; I'm impressed by his work and he's well ahead of schedule. A thought I have makes me smile. I bet if Jenny was still living with me she wouldn't agree. She'd be going on and on at me about something or the other that, in her opinion, isn't right, and she'd probably want another extension started for a nursery and playroom, and for good measure the pool filled in to stop a potential accident in the future. I've spent enough of my hard earned cash on this place already, and although concreting in the swimming pool isn't such a bad idea - because I won't use it - I'm not wasting any more of my cash.

I'm giving Brad's idea some serious thought. For a long time, I have longed to own a house of distinction. A Victorian manor house will do nicely. The magnificent country retreat he's introduced me to is an offer I can't refuse. It's crying out to be bought by someone who will love and cherish it. I am that person, and I'd be incredibly stupid to let this opportunity slip from my grasp.

A secret place where I can go to relax, get away from the pressures of life; a place where no one will bother me. The money required to buy and renovate the manor house is not important. I want the place. It's an investment for the future, and on those grounds, I will own it!

Chapter ten

Sunday, 31 January 1988

Last night, while I paced the house, watching the time slowly tick by, it occurred to me that once Brad had left, and I could pick up the boat keys from the agreed drop, I'd need to get them copied. This morning there's a need to get inside the cabin and clean up after yesterday's excursion, remove, and destroy any evidence Brad and his friend may have left behind. Overcautious, perhaps, but I must do what's necessary to cover my back, just in case I have unexpected and unwelcome visitors.

Ed will want the master set back first thing Monday in order to finish the work he's started. I'm not sure how I'm going to explain away the new batteries I fitted. To complete that work, Ed will want access to his tools; to do that he'll need his workshop key returned. Sadly, and this epitomises country life, getting something done around here on a Sunday - like having keys cut - is a non-starter.

A couple of years ago, when Richard's security advisory service was in its infancy and no more than an idea on paper, we took the opportunity to watch how key pressing moulds were made. Richard was impressed by the simplicity of the process and he ordered himself the full kit. Unbeknown to him, when I signed the purchase order, I doubled the quantity.

The road to Cardiff is quiet, this morning. Secure in the knowledge that Brad is off my boat and Ed's keys are lying on the floor of his hallway, I set off early in the hope of returning in good time to tidy up my boat. I'm too well organised today, there must be something I've overlooked!

High profile, someone everyone knows and respects, that's what Brad had said to me. I've taken him literally. After standing outside Stephen Jones's house for several hours in the freezing cold - taking on board the delicious aromas of Sunday lunches drifting on the breeze - not a single person has acknowledged me. Even the curtain twitching has stopped.

Being a top private detective isn't quite the same as being a well-known politician. They spend hundreds and thousands of pounds promoting their party views, boasting what they can and will do for the local community. Their pretty faces brighten our day, smiling down at us from the billboards as we queue for hours in the traffic jams they promised to fix.

They smile dutifully and talk to anyone they meet; people from all walks of life. The only people who recognise me come from the wrong side of the street, and want more than just a quick chat and a shake of their hand. Maybe being high profile isn't such a good idea.

I could sit inside my car, start the engine and warm myself up. But I know if I do that - through the lack of sleep last night - I would nod off within minutes, and Stephen would be away.

I'm becoming desperate for a call of nature. Worse still, I'm rapidly running out of cigarettes. Bringing a bloody thermos flask of hot coffee with me would have been a very good idea, too. I'd crucify one of my agents if they left the office as unprepared as this and had to give up a stake-out for any of those reasons. I knew today had started too well.

Stephen Jones knows I'm outside his house. I've seen him peering at me from across the road through the net curtains of his lounge window. I don't want to knock on his front door. If, for some unexplainable reason he opened the door when I knocked, he'd slam it closed in my face, anyway. Surrounded by all his creature comforts inside his castle, he is safe. My intention is to draw him out into the street where he is vulnerable and alone, where I am the king and boss.

As I see this, there is one small problem: what if the postman hasn't delivered the tax bill I sent Stephen? I haven't followed that up, and I have no way of knowing. That is a mistake, and extremely inconvenient, because it's my very reason for being here. I've no way of proving the letters were delivered, and I could be wasting my valuable time standing out here in the cold. Those two things; wasting time and being cold are my pet hates. Whoever it was that said the life of a private detective is a glamorous one is a born liar - I'd disagree, fervently.

I didn't plan this very well. Actually, I made no plans at all. To say today was on the spur of the moment would be wrong. Mentally, I knew what I wanted to achieve work-wise, and blaming Brad or Jenny for my deficiencies is the easy option. I am supposedly a professional. This is something I've done a thousand times, and preparation for a stake-out should be second nature. I should have taken greater care. There is no excuse for not being prepared. I guess I thought Stephen Jones would dash out into the street begging for my help the moment he saw me. It's dangerous to assume, and now I'm paying the penalty for my stupidity.

My resolve is being severely tested. My patience is running out and my morale has reached an all-time low. This nothing of a day, after the challenging one yesterday, has me questioning my direction. Is this the sort of work I really want to be doing: sat outside someone's house for hours, in the cold? Or is the excitement of what Brad is offering more suited to my talent? Right now, the latter has the greater appeal and attraction. I just don't know if the two will mix. Can I be the business partner Brad wants, and still run my own business? There aren't enough hours in the day, already, to do all the things I need to be doing, some of which are important. At the end of the day, any decision I make comes down to money, when it shouldn't. I've worked long and hard to build up my business; eighteen years' worth will be hard to walk away from, and I'll let many good friends and colleagues down if I do. That will be selfish, but to get anywhere in life, one has to be. I don't want to let my close friends down, they are important to me. I'm beginning to wish I'd never responded to that advert of Brad's in the paper.

My day suddenly takes a turn for the better. The very second Stephen Jones opens his front door I'm on his case like a frustrated *Action Man*. Wearing a thick warm puffer jacket, ideal for the weather conditions, accompanied by a look of contentment on his face, Stephen ambles along the path toward me.

'You don't give up easily, Mr. Thompson, do you?' he asks cheerily, his belly, no doubt, satisfied by a lovely Sunday roast dinner. 'You must be freezing, stood out here all this time.'

'Nice of you to show concern, but I'm used to this,' I reply. *If only he knew the truth*, I think.

'What do you want, Mr. Thompson? Got some more pictures to show me?' he churlishly says.

That pisses me off even more. I'll wipe that smug look off his face.

'Where are your reinforcements?' he continues, deliberately taking his time to look up and down the street.

Last time I was here, I told him I'd return with someone. More a threat really, suggesting that it would be over for him. Assuming I've failed Stephen is taking great pleasure putting me in my place.

'I've got to confess, they're good. Are they wearing combat fatigues, because I can't see anyone?'

'You're in luck,' I respond. The heavy mob have more important people to deal with today. Then again, I personally don't need their services.'

'You really like yourself, don't you? Fancy your chances do you?' he says, goading me.

'Oh, I won't need to get violent or physical. You might though, when you've heard what I have to say. I now know exactly what happened that day on *Ten-Acre Farm*. By the time I've finished, you'll be begging me for help.'

Stephen laughs my suggestion off, nervously.

With him questioning my sincerity, it's high time I really gave him something to think about. 'I've spoken to the train driver involved that day. Surprising how much he remembered when I told him I could help. Mr. Reece was most obliging when I interviewed him.'

'You're lying,' he blurts in my face.

'Am I? Let me jog your memory a little more. I also know how you manage to live in such a nice area. Trust me when I say I know it's not on the combined wages you and your wife bring into the house.'

'We put the deposit down on this house with money my wife inherited,' he snaps.

'No you didn't. I checked.'

Stephen steps back, looking down at the pavement and avoiding eye contact, he pushes a cigarette butt around with his foot. It's probably one of mine. 'That's personal information, Mr. Thompson. You've no right to pry,' he mumbles, looking at the paving slabs.

'A young man died, Stephen. I have every right.'

'The train driver said David ran out in front of him. That's what I'm told happened. I wasn't with him and I didn't see it!'

'But you do know why?' I pause for a moment as Stephen raises his gaze. 'You're only making the situation worse for yourself. You have a large mortgage, which is paid for by monies you receive from Gavin Thomas, as a sleeping director of his companies, and before you deny it, yes, I can prove it. Using your wife's maiden name was cute, but not cute enough for an old hand like me. Was that your idea, or Gavin's?' I ask, trying to provoke a response.

Stephen chooses to remain silent, staring at me. The information I've divulged, most of which I can prove, will be hard for him to deny. It's how he deals with it that interests me. He has the chance right here and now to tell me the truth. It's time to help him with his decision-making.

'You're young, Stephen; you have many years ahead of you in which you can rebuild your life. Tell me the truth before Gavin Thomas and Reginald Moss drag you deeper into this mess. Trust me, they are bigger players than you are, and they will shit on you to save themselves. Don't give them that chance. Think of your wife, and your unborn child. How will they cope if you're not around?'

Stephen sighs in resignation. 'You'd better come inside.

Stephen quietly gives me his version of what happened that day on *Ten-Acre Farm*. My small tape recorder rests, whirring away on the coffee table that sits between us. I'm recording his every word.

Like Mr. Reece, Stephen is keen to point out his innocence. There's an underlying problem with that, and I caught Mr. Reece out in the end. At the beginning, he did nothing but lie to me. If I'm to believe Stephen - and he's doing his best to convince me - David's death was no more than a tragic accident, compounded, that day, by Mr. Reece the train driver, with his act of gross negligence.

The act of hunt sabotage in which Gavin's son, David, appears to have been involved doesn't make sense. The hunt meet was on his father's land. David's father was making money from the enterprise. Why mess it up for him?

Stephen will only talk about, or refer to his part in that day. When I ask him personal questions about Gavin and David, he tells me that he'd only met them that day, didn't know them, and that he was there to sabotage the hunt on the request of Reginald Moss, who he'd met at a protest march a few weeks earlier.

I get the feeling Stephen is trying to play me. I've given him too much time to think about his story, and apart from a few minor details here and there, it's pretty much on par with his statement. There's rigidity to it, a line he's so closely following that it's parrot fashion. There's little doubt that in the way he's speaking, Stephen has taken advice. Threatened, most likely, that the nice little earner he receives on a monthly basis will be withdrawn if he sings.

David's death was someone's fault, and that may turn out to be Mr. Reece's, but he, as far as we've currently established, isn't on the payroll. Like he suggested to me, someone was looking for a scapegoat back then, and that someone is responsible for David's death.

'Stephen, if I'm to believe that what you're telling me is the truth, then why is Gavin Thomas paying you? I suggest to you that's because you know more, and he's paying for your silence. I'm right in thinking that, aren't I? Without your monthly income from him, this luxury you live in would go. So far I've been very patient with you, but I've reached the point where, if you don't tell me what I want to know, then I will go to the police with the information I have. I'm going to give you one last chance to tell me the truth. If you are innocent, forget the money and look after number one.'

The hunt saboteur movement is gaining momentum. Dairy farmer Tom and I have had many conversations about the very topic. It seems the control of vermin and wildlife is just one of the country's practices misunderstood. Wildlife damage valuable crops and spread disease. The loss of one cow through

TB can cause great hardship; the loss of an entire herd is to the farmer devastating, and that is just one of the many problems they face daily. Farming is tough enough when controlled. Not being in a position to manage one's life-long work, effectively, can produce a disastrous outcome. It's a tough call.

'I didn't see it happen.'

'Then please tell me what you did see, and what you know.'

'David should have been at college. I was originally told that he'd agreed to help Reginald Moss because he didn't agree with his father's view on hunting. I was roughly the same age as David and sympathised with his feelings towards fox hunting.

'The instruction to open the crossing gate came from Reginald Moss, but not originally. Prior to the order being given, I saw Moss talking to Gavin Thomas. I didn't hear all of what was being said, but they were pointing and looking in the direction of the crossing. David was close by when Moss gave the instruction, and volunteered. He knew exactly where the gate was and how it opened. David could complete the job quickly, lay a false scent trail across the track, and be away before the hunt appeared. The hunt was bearing down on us and timing was of the utmost importance. There wasn't the time to argue. I offered to help but Moss had something else for me to attend to, and David seemed happy enough to carry out the task on his own. I was told by Moss that David knew the train timetable off by heart and nothing was due to pass for at least half an hour. As far as everyone was concerned, there wasn't a risk. Moss assured me that David would be back in ten minutes, tops, to help me, but no one knew of the problems British Rail was experiencing that day. We were totally unaware of the unscheduled train movements to correct a failure. That was the last time I saw David alive.'

'This doesn't make sense. Are you suggesting that the order to open the crossing gate came from Gavin Thomas?'

'Yes I am. They knew I'd seen them talking shortly before the accident. Why else do you think Gavin is paying me to keep quiet? And there's something else, Mr. Thompson. Later in the day, after the accident, I learnt that David was absent from college because he'd been unwell. The previous weekend, while playing rugby for the college, he received a hefty blow to the right side of his head. The resulting injury left him concussed for a short period, and the subsequent swelling caused deafness on his right side. I believe tinnitus in his left ear had temporarily left him virtually deaf. It's little wonder he didn't hear the train coming.'

I leave Stephen alone. He has given me a lot to chew over, and I guess he has to think, too. For his part in what went on that day, if he is indeed telling me the truth, I'd say he is innocent of any wrongdoing. He claims he didn't open the gates, and he didn't tell David to open them. His crime was in not telling the truth at the inquest, and then accepting money to keep quiet. He, for all I know, may have been threatened at the time, like Mr. Reece.

Why, though, did Gavin Thomas instruct Reginald Moss to open the gates? From the outside, looking in, they appear to be in conflict with one another. Gavin pro-hunting, allowing his land to be used by the local hunt, and Moss, anti-hunt, trying to stop the potentially gruesome sport taking place, at all. Yet for some unexplainable reason, they appear to be in this together. I've overlooked something that might help: the hunt organiser. He, or she, might just have the answers I'm looking for.

Arriving back at the builder's yard of a house, I have but one thing on my mind: food! My stomach must think that my throat has been cut. I've not eaten, or drunk anything all day and I'm famished. A blank, brown envelope, lying on the floor by the front door catches my eye. I pick it up and head directly for the kitchen. There are more important things to deal with before opening the blank envelope - it's probably junk mail, anyway.

After abandoning my gear on the nearest flat surface, I head directly for the fridge. The new refrigerator door swings smoothly open in my hand. Relieved by the fact that I now have the opportunity to eat, I peer inside to choose the goodies I fancy for tea. The bloody fridge is empty! I haven't done a weekly shop. How remiss of me, and I've overlooked the fact that the home help, Jan, refuses to undertake the laborious task for me. She has got to go. First thing in the morning, I'll give her two months' notice. That should be enough time to see the job to a conclusion.

I can't remember when I last went grocery shopping. I've not been here a great deal recently and the need to shop hasn't arisen before this moment. I'll grab a quick coffee, and then head down into town for a bite to eat. Saves cooking.

Switching on the kettle and reaching for my cigarettes, I clap eyes on the unmarked brown envelope once more. Ever curious, I rip the seal open. Inside, a brief three-word handwritten note informs me that my presence is required elsewhere. 'Mansion. Will wait', is all the note says. The content of which is fully understood of course. For some reason, Brad wants to meet me at the Victorian mansion I'd viewed near Carmarthen.

This is a ludicrous situation; not half an hour ago, I past within two miles of the place. If it weren't for one minor detail, I'd leave him there all night to stew. Brad hasn't coughed up the dosh yet, and as the job is now complete, it's high time he did.

It's deathly silent in the grounds of the mansion. Pushing the car door gently shut, I pause, looking at the mansions mysterious silhouette, carefully listening as I wait for unusual or threatening sounds. The night is still, dark, and clear. What on earth am I doing here at this late hour? Potentially, this is a dangerous situation to have willingly placed myself in. Anything could happen, and no one would be any the wiser. Money! It's always about money and personal greed.

A noise coming from the direction of the stable block away to my left gets my immediate attention. The very least I should have done was to bring a torch with me, but then, it's been a day for being ill-prepared, which ultimately could cost me dearly.

I took it for granted that the note through my door was from Brad. For all the professional attributes I possess, I certainly cancel them out in style on occasions with some dumb decision-making. Don't do as I do; do as I say. Whoever penned that must have had me in mind. If I took as much care of my own well-being as I do for my staff - wouldn't life be boring? But probably far less stressful.

'Drive your car around the back, out of sight, Nick'.

I'm not given the time to answer before the glimpse I have of Brad's ghostly figure disappears from sight. Knowing I've called this right, I exhale deeply with relief, but this is far from over. Even now, I feel this could all be part of an elaborate set-up.

In the clear moonlit sky I can see the wispy smoke rising from the cottage chimney drifting lazily skyward into the cool night air. An inviting orange glow emanates from within the cottage. Brad has made himself at home.

In this light the cottage looks to be in poor repair, I hope that's not indicative. The tiny, low-beamed, green coloured, entrance door creaks and groans as I push it inward. The base of the door struggles defiantly to win the battle of freedom with the red, stone, floor tiles. With similar problems, the ill-fitting internal door allows light in to the small entrance lobby. The narrow and bare wooden staircase rises steeply in front of me up to the first floor. The steps look damp, and any remaining wallpaper clings defiantly to the wall, despite the mass of fungi.

'In here,' Brad's voice echo's in the silence from behind the door to my left. Stepping into what I understand to be the kitchen, he speaks again. 'You took your time. Where the hell have you been all day?'

'You're not my keeper, so let's not go there,' I reply.

Once inside I see that Brad has found a couple of old beer crates from somewhere, and placed them on the floor in front of the old range. Apart from those, an old Belfast china sink supported on metal legs, and the rusting old range, the kitchen is bare. The range is the same make as the one Tom and Mother have up at the farm, but around half the physical size. Serviceable, it still chucks out some heat. Brad has obviously been here some time waiting for me. The heat in the old kitchen suggests the fire was lit hours ago, and the pile of wood that lay to one side wasn't collected in a hurry.

'I was beginning to think you weren't coming,' Brad says.

'I've been working. This isn't some cosy 9-to-5 weekday job I have. Where's your mate, then?'
'Safely delivered, thank you.'
'I guess that means we've been paid?' I reply, rubbing my hands together in anticipation.
'All in good time.'
'I think now is as good a time as any.'
'A couple of days.'
'What do you mean, "a couple of days"? What's going on, Brad, and why here?'
'Would you have driven up to my place, tonight?'
'Probably not,' I tell him, and sit down on one of the beer crates in front of the fire. 'I've had a long day and I'm tired, but we're not here to talk about my day are we? 'What is going on? One minute you're telling me you're freelance; the next, you're jumping through hoops because someone in the Home Office says so.'
'Who said it was someone from the Home Office?'
'Call that an educated guess. If what you've told me about starting again with a new identity were true, then achieving that would only be made possible with the help of the hierarchy of that department. And from where I'm sitting, I'd say your freedom comes at a price.'
Sighing loudly, Brad sits down next to me on the other beer crate and throws a few more logs on to the fire in the range. He sits motionless for a moment or two once he's done, staring at the dancing flames of the fire.
'Buying this house is important to me. With its purchase, and some personal business finally taken care of, I can disappear off the face of the earth; start to live my life the way I want to.'
'What does this personal business you're talking of involve?'
'What I must do is none of your business, so don't involve yourself.'
'Here we go again, more bollocks!'
'I can assure you, it's not bollocks.'
'I can't be doing with this. Every time we get into a conversation, we disagree or argue over something or other. You want us to form a working partnership and yet you're very reluctant to meet me half way. I'm here, Brad, at your request, giving this my best shot, when I really should be at home taking care of my own business. Heaven knows it needs my full attention, right now. And while I'm in the chair, how many more times are you going to tell me I don't need to know, and I'm not to involve myself? I do need to know, and I can assure you things cannot go on this way if you want our partnership to be successful. Truth is, the partnership can't continue unless you let me into your world.'
'I need time. I told you that.'
'Well, right now is all the time you have left. If I walk out of here without knowing what your future intentions are, then you can forget the partnership thing. I'll live with not being paid, and the few quid I spent on diesel won't break the bank. That's where we're at. Like it or not, you have got to make a decision. Tell me, or forget it!'
'I can't. Yes I want our partnership to continue, and yes I want it to be successful, but I can't involve you in what I must do!'
'Fine,' I respond, and stand up. All of a sudden, my hunger pains are my number one concern. This isn't going to work, and more fool me if I thought it had a chance.
'All right! But you have got to understand that once I've told you, there's no going back. The other day, I joked about having to silence you. This is where the joking ends and reality kicks in. Can you live with that?'
'That sounds like a threat?'
'It's not a threat, it's a promise, and don't for one second think I wouldn't do what is necessary. I am a survivor and I will survive.'
'I'm listening,' I say, rejoining Brad in front of the fire.
'This is serious shit; are you sure you want to hear it?'

I'm not sure, but I gently nod my head to confirm I'm ready.

'At nineteen, I was drummed out of the army on some trumped-up charges. They were, of course, false because someone had plans for me. In the eighteen months since signing on, I had excelled in everything I turned my hands to. That was a personal, because that's the way I am. I love winning and I want to win - fuck the cost.

'What I achieved in a short space of time got me noticed, and one man became my mentor and trainer. With false service papers and a totally new identity, which could be checked and verified on their records, I walked through the elite, squadron entrance program and became a fully-fledged member of the SAS.

'I did my job for that man, and when things went wrong he eliminated the John Doe I was. The John Doe who served him well in Northern Ireland never existed. The boy who was drummed out of the army at nineteen died in a motorbike accident three days after his dishonourable discharge.

'Today, with new papers and a brand new ID, with no military background, one man stands between me, and total anonymity. He is pulling my strings, telling me what to do, because he is in a position of power to do so. He owns me, and the time has come to put an end to his domination of my life. I am going to take him out, and use my anonymity to its fullest potential. I only have one chance to get this right, and should I fail then the game is over for me, as it will be for those that they associate with me. See what you've done, by insisting I told you the truth.'

I'm sitting next to one of Britain's most evil products of the home defence system. The man is a highly trained and licensed cold-blooded killing machine. Someone like Brad has no thought or compassion for human life. In his dog-eat-dog world, earning his daily crust means only the toughest and fittest survive to collect.

I don't agree with his plans, but in his world, I guess it's an accepted outcome to life. In that sense, we're no different. I'm not like Brad; I'm not violent to the extreme, or otherwise, but there are those out there who would reciprocate with pleasure and terminate my very existence, and I have to be prepared for that. Confronted with that situation I wonder how would I react, and when all else has failed, would I pull the trigger first?

Brad has cleverly drawn me in. I can identify him, I know where he lives, and I'm party to helping him bring an illegal immigrant into the country. I now know he intends to rid himself of the noose around his neck, and I know his old army colleagues would love to meet him. With the information he's provided me with, he's sucked me in, and there's no way out, but why? If no one knows of his existence, then why does he need me?

'You haven't left me with much of a choice, have you?'

'You pushed me.'

'Under the circumstances, I think I had every right to push you for answers.'

'But it wasn't what you wanted to hear, was it? Because you pushed, you're now an honorary member of my hit list. You know too much, Nick. If you walk away from our arrangement, you'll leave me little choice in the matter.'

'I don't think you'd want to do that; you need me too much.'

'You're quite correct with your assumption, but think on. If I can push the button and blow up six of my army colleagues, just to survive, doesn't that tell you that I'm capable of anything.'

Walking away from the prospect of earning money is extremely foreign to me. Placing myself in danger is becoming all the more frequent. As I stand up, ready to leave Brad in his secret world of espionage, both thoughts are foremost in my mind. I'm tired, and past caring about the consequences I may suffer as a result of my action. After eighteen tough years of making my own decisions and taking risks, I'm not going to change my lifestyle because someone wants me to – that's part of the reason for being here in the first instance.

'You must do what you must do, Brad,' I inform him, matter-of-factually. 'You know where you can find me.'

'You're making a big mistake, Nick.'

'We'll see. Before I leave, there's one question I'd like you to answer for me: why do you need me, if, as you say, you don't exist?'

Chapter eleven

Monday, 1 February 1988

'Autopilot', and running on empty tanks' are phrases most will associate with. I'm not giving it a thought, but that's the way it is. All I'm concerned with, this morning, is organising my notes and putting this David Thomas job finally to bed. Stephen Jones and David Reece's statements need typing up and there's an urgent requirement to speak to the hunt organiser.

To add to my woes, the month of February begins today, and on behalf of the lovely Victoria Jackson, Richard is placing me under pressure to deal with Reginald Moss accordingly. To cap the start of my day, Lord Brock - Mal - has phoned and wants to meet later to discuss the first chapter of his book. I could go on and on, what with the building works, Jenny, and the problem Brad has left me with. What a position to find myself in.

I'm exhausted and for the first time I'm beginning to feel the pressure I'm under. Driving myself forward to achieve results, splitting my time as equally as I can, I'm desperately trying not to let anyone down. Constantly flitting from job to job, from task to task, I'm flirting with the inevitable. When I do finally hit the wall, and even I can see the possibility arising, will I get up and carry on?

Amongst the paperwork on the police file I'd photocopied is the name and number of the hunt master. Donald Bradshaw is a lawyer based in Cardigan and according to his secretary; if I wish to speak to him then I need to make an appointment. I use to like driving, but having to be in Cardigan by eleven o'clock does not fill my heart with any great joy.

As seems to be the norm these days, time is of the essence. Wanting to be in Cardigan in good time, I forgo breakfast. I've not eaten for over twenty-four hours, and although I've gone past the stage of feeling hungry, I'm positive that not eating a solid meal for that length of time can't be good for me.

Donald Bradshaw is a big man, tall and overweight. His bald scalp and round face, supported by the half glasses perched on the end of his nose, are close to how I imagined him. It's clear he is a man who likes the good things in life, and he is the perfect advert.

Men like Donald Bradshaw are clever. Having recovered from being upstaged by Brad, I must take great care what I say this morning. I don't recall seeing a statement of his in the police file, but few I did read supported the fact that he was present on the day of the hunt. Donald Bradshaw could be involved in the cover up.

'Now then, Mr. Thompson, how can I be of assistance?' Donald Bradshaw beams while I sit down in a plush leather chair, opposite him.

'I'd like to ask you a few questions, Mr. Bradshaw, if I may, about an incident that occurred seven years ago.'

'Fascinating!' he responds and leans forward in his chair, resting by his elbows on his desk. 'Please call me Don. So what, may I ask, does the eminent Nick Thompson wish his humble servant to divulge?'

Patronising git, I think.

'I've heard a lot about you. All good, I'm pleased to say, and it's a real pleasure to place a face to the name. If I can help, it will be my honour.'

'I'd like you to cast your mind back for me if you will, to the spring of 1981, and to the Pembrokeshire hunt held on *Ten-Acre Farm*. A farmer's young lad was struck and killed by a passing train; David Thomas was his name. My enquiries inform me that you were the Master of the Hunt, and I'd like to hear your version of what happened that day?'

'Tragic…tragic…' Don whispers, shaking his head. 'The inquest ruled it was an accident, if I remember correctly?'

'Death by misadventure,' I inform him. 'The land you were hunting on belonged to his father, Gavin Thomas. As the Master of the Hunt, I assume you must have had dealings with Gavin prior to the hunt day. What can you tell me of him?'

'Mr. Thompson, I had dealings with the man back then most certainly, but I don't consider him an associate, nor is he on my Christmas mailing list.'

Don's sudden formality suggests that he's gone on the defensive. Every single person I've interviewed on this case has done exactly the same. Makes me wonder.

'Since the incident,' Don continues, 'and I refer to *Ten-Acre Farm* when I say that, we've not spoken and nor will we. My hunt has not used, nor will be using, his services again.'

'What you're suggesting to me, then, is that you only dealt with Gavin Thomas on a business level, and nothing else?'

'That is exactly what I'm saying.'

'If you don't mind me saying, you appear a little agitated. Has Gavin Thomas got something over you, Mr. Bradshaw?'

'Not in the slightest!' he snaps at me. 'That horrible man left a nasty taste in my mouth, and if you don't mind, I'd sooner forget him. That tragic incident ruined what was turning out to be a wonderful day's fox hunting. Many of my members held me responsible, and the man had the confounded cheek to charge me in full for the day's sport. I think you will understand why I'm a little agitated.'

'So there was a charge involved here?'

'For the use of his land there was a nominal fee, most landowners do the same. It's the sundries, the little extras, where the likes of Gavin Thomas make their money. The more lavish one wants the meet to be, the more it costs. Things like refreshments, luncheons, grooming facilities, and stabling are all chargeable extras, and he hit me with the lot. Legally, my hands were tied; we'd struck a deal and signed a contract to that affect. I tried to argue the point, as you may imagine a man in my position would. The fact that my members were extremely upset by the young man's death and left early, thus not making full use of his facilities and hospitality carried no weight.'

'Did Gavin Thomas get paid?'

'In full, Mr. Thompson.'

'I assume the contract you had with him was a simple affair, with no hidden anomalies?'

'Absolutely! I wouldn't have it any other way. But I did reduce the initial cost of the contract by removing what I considered to be unnecessary items.'

'Such as?'

'I forget them all, but I do recall one of the more expensive items he insisted upon was for security. In hindsight, probably one of his better ideas.'

'Is security normal for an event such as yours?'

'Not at all! Gavin Thomas claimed, when I failed to agree on the terms, that he had it on good authority the hunt saboteurs would ruin our day, and we should not ignore the possibility of trouble. And he wasn't wrong, was he?'

'And you've never questioned him on how he knew?'

'Why should I have done? Sadly, hunt saboteurs are a fact of life in these times, and we as huntsmen deal with that in the best way we can.'

'Do you remember the name of the company he wanted to employ for that job?'

'No, but I could probably find out. I keep all the society's records and invoices here in the office.'

'Mr. Bradshaw, would it surprise you to learn that Gavin Thomas is a secret partner in a security company, who incidentally, specialise in country affairs such as hunting and shooting events?'

'You're joking with me?'

'Unfortunately not, and it's my belief that the hunt saboteurs were brought in to promote and enhance his own security business at your expense. Tragically, he lost a son that day, but if you set that aside, financially he lost nothing and gained a great deal from his actions.'

'I hope you're right, because if you are I'll sue him for every penny he has. Do you need a good lawyer?'

'No, thank you, I already have a good one on a retainer. Before I go, I'd like to ask, would it be possible to send me the original quote, and invoice, Gavin Thomas sent you? The finer details could be vital in gaining a conviction, and for your information, my lawyer will deal with any claims against Gavin Thomas you might have, so don't go having any unprofessional ideas; the job is already contracted. I'd like your statement of our conversation, and the quotes Gavin sent you on my desk by Friday, Mr. Bradshaw. Please see to it,' I tell him, and rise to my feet. Dropping my business card on the desk in front of him, I leave before he charges me for his time. The poor, hard done by, pompous ass.

Maggie Davies runs our accounts office with a road of iron. She is a ferocious lady whose bark is as bad as her bite. The every day matters of the company are her responsibility. Ultimately, the financial control is first Graham's, then the Board's. Even I have to be accountable. Graham knows exactly how much I earn and how much I earn the company; he even looks after my taxation for me. So, you might ask, why do I need my very own personal accountant?

Very simple. Since day one, I've siphoned off some of the money I've earned. For every ten jobs I do, one doesn't go through the books. 'Everyone does it', I was told way back then, and I have kept up the tradition for the past eighteen years.

My personal work isn't easily defined or distinguished, because I do flit from one job to another, which confuses the best of them - and me, at times. Being the boss is an advantage, too. Who is going to question me? My personal accountant manages the fund, pays the taxes due and makes interest for me.

I dropped in to see him on the way back to the office and asked him to transfer one hundred and fifty thousand pounds into a Swiss bank account by Thursday. A large slice of what I have saved. Brad and I settled our business differences last night, and I've agreed to go ahead with the purchase of the mansion near Carmarthen. There are a number of i's to dot and "t's" to cross, but we are making steady progress on that front.

The money my accountant manages was originally set aside as a fall back if the business failed in its infancy. Today, it acts as my pension fund. I've just made a huge hole in that, but I think the mansion is a safe investment, and in the long term, I should profit from the purchase. The only risk is Brad, but if all goes well, the mansion will be ours by Saturday.

James pounces on me the moment I walk into the main office reception area. He is excited over a discovery he's made, and can't wait to share the news with me. I tell him to give me ten minutes to settle in and inform Richard of the meeting. Before I can move, Sue takes hold of my arm.

'There's a Stephen Jones waiting to see you,' she says. 'He's just gone across to the town to get something to eat. He's been sat waiting for you since eleven o'clock. Wouldn't speak to anyone else.'

Now there's an interesting development. I wonder what he has on his mind? 'Let me know the second he returns, Sue. I'll be in my office.'

Pausing in the doorway of my office, looking objectively in for the first time, the state I've left it in actually embarrasses me. Everywhere one cares to casts one's eye there's a mess. James will have a moan when we convene but I haven't the time too do much about that now, and God knows what Stephen Jones will think. Time has come to change the habits of a lifetime. I will knuckle down and sort this unsightly mess out, when the current workload allows.

The state my office is in has got to be sending the wrong message to my employees. I demand perfection from them, and yet I allow them to see what a slob I am. The boss, of what Graham describes as a 'multi-million pound company', should lead by example; set the standards he expects his employees to follow. Visually, I'm highly unprofessional in my attitude and housekeeping, which in the long term could rub off on others. Hiding behind the pretence of not having the time isn't good enough. I wouldn't tolerate it from them.

I knock on Richard's door with the intention of changing the meeting venue. Sat behind his desk in his tidy and clean office, he beckons me inside while he continues his phone conversation.

Richard's view from the window isn't a patch on mine. He can see most of the harbour from here and if one cranes one's neck, or opens the window wide, one can see a small amount of the town. Bad luck, I'd call that.

Waiting for Richard to finish on the blower, I realise that my boat isn't tied up at its mooring. Ed had better be responsible for that, or there will be trouble! His lackadaisical approach to security has already been noted. It is possible that he's taken her out for a test run, as he said he would, but of course, that will generate a number of awkward questions, like, for instance, where did I get the batteries? Why did I bother when I knew he had ordered a new set? There is a plus side to this: having spent several pleasant and informative hours at sea with Brad, I know there isn't too much wrong with the old girl, bar a couple of scratches along the starboard side. If Ed's pissed, I can blame them on the way he parked it!

'Are you ready, Richard? The old man will…' James blurts out before he sees me. '…Ah you're here boss?'

'"The old man will" what, James? Have your guts for garters? Sack you for being late? Or perhaps not sign off your quarterly bonus. Which would you prefer?'

'I'm sorry, boss. None of those choices as it happens.'

'Do you know what? I'm not sure which of your annoying expressions regarding my persona I detest the most? "Boss" is technically correct, and "old man" is something I call my father. May I be as bold to suggest that if you want to be politically correct, then "Mister Thompson" is fine? But, James, we're one big happy family in this office, aren't we, and I like my Christian name. You have my permission, and my blessing to call me "Nick" in future.'

'Are you sure…Nick?'

'Shall we get on?' I suggest to them both. 'I have someone downstairs waiting to see me.'

As we pull up our chairs to begin, Richard's phone rings. At this rate we'll be here all afternoon trying to conduct a five-minute meeting. The receiver is thrust into my hand.

'For you,' Richard scowls.

'Hello,' I say, placing the receiver to my left ear while sitting on the edge of Richard's desk.

'Nick! Don Bradshaw here. I've some news for you', the voice on the other end informs me.

'That was quick,' I suggest, in reply.

'We lawyers are noted for our prompt action; you should know that!'

'Only when it's to your financial benefit. What have you got, Don?'

'The company Gavin Thomas recommended to do the security was called Sandfords. Is that of any help?'

'Excellent work, Don, and thank you. Yes it may be of some help,' I tell him before reminding him to send me his written statement and hunt-day receipts before Friday.

'Don?' Richard asks as I pass the receiver back.

'Don Bradshaw. Master of the hunt on the day David Thomas was killed. Gavin Thomas tried to sell him security for the day, in the shape of Sandfords. Needless to say, Mr. Bradshaw didn't take up the option. The whole thing was a scam, Richard, and Moss played his part. They were in it together to make sure security for such events was high on the must have list in the future, only now, and because of the risks, at a far higher price. Very smart if you ask me, and easy pickings on those they know can afford the extra cost. The one thing I can't come to grips with, is why Gavin felt he had to cover up his own son's death and pay those who knew the truth to keep quiet?'

'I might be in a position to answer that, boss,' James adds, from the comfort of Richard's client's chair.

Strange how he'll sit down on Richard's furniture, and not mine.

'Max Walker. Remember, how I asked you both if the name meant anything? I suggested that

Max Walker and Gavin Thomas were one of the same. Well, I've no proof, but whoever Max Walker is, he is a very sick man who just happens to live at *Ten-Acre Farm.*'

'What are you suggesting, James?' Richard asks, before I do.

'I'm suggesting that Max Walker is David Thomas.'

'And your reason for coming to that conclusion?' Richard adds.

'Complicated, but hear me out.' James asks. 'I hope you don't mind, boss, but I borrowed the notes you copied from the police file. Did you know that no one positively identified the body after the accident? There is no actual proof that it was David, and hardly surprising. Body parts were found strewn over a two-hundred-yard stretch of track. Dental records couldn't be matched because the head and upper torso were so badly mutilated. It was assumed, because David was missing after the accident, that it was he.'

'Not conclusive enough, James,' Richard interrupts.

'James, why did you take the notes off my desk?' I ask. 'You must have had good reason.'

'I did, boss. Through a few old school pals of mine, I discovered that David Thomas had been suspended from college. It appears to have been involved in some sort of fracas during a very important college rugby match. As a result he was asked to give a blood sample, and was found to have traces of muscle enhancing substances in his blood stream.'

'Steroids?' Richard asks.

'Very similar. Only, the traces found in David's blood sample are more commonly used for treating multiple sclerosis, which brings me neatly back to the very sick Max Walker, who it appears is suffering from the very same muscle-wasting disease, and who has had thousands of pounds spent on medical equipment on his behalf.'

'If what you are suggesting is right, James, and I'm not sure I buy it,' Richard says, leaning across his desk, 'who the hell was hit by the train?'

'I have to agree with Richard here. It is a touch drastic just to cover up your own son's drug habit, whether or not it is for all the right reasons,' I add.

'Normally, I would agree with you, that's why I dug a little deeper. David did receive a blow to the head playing rugby, but it was no accident. The blow he suffered was an act of retaliation for something David did during the rugby match. David was guilty of a high and dangerous tackle on an opponent. He caught the opposing fly half under the chin with his forearm; the blow was sufficient to break the young man's neck. I understand he was left paralysed from the neck down after the incident, and will remain so for the rest of his life. From what I gather, there was a history between David and this young man, and it has been suggested to me that it was deliberate, intentional on David's behalf.'

'And allegedly,' I say softly, thinking aloud, 'a few days later we are to assume, David was struck and killed by a train.

'It's only a theory, but there are ways of proving this,' James offers.

I rise to my feet and stand looking out of the window. I do this a lot, not in Richard's office, naturally, but in my own. The calming influence of the ocean helps me think rationally, filter out the fiction until only the facts remain. Richard sits down on the windowsill beside me.

'Brilliant, isn't it?' I tell him.

'What is? Murdering some poor unsuspecting lad to cover your sons arse?'

'Is that what happened, Richard? Or did Gavin Thomas seize upon the opportunity when it presented itself?'

'Why? What did he hope to gain?'

'I would have thought that was obvious. I have no reason to doubt that what James has told us about David Thomas is true. That agreed, then, David's promising rugby career was over before it had begun, and he was facing criminal prosecution for his momentary act of stupidity. Gavin probably sought legal advice on his son's behalf, and knew that without his son's testimony there was no case to answer. Had they faced up to the consequences of his actions, the legal and financial implications could have been crippling. I ask you, Richard, what would you have done in Gavin's position? Especially if you already knew your son was dying from multiple sclerosis, and was perhaps facing a stretch.'

'Told the truth.'

'I doubt that. Blood is thicker than water; you'd look after your own first.'

'Then you don't know me as well as you think you do. I would not walk away and leave someone to suffer. And I'm still not sure I'm buying, because if you're right, how come no one has reported their son missing?'

'Real world, Richard! Next time you speak to Reg Wallace, ask him for a current list of missing persons. I guarantee it'll take you half a day to read,' I snap, and turn to face James. 'These friends of yours, did any of them see what happened?'

'One of them - Nathan - was playing for the opposition. Michael was watching.'

'Did you get statements from them?'

'No.'

'Can you?'

'Yes, boss.'

'Then please do. I want this wrapped up by Friday. Oh, and James, well done.'

'Thank you, boss.'

Turning back to look out of the window my boat, named *Linda*, comes into view with Ed at the helm. I'm looking forward to hearing what he has to say about the condition she's in. In a rare moment Ed must be sober, because he carefully and diligently takes her alongside and ties her up. Damn it!

Richard's phone rings. Without saying a word, he thrusts the receiver into my hand for a second time. Stephen Jones has returned.

My original plan was to interview Stephen in front of Richard. I've changed my mind. To drive over here from Cardiff, Stephen must have something important on his mind, and talking to him in front of Richard might inhibit him. Grabbing a coffee from the kitchenette, I meet Stephen, down in reception, and suggest we take a walk along the quay.

Fine misty drizzle swirls around in the stiffening breeze. Stopping for a moment, I place my coffee on the ground and lift my collar, zipping up my jacket to keep the rain out.

To begin with our idle chat is centred on the village and harbour. I'm in no hurry, and I want Stephen to be relaxed enough to volunteer whatever it is he came here to tell me.

I time our stroll along the quay to miss Ed's return passage to his workshop. Any conversation I have with Ed regarding my boat should be conducted in private. He understands my wish for privacy, although others are not so accommodating. I'm truly amazed by the number of people who, over the years, have stepped forward and told me where I'm going before I know.

'I bet you own one of these?' Stephen suggests, gesturing toward the line of moored boats below us bobbing up and down on the ebbing tide. 'When you're bored, and the weather's fine, you simply untie the ropes, turn a key, and sail away. Wonderful. If I sound jealous, it's because I am. I have dreams too, Mr. Thompson, and why not? Everyone should. You're destroying mine, and I've decided not to let you.'

Stephen stops. 'I'm withdrawing my statement. I didn't make it, and you can't use it.'

'Too late,' I reply. 'And why drive all this way just to tell me that? You've been to see Gavin Thomas, what's he promised you, now? More money to fulfil your dreams? You were right about me having a boat, Stephen. Beauty, isn't she,' I gloat, standing over my forty-foot motor launch while checking that Ed has tied her up correctly.

'I want to make a fresh statement,' Stephen continues. 'I'm denying everything I said because you pressured me into making a false confession.'

'You, Stephen, can do what you like. However, we both know that's not true. You see, I no longer require your personal statement to get a result. Most of what you told me was a lie, anyway! Do you know, I think I might go fishing on the week-end. I'd ask you along, but I fear you'll be otherwise engaged.'

'You don't frighten me, Mr. Thompson,' he growls in a threatening manner. 'Without my statement you've got nothing.'

'I've decided to apply to have David's body exhumed,' I announce out of the blue. It's a total fabrication of course.

Last night, I spoke with Tom Morgan, and he confirmed that David Thomas was buried. Tom had, in fact, attended the funeral and witnessed the coffin being lowered into the ground.

'I'm not exactly sure when this will take place, Stephen, because these things take time, but I will tell you, we have good reason to believe that the body buried seven years ago at St. Martin's church was not David's. New technology will enable us to prove that. So you see, it's out of my hands, now. And speak of the devil, here comes the man who can help me with my request.'

Reg Wallace is walking purposefully along the quayside towards us. Stephen may not know him but the thought of the police becoming involved very quickly changes his attitude.

'Don't do this, Mr. Thompson, please?'

'Give me one good reason as to why I shouldn't?'

'If you promise to keep me out of this, I'll tell you all I know.'

'I can't make you a promise like that. Like it or not, you are involved. What you can do is make life easier for yourself, and no more lying to me. Inspector Wallace will be here in a matter of seconds, have we got ourselves a deal?'

Stephen nods his head vigorously. Stepping away, I intercept Reg before he has the chance to speak with Stephen. Reg Wallace will be told, but there is one last deal to be done.

'I'm busy, what do you want?' After eighteen years, it still gives me pleasure being blunt and aggressive with Reg. Sometimes it's the only way to be with him!

'Who's that?' he immediately asks, looking over my shoulder at Stephen.

'None of your Goddamn business! Now, what do you want?'

'All right, have it your own way,' he responds. 'I've had a complaint about you which I must act upon,' he adds, smugly.

'Don't be ridiculous.'

'From Tony Morris. He claims you're hassling Jenny over the baby.'

'Hassling Jenny? That's absurd. Why should I want to do that?'

'I'm told it's because you believe that the child she's carrying could be yours. Is that correct?'

'You tell me?' I reply, deciding not to say too much. Reg doesn't need to know my personal business and feelings.

'I'm not here to discuss whether the baby is yours or not. I'm here to tell you to stay away from Jenny, and that includes her doctor. Accept this as a friendly warning; don't push me into doing something official about this.'

Reg's warning is perfectly clear. It also starts me wondering. Trouble is like water off a duck's back to Tony Morris, and in time, his attitude to authority will rub off on Jenny, but my involvement in her pregnancy has scared them both. I'm more convinced than ever by this that Jenny and Tony have got something to hide.

I catch Reg staring over my shoulder again, puzzling over Stephen. He's grinding his teeth again - he's thinking. Reg should leave that to those who can!

'Where have I seen that guy before?' he asks.

'Could be anywhere. He's a localish lad,' I tell him, which he seems to accept. 'He's looking for work. I'm in the process of interviewing him. I like to test possible job candidates on their powers of observation. It's served me well in the past.'

Accepting my explanation, Reg has one last warning for me before he leaves. 'I hope I've made myself clear. Stay away from Jenny,' he adds, and walks away.

'Message understood, Reg,' I shout after him.

Stephen Jones rejoins me. He waits until Reg is way out of earshot, before speaking.

'There's something I think you should see. Perhaps then you will understand,' he says softly.

Chapter twelve

Monday, 1 February 1988

I've committed a cardinal sin. The number one rule in our business is let someone know where you're going. In a hurry to conclude my business with Stephen, I've omitted to do that.

We left Stephen's car parked outside the office and took mine for the short drive over to *Ten-Acre Farm*. I like to be in control of my own destiny, and leaving Stephen's car behind guarantees him returning to Saundersby to collect it. A weak excuse for justification of not informing a soul of my intentions.

The main house on *Ten-Acre Farm* is set aside from the working farm, and is by no means typical of this area. With well-laid and tendered gardens, the Edwardian-style house gives one the impression of grandeur: a house owned by someone who deludes to be member of the gentry, but is not quite there, or perhaps has no wish to show their wealth for financial reasons.

As we approach the house, driving slowly up the shingle driveway, a man appears in the main doorway. I recognise him immediately from the few photographs we have of him. Gavin Thomas in person. I'm surprised by his casual acceptance on seeing me, here. I worry now that I've been set up, and I've walked right into his trap.

'We meet at last, Mr. Thompson. Please follow me,' Gavin instructs. I hesitate while he disappears. There's a conflict. Following Gavin inside, I may find the answers I'm looking for. I may also place myself in great danger by doing so. Once I step inside Gavin's house, I'm at his mercy.

Stephen is keen for me to do as I'm instructed, insisting politely that it is for our mutual benefit. Against my better judgement, we follow Gavin through the house and out into a new annex at the rear, coming to a halt in front of a lift. While we wait in silence, I notice beyond the lift, in the annex, the space opens out into a huge games room where a full size snooker table dominates the luxuriously furnished space.

The short ride in the lift, up to the next floor, is also conducted in total silence. Stepping out into a large hallway with clinically clean linoleum on the floor, two hefty swing doors to our right form a barrier.

James appears to be spot on with his prediction. Once through the swing doors, I am confronted with the largest private hospital ward one will perhaps ever come across. It has everything one would expect to see in a modern National Health hospital, from the most expensive and latest monitoring machines, whirring away, to just about every exercise contraption one could imagine possible. Not a penny has been spared equipping this room.

While I stand rooted to the spot, ogling the fixtures and fittings, mentally guessing at the cost, Gavin walks on ahead. I have no reason to be jealous of Gavin's wealth. By now I should be the co-owner of a rather splendid, if slightly run-down manor house. This though, is not something I will witnesses every day - particularly in a private dwelling – and I cannot help but be impressed by what I see.

Gavin is stood beside the one bed in the room, talking to a middle-aged lady wearing a white doctor's coat over her normal everyday clothing. Hooked up to all manner of technical gismos pumping and wheezing with monotonous regularity a motionless body lies in the bed. The equipment, no doubt, keeping him alive.

'Your son, David?' I ask. 'Or does he prefer Max?'

'Very astute of you, Mr. Thompson. Yes, this is my son David.'

The nurse smiles sweetly and leaves, prompting Gavin to sit on the bed and stroke his son's face. 'I've made his short life as comfortable as I can.'

His attitude rubs me up wrong way. As long as his son receives the best that money can buy, that's all right - and sod the rest! Even so, I can't help but have sympathy for Gavin. Life isn't supposed to be like this. In the perfect world, children should out-live their parents. Tragically, the one we live in isn't that perfect!

My thoughts momentarily turn to Jenny, and the child she's carrying. She and Tony know that I will not stop in my search for the truth, no matter how long it takes. The harsh reality of that particular situation is that, discovering the truth could take years, and if I'm proven right in the end, how much will I have personally sacrificed? A parent should be there to see their children grow up, love and support them through thick and thin. Guide and advise them through the trials of life. Watching Gavin and seeing what he's done for his son; where Jenny's concerned I can't help but feel that I'm being cheated of the opportunity to fulfil my obligation.

David looks peaceful and well cared for. It's clear from what I'm witnessing here today that despite Gavin's attentive parenting, and disregard of cost, David is close to death. I'm sure, though, that they shared better times, and Gavin will cherish those fond memories of his son for the rest of his life.

The pity I feel toward Gavin, toward David, is short lived. Out there somewhere, a mother, a father, a brother or sister perhaps, wait in hope for the return of their loved one, praying that today will be the day he walks in the through the door as if nothing has happened. That's the part I find hard to digest. It shows a side of Gavin Thomas not evident in this room. A callous, scheming bastard, whose own world is far more important.

'Who was the lad killed on the level crossing?' I finally get around to asking Gavin. 'My business partner is of the opinion that someone must be missing him.'

'I doubt that,' Gavin responds with an air of 'I couldn't care a less' conveyed in his voice.

'So you didn't know him?'

'Personally, no. Reg supplies the misfits to do the dirty work.'

'That would be Reginald Moss, I assume?'

'Your information is good, Mr. Thompson. Reginald Moss knows all their haunts, and you'd be surprised what the down and outs will do for a few quid in their pockets to fuel their habits. As long as he gets the job done, I don't care where he gets the hired help from.'

Wandering around the room, filling my head with all the information at hand, I continue with my quest for the truth. What I'm seeing and what I'm hearing compares with the saying, 'trying to fit a square pin into a round hole'. It just doesn't fit. I see a man full of compassion and love for another human being: his dying son. Yet, he's a man who doesn't give a toss about the lad killed by a train on his land.

'Did you plan it?' I ask, coming to stop at the foot of the bed, where it would be easy to become emotionally involved by what I see. I've overcome my personal involvement, because I believe this is an attempt to soften me up. 'You see, with the trouble David was facing, I think you did.'

'You have no idea, have you? David is all I care about. He is my life. As his father, I couldn't let him suffer anymore than he already was.'

'That wasn't your decision,' I respond. 'What about the lad from college? How do you think the parents of the young man killed on your level crossing are feeling, right now? You're not unique, Mr. Thomas. You're not the only one who feels pain.'

'I don't give a toss about their feelings! David is the only one that matters here. The lad involved was a junkie, a drain on society, and permanently stoned out of his head. He had no future.'

'And that makes it okay does it? Because he was a down and out druggie, his death didn't matter. One less addict for the state to take care of.'

'That's about the size of it, yes.'

'You make me sick,' I shout at him, in anger.

Stephen Jones, who up until now has been stood by the door listening, finds it necessary to voice his opinion. 'It was an accident, Mr. Thompson. The lad was totally out of his head on something and being a real pain in the arse. He could have fucked things up for us so we found something useful for him to do to get him out of the way. David went with him and showed him what to do, then came back to give me a hand. We honestly didn't know about the irregular train movements that day.'

'You're right,' Gavin informs me, joining me at the foot of the bed. 'We were deep in the brown stuff. I reacted on impulse. When we told this lad what we wanted him to do, he shot off across the field toward the crossing, prancing around like some demented delinquent. What everyone else saw, was David heading toward the crossing with the gunk to lay the false scent. By the time David got back, I was alone. Nobody saw him return.

'We were distracted by something or other, and by the time we heard the train it was too late to do anything. It was obvious what had taken place, and we knew who was involved. Thinking clearly, to protect my son you understand, I sent David back to the house. My initial decision was taken to save him from seeing the result of the accident. God knows, his mind was already a mess with everything else he had to deal with. When we realised the extent of the tragic accident, and people around me assumed it was David, the idea came to me. I played along. I sent Stephen back to the house to tell David what I had in mind, and that meant David staying out of sight until I said otherwise. Call it what you like, but when I saw the state of the lad's body; I knew no one would ever identify him. It was an accident, but I've always believed that one should never kick the gift horse in the mouth. Yes, it was callous, and no, I don't have any feelings for the lad, because as a parent, first and foremost, my job was to protect my son.'

Having said his piece, Gavin returns to his son's side.

I aim my anger at Stephen. 'Are you at ease with your conscience, accepting bloody money to keep quiet? I guess Bill Marchant and Reginald Moss are included in that exclusive club, too?'

'My brother-in-law is a bumbling, drunken waste of space,' Gavin pipes up. 'Unfortunately, for me, the pathetic specimen of a human being actually got something right for a change. He knew it wasn't David, because the shoes the lad was wearing were nothing like the ones David had on. Sadly, he left me with no choice; I had to pay him off to keep him quiet. Trust me, Mr. Thompson, when I tell you that that went against the grain. I can't stand the man.'

'My heart bleeds for you. So much so, that it's time to stitch you up.'

'What do you mean by that?' Gavin snaps in response?

'This isn't a social call to pay my last respects to David. What do you think I'm going to do? You know I can't ignore this!'

'Now wait a minute! I asked Stephen to bring you here so I could explain, so you'd understand. No harm has been done; you can see that. Why don't we leave it there?'

'No harm's been done! Just where do you get off on this?' I ask Gavin. Turning towards the exit, I push Stephen aside so vigorously that he falls back over linen basket onto the floor.

'I can't let you do this,' Gavin shouts, as I pass thorough the door and press the button for the lift.

This is going to turn nasty on me and my priority is to leave before events take a turn for the worse. I've achieved my goal; all I must do now is live long enough to tell someone.

When the lift doors open, I'm inside in a flash, and tapping my right index finger on the down button in what resembles a panic sending of the Morse code 'SOS' message. The lift doors close and I begin the slow, laborious, nerve-racking decent to the ground floor, alone. A fit and healthy man could reach the stairs in the old house, beating this heap of technical junk to the ground floor, hands down.

Blindly searching for a way out, I stumble out through a fire exit into a courtyard at the rear of the house. In the time it's taken me to get this far, I've managed to put the fear of God into myself. I'm scared, and have good reason to be. Farmers are unpredictable folk. This particular farmer has proven that he is capable of anything.

My car is not hard to find, but I'm having trouble with the keys. Fumbling around in my pockets to locate them, I become aware of a person standing a few yards in front of me. The click of a shotgun being locked into the firing position echo's menacingly in my ears.

'Lets not do anything hasty here, Mr. Thomas,' I utter, when I look up to see Gavin Thomas holding a double-barrelled shotgun aimed at my midriff. This could get real messy. 'My colleagues know I'm here. It's only a matter of time before they come looking for me.'

As I speak, I can hear the tension in my own voice. I'm trembling with fear – who wouldn't be in this situation? - frozen rigid to the spot. One false move; one moment's lack of concentration and I could be torn to shreds. Right now, my survival prospects don't look all that promising.

'I can't let you leave, Mr. Thompson. Not now, not ever! You know too much. That's your downfall: you ask too many questions.'

Taking tiny, slow steps backwards, sliding my feet over the grass away from Gavin, I glance around, weighing up my options. My car is definitely out of the question, but Tom's place isn't that far from here. If I make a dash for it I might just get away unscathed and make it across the fields to the safety of his farm.

Gavin's facial expression changes dramatically when he realises I'm moving slowly away from him. I've seen a similar look of hatred on a man's face before, and it didn't turn out the way I'd hoped for, that time.

My decision to make a break for freedom is instant. The horrifying sound of a shotgun being fired, quicker still.

Chapter thirteen

Friday, 12 February 1988

Sight is the most precious sense the human being possesses. Most of what we learn in life is gathered through our ability to see. The most incredible part of that is, our brain then digests and retains that visual information for future reference.

I've woken this morning with a problem: my sight is more than a tad bleary, it seems. I have no definition, only light, and that light is becoming brighter by the second, dazzling me in fact. I guess we had another heavy session in the pub last night. If only I could remember.

My body isn't responding to the messages my brain is dishing out. Most peculiar, but not altogether unusual. Last night must have been a real humdinger. As a matter of interest, nothing appears to be working at all, and now, some twat thinks it's funny to shine a bright light in my eyes.

'How are you feeling this morning, Mr. Thompson?' A man with a very polite bedside manner asks.

It's nice of someone to show concern, but who the fuck is he, and what is he doing in my bedroom? Oh, God! I hope I didn't make an arse of myself last night, and that is not in the least bit funny!

'My name's Doctor Ingram, I've been looking after you for the past few days.'

Doctor! I gasp, but nothing vocally resonates from my voice box. If it did, I certainly couldn't hear my own voice. Bloody hell! Not only am I paralysed, I'm dumb and blind as well! It's little wonder the doctor's here looking after me. What the hells going on?

With one last super human effort, I try to sit up. The pain is intense. My shoulders, my back, my thighs, and legs all throb like hell. I collapse back onto the pillow, aided by what feels like the doctor's forefinger pressing against my forehead.

'Just relax. You'll do more harm than good if you try to move on your own. Give the sedatives time to wear off and we'll see where we are.'

I want to ask him why I'm taking sedatives, but I can't. I know I've not slept that well of late - not surprisingly, given the pressures I've been under - but I feel that's a little drastic just so I can catch up on a few hours shut-eye.

'I'll pop back a little later to see how you are. And no trying to get up,' the doctor adds.

I can't lie here all day; I have work to do.

That bloody light is back!

'How are we doing?' the good doctor asks.

That was quick. This Doctor Ingram chap is extremely diligent.

'That looks better,' he adds, as a light sweeps from side to side in front of my eyes.

If he's not careful, I won't be held responsible for where his smart pencil-thin torch will finish up. Please, do me a favour, get that fucking light out of my eyes! While we're on the subject of eyes, can you please remove your finger?

'Can you see my finger, Mr. Thompson?'

Not that close up, I think. Actually, I can, wonderful! Because I can't speak, I nod my head. Shit! That hurts.

'Lay still, please, just until we've made a full assessment of your current condition,'

Once again, Doctor Ingram gently pressing my head back down onto the pillow by way of his forefinger in the middle of my forehead.

'You have a particularly nasty shotgun wound to your right shoulder and upper back region. It made quite a mess. For a while, our resident vascular surgeon thought you might lose your right arm, but Mr.

Webb is an exceptionally talented man, and has worked a miracle on your behalf. We're reasonably confident at this stage, with your co-operation, and with physio, that you should make a full recovery.'

'What are you talking about?' I croak. Thank God! I haven't lost the ability to speak.

'Do you know where you are, Mr. Thompson?' Dr. Ingram responds.

'No.'

'You're in Swansea hospital. You were shot twice with a twelve-bore shotgun. Had you been any closer to that gun when it was emptied, then I'm afraid to say the state of your shoulder would have been the least of your worries? You were a very lucky man.'

I've never come to terms with that expression. Where's the luck in being shot. If what Dr. Ingram is suggesting is good luck, then I'll sure as hell give the bad sort a very wide berth in future.

With my vision returning to a level resembling normal, I can at last place a face to the name. Dr. Ingram is quite young, late twenties or early thirties, I would guess. His neatly cut, short jet-black hair, and tanned complexion give him the appearance of being Mediterranean in origin. His accent, though, suggests he's from north Wales. Clearing my throat to speak, an excruciating pain grips my entire body once more. This is unbearable. I do hope the assessment Dr. Ingram mentioned doesn't take too long; I'd like to go back on the sedatives as quick as possible.

Lying motionless on the hard, unforgiving, hospital bed, I'm racking my brain as to how I've found myself in this mess. Thankfully, the drugs administered by Doctor Ingram have slowly begun to deal with the pain. I can recall some of the details of yesterday. I was up at *Ten-Acre Farm* when Gavin Thomas came at me with a shotgun. I remember thinking then, as he pointed the shotgun at me, that he was capable of doing absolutely anything to protect his son, and he clearly was. The bastard did shoot me, then – twice, I understand!

'What other parts of my body are hanging off, Doctor?' I ask, with great concern for my own well-being.

'Nothing is hanging off, but some off the buckshot did penetrate your back and lodge dangerously close to your spinal cord. We kept you sedated for a few days while your wounds healed sufficiently enough to minimise the risk to you. You were on the operating table for six hours, and having spent that much time and effort on you, we don't want you undoing all our good work. Most of your wounds are showing early signs of healing nicely, but you have one or two open wounds that we believe will benefit from being exposed to the air.'

'You said a few days: what day is it?'

'It's Friday today,' he responds. 'Friday, the twelfth of February. I've been asked by number of your friends and colleagues to let them know when you're well enough to see them. Do you feel well enough to receive visitors?'

'Sod the visitors! I need to get out of here, I have work to do.'

'Mr. Thompson!' Dr. Ingram shouts at me, gently placing his hands on my wrists to restrain my movement. 'Even if I gave you permission to leave, you wouldn't take two steps before you collapsed. Regretfully, I have to inform you that your right thigh took the full force of the second blast. It too is a mess, and recovery from the gunshot will take a huge amount of dedication on your part, and the physio department, to repair. So, if I were you I'd lie still and rest while you have the chance, and forget all about work for the time being. We'll talk in more detail, later on. But I'll warn you now; you, sir, face a very long and difficult few months.'

'You really know how to cheer a person up, don't you? How long are we talking about here?' I ask the good doctor.

'Months, rather than weeks, a lot depends on you.'

Heavily sedated, and unable to recall the exact events at *Ten-Acre Farm* it's taken a lot of convincing by Dr. Ingram for me to come to terms with just how bad my injuries are. From the way he's described my injuries, my back must resemble a colander.

A dedicated team of surgeons, led by Mr. Webb, painstakingly spent six hours patching me up; not necessarily saving my life by what they achieved, but they certainly saved my weary, ageing body from lasting debilitating injuries. The test of how good Mr. Webb's work is, as Dr. Ingram suggests, is all down to me from here on in. I guess I should be grateful to him for giving me a second chance.

I've lost eleven days of my life lying here in hospital. In that time, I may have lost one hundred and fifty grand. My need to see and speak to Brad is foremost in my thoughts. Has he bought that mansion near Carmarthen as promised? Has he done a runner with my pension fund? I'm not in a position to ask anyone to assist me with this, and that's not entirely because of our so-called pact. I could face a number of very awkward questions if I were to disclose the sum of money involved. Put very simply, I'm fucked - in more ways than one.

Epilogue

Friday, 13 May 1988

Looking back on that life-changing meeting with Brad in January 1988, I should have realised I was taking on far more than any one could. It was then, and still is, my obsession with money – my greed – that pushed me into making that rash decision. There were numerous other reasons, like Jenny and her pregnancy, and I saw my new association with Brad as a distraction, a reason to forget them. I pushed my problems aside with total disregard to the consequences, hoping that others would cope with the mess I'd left behind, and my problems would simply disappear. Graham and Richard bore the brunt of my unreasonable behaviour, because I naively thought they were ready to take on the extra responsibilities. I grossly underestimated their abilities, and then ignored their constant demands for assistance. On reflection, they were right to complain. Why should I have left them to deal with my personal and professional problems? All the time, I was ignoring my own person problems – not dealing with them, as I should have done. Inside, I was simmering volcano, boiling over and close to erupting. Soon, nature would show her disapproval.

I viewed the fledgling partnership with Brad the new beginning - a fresh challenge, and the next step in life's rich tapestry. This was to be a brand new chapter in my life, where the rewards were more than worth the risks taken. For some time, I had felt that my life had gone stale, and I shared in Brad's excitement in unlocking the world's riches. I should have known from my own past experiences, that when the pot's overflowing with gold, the stakes and risks are much, much higher.

I wasn't prepared mentally for the meticulous planning required to undertake such work, and having to do the correct thing at the right time. Trying to be the ultimate professional, almost overnight, created its own problems. The stress involved, that came with the demands made, both mentally and physically, very quickly took their toll on my health.

I hadn't once stopped to think what I was actually getting myself into, nor at the time did it matter. Being busy and involved, earning money has always been a priority. I was thirty-five years old and in the prime of my life, I could handle anything life threw at me - so I thought.

It happened because my plan was to retire at fifty, so there was little time to waste faffing around waiting for the big one to materialise. I was on schedule with my financial target to retire, although initially my finances would be stretched, but anything to speed up that process – or make retirement more comfortable – was up for serious consideration.

I was abusing my body by drinking heavily, smoking anywhere up to forty cigarettes a day, eating all the wrong fatty convenience foods, at irregular intervals, and taking little exercise. All those bad habits – mixed nicely together in the melting pot – made the perfect recipe for disaster.

My own attitude didn't help. It masked the long-term damage I was doing. I believed I was indestructible, that I could worry about my health tomorrow, or the next day when I might have the time. When you believe you're invincible, when you think that if you don't take full advantage of what's on offer, you may miss out, and live to regret your decision. That pressure to succeed creeps up on you, progressively becoming unmanageable, and blinded by the blasé statement 'in the prime of your life' you press on regardless, believing that your body can cope with the ever-increasing demands placed upon it. My state of mind, at the time, believing I could cope with my lifestyle, and tomorrow would be better, was yet to show.

Three days before I regained consciousness, David Thomas lost his long battle against multiple sclerosis and died on the 9th February 1988: Officially, from pneumonia. Four days after his son's death Gavin was charged with perverting the course of justice - on two separate counts – and on one count of attempted murder. Stephen Jones, Reginald Moss and William Marchant all face similar charges - a satisfactory result for the rapidly rising star that is Inspector Wallace.

Train driver, David Reece, wasn't charged. It's my belief that Mr. Reece's actions, leading up to the accident, were highly unprofessional. He may not have been in a position to change the outcome, but Mr. Reece was preoccupied and not concentrating one hundred percent on the job, and because of that, a young man died. In my opinion, he should shoulder some of the blame, but for some bizarre reason, Reg Wallace, and his admiring team, chose not to pursue that particular course of action. When I asked why that was, I was told to mind my own business. I understand British Rail has since reopened their inquiry into the accident, and I'm hopeful a prosecution will follow.

Mac and his crew have finished the building work on my house. I'm pleased, and impressed with the finished article, and mightily relieved it's all over. Taking my time on deciding on who was my preferred builder was totally justified, despite the end cost. If I were asked to pick one fault, or name something I didn't like, it would have to be the lack of thought in choosing the interior colour schemes. That's not Mac's fault; I chose the colours, but if Jenny had stayed, she would have seen to the trivial matters such as decorating, so it's fair to say she was to blame.

The expensive extension work has created a large modern family house with fantastic sea views, which I'm reliably informed has probably doubled in value. That's about the extent of the good news. Inside, I feel like a *petits pois* in an empty chest freezer, rattling around every time the door is opened and closed. At times, it's so quiet and lonely in the house that I've actually missed having Jan around, but I soon snapped out of that! Believe me, though, it's not much fun playing pool on your own in the well-equipped games room. Nor, it must be said, was spending loads of money on the four, surplus to requirements en-suite bedrooms, which incidentally, will never be used. But, hey-ho! That's progress.

The one plus, because the situation was forced upon me, is the swimming pool. Once my wounds had healed, and the physiotherapist could begin my treatment, in earnest, I made a point of swimming twice a day. At the start, my endeavours to glide effortlessly through the warm, pool water, gracefully, were extremely laboured. Very painful, in fact. Slowly, with single-minded determination, and totally dedication to repairing my damaged limbs, the all-round movement in my shoulder and thigh has returned. I'm not quite there yet, but because of the in-house swimming pool, the final push required to regain my full strength won't be so difficult to achieve. I thank Jenny for her foresight.

Mal - Lord Brock to give him his correct title – is doing well with the book. Baz left him alone as requested, to crack on, and he's predicting a publication date as early as August. My being laid up for several months has enabled a rapid progression towards the book's completion.

In fairness to Mal, he's helped me to remain focussed and sane in what proved to be a very traumatic time in my life. The period in my life that his book is based on was exciting, eventful, and fun. Recalling those halcyon days cheered me up no end. I'm comfortable with the way Mal has set about the task. Not too personal or revealing, and wildly inaccurate in places, but isn't that story-telling? All the basic facts of my early life in Wales are there in his writing, and throughout the meandering story line he's portrayed me as being almost human. On reflection, it's a fair analysis.

I drove for the first time yesterday since the accident. I like to consider what happened that day at *Ten-Acre Farm* an accident; it's far less personal. Climbing in behind the driving wheel again and driving on my own, after a three-month absence, was a weird experience, but it's like riding a bike - you don't forget; it is the lack of confidence one has to overcome. The belief in one's own ability to move on positively after a horrendous and life-threatening period is paramount in one's life. No guesses as to where I went? The manor house near Carmarthen. The only difference of note were the sold signs, otherwise it looked much the same. I'm reliably informed that an English property developer acquired the site and plans to divide the place up into four luxury apartments. Good luck to him.

Further research declared that, hours after reaching a Swiss bank account, my £150, 000 disappeared without trace. Gone, and lost forever. Much the same as Brad - or whatever his name was. The rented cottage he lived in now lies empty. I beat myself up on a daily basis for not running a check on him. Boy, what a fool I've been! Hoodwinked by a slimy, lying, and very convincing fraudster. My pension fund will not recover from such a huge loss. Eighteen years of blood, sweat, and toil down the pan, and after what has happened, I may not have the gumption or desire to start again and rectify my naivety. What was it all for in the end? Greed!

All I have to show for a few days of madness are a peppering of white coloured shot wounds in my thigh, and a shoulder, that resembles a patchwork quilt. I no longer stand in front of the full-length mirror to admire my physique, and in the future, I won't be so quick to whip off my tee shirt when the sun shines. Physically, my recovery has gone well. Mentally, I have a long, long journey ahead of me. I have lost weight, which can only be good.

A few weeks back, I was in Saundersby, conducting some retail therapy, when a passing motorbike backfired. I hit the deck quicker than one can say 'jump', and cowered in the doorway of a shop, shaking like a leaf for some twenty minutes afterwards. I don't mind admitting I was petrified. That sudden explosive noise will haunt me for the rest of my life.

No amount of persuasion, by those good willed passers-by who saw me dive for cover, could convince me otherwise that the noise I heard was just a passing motor bike. Someone who knew me went across to the office to get help. Even then, Richard had his work cut out, but his calm and patient nature shone through and he eventually coerced me into returning to the office with him.

A motorbike backfiring in the street like that will make a lot of people jump. It's unexpected, so it's a natural reaction. To me, it's more than a simple bone-shaking, nerve jangling fright. It spells disaster, and evokes lasting and painful memories. A situation I must learn to cope with, or my life from here on in will be very different.

Jenny came up to see me the other day. Tony was out of town on business. I didn't ask what sort of business. She did her best to hide the bump as we sat talking and drinking coffee out on my new patio. All I have to say on her appearance is that she was conveniently over dressed for the middle of May. For someone who's only six months pregnant, she was awfully large out front. Water retention, she claimed. I'll reserve judgement for the time being, but watch this space. She looked well though.

Ultimately, it was Gavin Thomas with his twelve-bore shotgun that has brought me to this time and place. There were many other factors. My lifestyle for one, and my driven passion to win at all cost. The lack of sleep and woefully inadequate diet didn't help. The pressure of work, the extension, and of course Jenny, all blended nicely into the mix. Coupled with high blood pressure, the new office in Great Malvern, drinking to excess, and smoking forty a day, I was a disaster waiting to happen. The icing on the cake was Brad, what I thought he had to offer, and what I would have to sacrifice if I were to choose that route.

At thirty-five, I'm not an old man, but I was treating my body in the same way I did when I were in my early twenties. Age, too, had become an important issue. Because youth was still part of my outlook I was unaware of what I was doing to my body, and so very nearly paid the ultimate price. If I've learnt anything from the experience, I know it's time to slow down; time to reflect and take stock. Brad hasn't made that easy. A loss of £150,000 computes to many more hours of unselfish work.

In conclusion, if I'm honest with myself, Dr. Ingram was right: I was lucky, but this is far from finished. My lifestyle must change, I'm very aware of that, but my circumstances haven't. That is the challenge I face. I still live on top of the hill in a house big enough to accommodate six people comfortably. The loneliness still exists, and the friends who gave their time freely, to help me through those difficult days, stepped back as my health improved. Other than my financial loss, nothing much else has changed. Is it all worth the effort?

Printed in Great Britain
by Amazon